"I like *you*, Celeste, even when you're angry with me."

Warmth flooded through her. The heat of desire. Lust. Sin.

"I don't care whether you like me or not. I am *not* leaving."

"Oh, yes, you are," he replied in that same low, seductive tone. "You can come quietly and obediently like a good little nun, or I'll have to carry you."

She must be strong. Her faith, her duty and her self-respect must make her so. "I will not allow you to drag me through the village like some chattel."

"I didn't say I'd drag you. I shall pick you up and carry you, like a groom does across the threshold."

She swallowed hard and fought to maintain her composure, such as it was. "I am a bride of Christ and shall never be a man's."

Author Note

I enjoy creating the main characters of my novels, but I also really like coming up with secondary characters, the best friends, second bananas and bit players. Sometimes I know from the planning stage who my secondary characters are going to be, especially if the character is a villain. Other times I realize in the writing that I need somebody for my hero or heroine to interact with. So sometimes very minor characters become more important.

Arnhelm and Verdan, who first appeared in *Bride for a Knight*, began as basic background characters. Then I realized I had more than one place where I had such characters. Why not combine them? Why not give them names?

Once they had names, I began to give them more to do. They were soldiers in the household of the heroine's uncle, so they would know her better than the hero, at least at first. Why not make them a sort of protective Greek chorus, wondering and worrying about her?

Then I made them brothers, and the minute I did that, I realized their friendly relationship could contrast that of Roland and his twin brother, Gerrard.

Being a romance writer, I couldn't resist giving Arnhelm and Verdan their own love interests, two female secondary characters who live in Dunborough. And I gave them a mother who is making a bit of trouble for them.

That's how secondary characters become just as real and vital to me as the hero and heroine of my story, and I hope for my readers, too.

Margaret Moore

Scoundrel of Dunborough

HARLEQUIN® HISTORICAL

Recycling programs
for this product may
not exist in your area.

ISBN-13: 978-0-373-29865-5

Scoundrel of Dunborough

Copyright © 2016 by Margaret Wilkins

This edition published by arrangement with Harlequin Books S.A.

For questions and comments about the quality of this book,
please contact us at CustomerService@Harlequin.com.

Printed in U.S.A.

Award-winning author **Margaret Moore** has written over fifty romance novels and novellas for Harlequin, Avon Books and HarperCollins Children's Books. Her stories have been set in the Dark Ages and medieval Britain, Restoration, Regency and Victorian England and pre–Civil War Massachusetts. Margaret lives in Ontario, Canada, with her husband and two cats. She can be found online at margaretmoore.com, margaretmoore.blogspot.com and @MargMooreAuthor on Twitter.

Books by Margaret Moore

Harlequin Historical

The Knights' Prizes

Warrior Series

Stand-Alone Novels

Harlequin Historical Undone! eBook

Visit the Author Profile page at Harlequin.com for more titles.

With thanks to my family and friends for their love and support, especially during times of crisis. It's appreciated more than words can say.

Chapter One

England, 1214

The November night had fallen, but inside Sir Melvin's hall, warmth and light dispelled the cold and gloom and provided a welcome shelter for the young woman dressed in the habit of a nun. She had been traveling many days, and it had been a long time since Celeste had enjoyed such comfort.

A fire blazed in the long central hearth and several torches lined the gray stone walls. Two beeswax candles in silver holders graced the trestle table covered in linen on the dais. Behind the high table where Celeste and the plump and prosperous Sir Melvin sat, a tapestry of knights and finely dressed ladies swayed. His wife, the calm and competent Lady Viola, was seated to his left. Servants male and female moved among the other tables, where the steward, a priest, retainers, senior servants and household guards prepared to eat the evening meal.

The elderly priest, who put Celeste in mind of Methuselah, finished the grace. Serving maids brought trenchers of stale bread to hold a thick beef stew. More bread sat in baskets on the table, and wine was poured into bronze goblets that gleamed with the reflected glow of the firelight.

"It's kind of you to offer me shelter and such a fine meal," Celeste said to her host, her voice soft and sincere.

"We're delighted to have you stay the night, Sister," Sir Melvin said with hearty good cheer and a broad smile. "Delighted!"

"We'll be happy to provide you with an escort for the rest of your journey," Lady Viola offered.

"I thank you," Celeste replied, "but I have not far to go. I should reach Dunborough tomorrow."

"Dunborough?" Sir Melvin couldn't have sounded more astonished if she'd announced she was going to the devil and happily so. "Why are you—"

He caught his wife's eye, cleared his throat and began again. "Dunborough, eh? I know the lord there. Sir Roland. He and his bride stopped here on their way from her home to Yorkshire. Lady Mavis of DeLac, she is."

Celeste stopped reaching for a small brown loaf from the basket of bread on the table. "Sir Roland is lord of Dunborough and he's married?" she asked, doing her best to hide her astonishment.

"His father and older brother died a short time ago and he is recently wed," Lady Viola supplied.

Celeste had to believe her, and yet she still found it hard to imagine.

"A fine fellow, a fine fellow!" Sir Melvin cried, picking up his eating knife to carve a piece of beef from the roasted loin a neatly dressed servant set before them.

"Quiet and a bit stern for my liking," he continued, "but I'm not the bride. Our byre caught on fire when they were here and she lost all her dower goods. He never asked for a penny in compensation."

"And he led the efforts to put it out," his wife noted.

"He's not in Dunborough now," Sir Melvin continued, unaware of the relief he was giving his guest with that information. "He's at DeLac. He was—"

Lady Viola touched her husband's arm and shook her head.

"Well, that's not a fit subject when we have a guest."

Celeste wondered where Roland was and why, although it didn't really matter. Her business was not with the lord of Dunborough.

"Have you been to Dunborough before?" Sir Melvin asked.

"I lived there until I went to the convent," she admitted.

"Ah!" Sir Melvin cried. "So you'll have seen Sir Roland. Grim fellow, isn't he?"

"Rather," she replied. Indeed, she remembered him very well, and his brothers, too. "He had a twin brother, too, I believe."

"Oh, yes, Gerrard." Sir Melvin's pleasant face darkened with a frown. "Quite a different sort, he is, even though they're twins."

Gerrard had always been very different from Roland.

"It's too bad he's a wastrel and a lecher, like his father, or so they say," Sir Melvin remarked. "From the stories I've heard, old Sir Blane was as bad as they come."

Worse, Celeste silently supplied. She could have told him stories about Sir Blane that would have made her host's beard fall out from shock.

She also could have told him how Sir Blane had raised his sons to hate each other and compete for any crumb of praise. He'd even kept the knowledge of which of the twins was the elder from everyone, including them, using it to goad or torment them, always dangling the hope that one of them could be the heir someday, should anything happen to their older brother, Broderick, before he married and had sons, as it had. Blane had made the twins bitter foes and rivals in a constant competition.

She could have described how the younger brothers had fought and quarreled and come to blows more than once when they were boys, and that only their stubbornness and their features were alike. Roland was hard, cold, stoic, a stickler for rules and duty. Gerrard was bold, merry and exciting.

As for what had happened to Gerrard in the years since she'd been gone, Celeste had only gossip and tales told by girls who'd arrived at Saint Agatha's for information. One story had been particularly upsetting. Esmerelda had claimed that Gerrard had lured her into the woods with a promise to meet her there. He'd failed to arrive and outlaws had found her instead. Esmerelda had barely survived. Her maidenhead had not.

"Have you family in Dunborough?" Lady Viola asked, bringing Celeste back to the present and this comfortable hall and the reason for her journey.

"Not anymore," she answered, turning away to hide her face before the sudden rush of sorrow became visible.

"I'm sorry, Sister," the older woman said sympathetically.

Clearly, Celeste realized, she had been too slow to keep her reaction from her features.

"It's all right," she replied, giving her hostess as much of a smile as she could muster. "My mother died shortly after I went to the convent and my father some years later. My only sister passed away recently. I have no brothers, so I'm on my way to Dunborough to see to her things and sell my parents' house."

"Oh, dear me! How sad!" Sir Melvin exclaimed. "Your sister must have been very young. Sickness is a terrible thing, a terrible thing!"

"She was murdered."

The moment the harsh and horrid truth escaped her lips, Celeste regretted saying it. She need not have used the same words with which the mother superior had informed her of Audrey's death and the manner of it. "Forgive me for being so blunt. I have only my weariness for an excuse."

"It's quite all right," Lady Viola hastened to assure her. "We're so very sorry about your sister."

"We'll speak no more of it," Sir Melvin said, his usually booming voice hushed with respect as he shut the door on any more talk of murder.

Or anything else to do with Dunborough and its inhabitants.

Shortly after noon the next day, Gerrard of Dunborough pulled his snow-white horse to a halt outside the stone fence surrounding the yard of the house that had belonged to the D'Orleaus. The soldiers of the patrol returning with him likewise reined in, exchanging puzzled glances at this sudden and unexpected halt.

"Seen something amiss, sir?" young Hedley asked the tall, broad-shouldered commander of the garrison.

"It may be nothing," Gerrard replied as he slipped from the saddle, "but the door to the house is open."

A few of the men gasped and more than one made the sign against ghosts and evil spirits. They all knew what had happened in that house and that it should be empty.

Gerrard did not believe in ghosts or evil spirits. He

did, however, believe in outlaws and thieves drawn by rumors that money and jewelry were hidden inside the D'Orleau house.

"Take some of the men and search the stables and outbuildings," he said to Hedley as he drew his sword. "Quick and quiet, though, so no warning given."

The young man nodded and Gerrard walked swiftly toward the house that had been built by Audrey D'Orleau's father, a prosperous wool merchant. The air was chill with the approach of winter, the sky gray as slate. Rain would come soon and wind from over the dales, bringing more cold and perhaps turning the rain to snow.

Gerrard's steps slowed as he neared the front entrance. No ordinary thief or outlaw should have been able to pick that lock, yet only a foolish one would have left the door visibly open while he pillaged inside.

Gerrard eased the door open farther with the tip of his sword and listened. Nothing. Not a whisper, not a sound, not even the soft scurrying of a mouse. It was as if the house, too, had died.

He stepped over the threshold. Still all was silent.

He continued to the main room. The last time he'd been in that chamber, many of the furnishings had been broken and strewn about, obvious signs of the struggle between poor Audrey and her attacker. Since then, the unbroken furniture had been righted, if not returned to its proper place, and the ruined pieces taken away. The horrible bloodstain, however—

He wasn't alone.

Someone else *was* there, swaddled in a long black cloak and standing still as a statue, looking down at the large, dark stain upon the floor, as if Death itself was brooding over the spot where Audrey's murdered body had lain.

Gripping his sword tighter, Gerrard moved closer, making a floorboard creak.

The intruder looked up.

It wasn't Death, or even a man. It was a woman in a nun's habit, her skin as pale as moonlight, the wimple surrounding her heart-shaped face white as his horse, her eyes large and green, her lips full and open in surprise. Her nose was straight and slender, her chin pointed...

"Celeste!" he cried, his hand moving instinctively to the collarbone she'd broken years ago.

Audrey's younger sister regarded him warily. "Who are..." Recognition dawned. "It's Gerrard, isn't it? Or is it Roland?"

"Gerrard," he answered, hiding his dismay that she hadn't been able to distinguish him from his twin. She had always been able to tell them apart when they were younger.

He reminded himself that ten years had passed since they had last been together and in that time more than their height had changed.

He was about to ask her what she was doing there when the obvious answer presented itself. She was there because Audrey was dead, and she was Audrey's only family. "We thought to see you days ago."

He saw the flicker of anguish cross her features, yet when she spoke, her voice was calm and even. "I was on a pilgrimage."

"An odd time of year for traveling."

"I came as soon as I was informed." She turned away and added, "Of course I would have come sooner had I known."

Silently cursing himself for speaking without thinking, Gerrard said, "If you'd sent word you were coming, I would have met you and escorted you to the castle. You need not have come here."

"I wanted to see," she replied, sounding exactly as she had when they were children and one of the hounds had caught and worried a badger to death. Gerrard had tried to keep her away, but she'd gotten past him and then stood staring at the torn and bleeding body, silent and white as a sheet, the same way she'd been staring at the floor moments ago.

"And now you have seen," he said with quiet compassion, nevertheless determined to get her away from this place with its blood-soaked floor and unhappy memories.

"How did Audrey die? The mother superior would only say that she'd been murdered."

God help him! He didn't want to have to describe what had happened to her sister. He didn't want to remember, either. "You don't need to know more than that, do you?"

"I would rather hear the truth, however terrible, than have my mind run wild with speculation. Some of the furniture is missing, other pieces are not in their proper place, and there is that," she said, pointing to the stain.

She regarded him with pleading eyes. "Please, Gerrard, tell me what happened here, or I will imagine a thousand awful things, each worse than the last."

He well recalled Celeste's vivid imagination. There had been times she'd frightened them all, even Roland, with tales of ghosts and demons, ogres and monsters.

Besides, she was Audrey's only relative, so he supposed she had a right to know. And she would likely hear the horrific details from someone else, anyway.

Better, perhaps, that he should tell her and as gently as he could. "She had a bodyguard, a Scot named Duncan MacHeath. Apparently the man was in love with her and fiercely jealous. One day when her servants were out of the house something happened between them and he attacked and killed her. She fought for her life, but in the end she lost it."

"Not easily, then," Celeste replied, with a catch in her voice. She bowed her head. "Not quick."

"No," Gerrard said softly.

After a moment of heavy silence, Celeste raised her head and looked at him with unexpected composure. Perhaps the knowledge of what had happened to Audrey—the main details of it, at least—had indeed brought her some peace.

"What of the bodyguard?" she asked. "Is he imprisoned, or has he already been hanged?"

That, fortunately, was an easy question to answer. "He's dead, drowned in the river after he was wounded attacking Roland."

Her green eyes widened. "He attacked your brother, too?"

"Aye. He thought Roland was Audrey's lover."

"Roland? That's ridiculous!" Celeste exclaimed. "Audrey didn't even like…"

She fell silent and her cheeks colored with a blush.

Gerrard had often wondered how Audrey really felt about Roland. Now he knew.

Nor was he particularly surprised. Roland was hardly the sort of man to appeal to Celeste's older sister, at least until he'd been named heir and lord of Dunborough. "Aye, Duncan was wrong about that, but he nearly killed Roland just the same. Roland wounded him and

Duncan fell into the river afterward, trying to flee, and drowned. Too easy a death for a man who'd…"

Gerrard hesitated and looked away, but not fast enough.

"There is more," Celeste said with certainty. She walked toward him, her steady, determined gaze holding his. "This MacHeath molested Audrey, didn't he? A man angry enough to kill would be angry enough to forcefully take what a woman would not willingly give."

Gerrard was sorry she was so perceptive, or his features so revealing. "If there is justice in the next life, he will burn in hell forever."

"Did no one see any signs that she should fear him?"

"He was a fierce-looking fellow, but nobody ever thought Duncan MacHeath would hurt her. Surely she didn't, either, or she would have sent him away."

"Then there was no sign of his feelings for her? No hint that he might be jealous?"

"The man gave no sign of any feelings at all. He was a silent, sullen fellow."

"Where did my sister meet him? How did she come to hire him?"

"York, I believe. I don't think she ever told anyone here in Dunborough how he came to be in her employ."

Gerrard braced himself for more questions that would be difficult or uncomfortable to answer, but fortunately, Celeste seemed satisfied. She began to move around the room, putting the remaining furniture back in place. With a sorrowful sigh that touched his heart, she ran her hand over the unfinished needlepoint on a stand beside the window. Audrey had been skilled at needlework, among other things.

He wondered what Celeste planned to do now. The

burial had been weeks ago. "I suppose you'll be returning to Saint Agatha's."

"Not for a few days," she replied. She made a graceful sweeping gesture. "I shall have to deal with all of this first."

Of course. The land was held by the lord of Dunborough, but the house and its contents were hers, with a portion to go to the overlord. "Roland might waive the heriot, considering."

"What should be paid will be paid, and the rest I shall give to the church."

"You're welcome to reside at the castle for as long as necessary."

She shook her head. "I thank you for the offer, but I don't wish to impose."

"I assure you, you won't be." He gave her a smile. "I'm happy to offer the hospitality of Dunborough to an old friend."

"Again I thank you, but I would rather stay here until the house is sold."

"You brought servants with you?"

"No, I need none."

"You came *alone*?"

"Yes."

"What the devil was your mother superior thinking?" he demanded, appalled. The roads and byways were dangerous for a woman alone, especially a beautiful one, even if she was a nun. "Did she have no fears for your safety?"

In spite of his shocked and angry tone, Celeste remained remarkably calm. "I was never in any danger, nor did I ever have to walk far. Many farmers and carters are happy to help a nun, and many a nobleman and innkeeper pleased to give one shelter while asking nothing in return, just as you have done."

Although it took considerable effort, Gerrard managed to subdue his temper. "Be that as it may, you can't stay here alone, and none of Audrey's servants will come back to the house. They think it's haunted."

"As I told you, I need no servant, and even if Audrey's spirit does still linger here, I am quite safe. Alive or dead, she would never hurt me."

Gerrard felt like a fool for mentioning any supernatural concern, especially when there were other, more worldly reasons she couldn't spend the night alone in that house. "Rumors of your father's hidden wealth might tempt outlaws and thieves."

She sighed, but otherwise remained the same. "I suppose that's to be expected. Nevertheless, I'm not leaving. The locks are strong and God will protect me."

God? God had not been here to save Audrey. "Just in case He is otherwise occupied, I must insist you come to the castle as my guest."

Her expression turned wary and suspicious, a look he unfortunately recognized. Women who'd heard the worst of him looked at him like that. Then he remembered who else was at Saint Agatha's.

"You will be quite safe there. I give you my word."

He steeled himself for another refusal.

That did not come. Instead, she spoke as if she'd been agreeable all along. "Very well, and thank you."

He tried not to show his relief as he held out his arm to escort her.

She did not take it.

Instead, with her expression as placid as if they were in a cathedral, she walked out of the chamber.

At least she'd finally seen sense, he told himself as

he followed her outside. He went to his men and ordered them to continue to the castle, and told the fair-haired Hedley to take Snow to the stable for him.

By the time he'd done that, Celeste was at an outbuilding at the far end of the yard.

As he hurried to join her, Gerrard still couldn't quite believe she was there. When she hadn't arrived in the days after Audrey's death, he'd assumed she never would. Now here she was, and staying in the castle, too.

He wasn't the only one who'd changed. Celeste had been a lively little elf of a child who skipped and danced more than she walked, and laughed and sang. She'd had freckles and long brown hair that curled as if it had a life of its own.

Maybe it was long under that cap, veil and wimple. Or maybe it had been shorn to the scalp.

Not that it mattered what her hair was like, or how beautiful she was, even if she was more lovely than Audrey had been, something he hadn't foreseen.

She was a nun here to sell her family's goods and house, and then she would return to the convent.

When he reached her, she regarded him quizzically. "Where is Audrey's horse? She liked to ride, so I'm sure she had one."

"She had two and they were taken to the castle stables for safekeeping until we learned what you wanted done with them. Roland was going to ask you."

"I'll pay you for their keep."

He gave her another smile as he shook his head. "No need. Roland can afford it." Gerrard held out his arm again. "It will be my pleasure to escort you to the castle."

She didn't decline, but neither did she touch the arm

he offered. Instead, she once again left him to fall into step beside her.

No doubt she wasn't used to walking with a man.

From his hiding place behind a tree at the side of the D'Orleau house, Lewis watched the smug, arrogant Gerrard and the nun walk toward the village. He'd seen the patrol stop and suspected they were looking for thieves.

If outlaws were inside, they'd be sorry they tried to steal from that accursed place, the slender youth thought. Whatever other people believed, Sir Roland or his brother probably wouldn't be any more merciful than their father.

He'd nearly fallen over when Gerrard had come out of the house with a nun. Then he remembered that Audrey D'Orleau had a sister who'd been sent to a convent because she'd dared to attack Gerrard for cutting off her hair. That was probably who it was.

Lewis left his hiding place and followed the couple to the village. He ducked into an alley and hurried past the buildings lining the green, including his father's shop. That way he was able to get ahead of them and come out near the smithy, where he could see her face.

She was beautiful! Even more beautiful than Audrey! Indeed, she was far too beautiful to be a nun.

Maybe she wasn't a nun and maybe she wasn't Audrey's sister. Maybe she was a thief in disguise, come to search for the treasure. Gerrard must not think so, though, or he would have had her taken to the dungeon. Or perhaps he wouldn't, since she was young and pretty.

Lewis glanced at the rogue and got another shock. Gerrard looked as stone-faced as his brother. Usually he was all easy, affable charm when he was with a pretty girl.

Maybe then she really was a nun. Lewis almost laughed aloud to think of how disappointed the lecherous Gerrard must be if that was so.

On the other hand, given what Gerrard's father had been like, the lout might still try to have his way with her although she was a bride of Christ.

He'd tried to warn Esmerelda about Gerrard and she'd ignored him. Audrey D'Orleau hadn't been worth his help, despite her beauty.

Surely, Lewis thought, it was his Christian duty to protect this pretty, holy woman, this lovely creature undoubtedly too innocent and naive to see Gerrard as he truly was, even if he was only the chandler's son.

Chapter Two

As Celeste and Gerrard walked through the village of Dunborough, she was very aware of the tall, broad-shouldered man striding so confidently beside her. He had always been a bold and merry fellow, ready with a smile, and laughter in his shining brown eyes. Now he looked more like the cold, stern Roland.

Given the passage of time since she had last seen either of them, change was to be expected. She had been twelve years old when she had left Dunborough, and Gerrard and Roland fifteen.

It was also surely to be expected that whispers of surprise and speculation would follow them like a breeze through bracken. No doubt many would wonder who she was and what she was doing there, especially with Gerrard. Some, perhaps, would recognize her, although it had been ten years since she'd been sent to Saint Agatha's.

She cast her gaze toward the castle. The stronghold had grown more massive in the time that she'd been gone. Even when she lived there, Gerrard's father had always been adding to it, building more walls and towers, raising the money from the tenants' labors and merchants' fees, as well as fines for almost any infraction, no matter how minor.

She tried not to think about Sir Blane or the old days as she walked past the stalls and shops of the village, the smithy with its gaggle of old men outside and the well with a similar group of matrons, all eyeing them with curiosity. A gaggle of children, laughing and giggling, chased an inflated pig's bladder down a nearby alley. She turned away, ignoring the little pang of loss. The lack of children was a small price to pay for the peace and security of the religious life.

Gerrard was still silent as they reached the outer walls and proceeded through the thick, bossed gates, the grassy outer ward, the inner gate and then the inner ward, beneath the portcullis and through the final gate into the cobblestoned courtyard.

She said nothing, either, even when they reached the great hall.

It was just as huge and barren as she recalled, awe-inspiring in a bone-chilling way. It wasn't only the size that made it so. There was a central hearth and stone pillars, but no ornamentation of any kind. No pennants, no tapestries, no paint, no carving. The floor was covered in rushes and she could smell the fleabane, but that was the only herb she could detect. There was no hint of rosemary or anything else to add a pleasant odor.

Hounds of various ages and sizes rushed up to Gerrard and he gave them each a pat before telling them to sit. They did, looking up at him like an adoring chorus about to burst into song.

He had been a favorite of the dogs when he was a boy, too, no doubt because he gave them ample attention of the sort he rarely received from anyone save Eua, a serving woman who had been his nurse, and who had praised and spoiled him.

Indeed, the hall was so little changed, Celeste half expected to see Sir Blane seated on the dais, with his cruel features and even crueler sneer while he berated his sons.

She removed her cloak as a maidservant appeared from the entrance to the kitchen. The woman was young and not unattractive, slender and with chestnut-brown hair, the sort of girl a parent would have kept far from the hall of Dunborough when Sir Blane and his eldest son, Broderick, were alive.

More surprising still, the maidservant merely nodded when Gerrard asked her to bring refreshments. She didn't blush or smile at him as she took Celeste's cloak.

Not that it mattered to her if Gerrard was carrying on with a servant. If he were, he would be no different from most men of his rank. As for the other things she'd heard about him, rumors were often exaggerations, if not outright lies.

And poor Esmerelda might have been mistaken about where she was to meet him, or if she was to meet him at all. Given her own youthful infatuation with the handsome, merry Gerrard, Celeste could easily imagine a girl misinterpreting his words or intentions.

"Now then, this is better, isn't it?" he said with a familiar smile as they sat on finely carved chairs on the dais and the maidservant brought wine, bread and cheese. "Please, have some wine. It's very good. I'm working my way through Father's cellar."

Celeste accepted the wine and took a grateful sip. It was indeed very good wine, which meant it was a hundred times better than anything she'd had at the convent.

The mother superior kept all the best wine for herself or her favorites. The rest got much cheaper fare.

"It's been a long time," Gerrard said after he took a drink of wine, fixing his brown-eyed gaze upon her in a way that made her grateful for the nun's habit she wore.

"I heard about your father and Broderick," she said, knowing better than to offer him any sympathy for their demise.

Gerrard gave a little shrug with his right shoulder, as he used to do when they were children. "Then I suppose you know Roland is lord of Dunborough now."

She was surprised at how calm he sounded. "Yes, I did hear that."

"And that Roland is married?"

"Yes."

She had been even more surprised by that news. Audrey had often said Roland would have to marry a statue to find a wife as cold and stern as he, and Celeste had not disagreed.

"He's not here at the moment. He's at his wife's estate recovering from the wounds he got fighting Audrey's killer."

Gerrard didn't sound overly concerned. Nevertheless, she remembered what he'd said at the house, about Audrey's bodyguard nearly killing Roland. She'd been too overwhelmed by all that he had told her to inquire about Roland's state then. "So he *will* recover?"

"Yes. I'm garrison commander in charge of Dunborough until he returns."

Being the temporary lord was better than nothing, she supposed, although she nevertheless found it hard to believe that Gerrard could be so apparently accepting of his lower status.

"Things are better between us now," he added.

Much better, it seemed. "So Roland won't be angry if you drink all the best wine."

Gerrard laughed softly. As much as she'd remembered, she had forgotten the sound of his laughter and the way it seemed to brighten everything around him.

"It would take years to do that," he assured her, "even if I drank as much as I used to."

She had heard that he drank to excess, among other sins, so that was not a surprise. The surprise was that he was willing to admit it.

"Enough of what's happened here in Dunborough," he said. "I have some questions of my own to ask."

The last thing she wanted was to be interrogated by Gerrard. It would be worse than facing the mother superior at her most irate.

Celeste got to her feet. "If you don't mind, Gerrard, I'm quite tired and would like to rest."

A flash of irritation crossed his leanly handsome features and she waited for a protest.

Instead, he rose and called to the maidservant who had brought the refreshments. "Lizabet, show Sister Celeste to Roland's chamber."

He turned back to regard her with those brilliant dark brown eyes. "Or are you Sister Something Else?"

She kept her composure and silently prayed for forgiveness for the lie she was about to tell, along with her other recent sins. "I am Sister Augustine now."

"Until later, then, Sister."

"Yes, until later," she agreed as she turned to follow the maidservant to the stairs leading to the family chambers.

Despite her answer, though, she had already decided she would not be joining Gerrard in the hall later, or at any time. When she was with him, the past crowded in on her, the memories fresh and vivid, both the good ones and the bad.

Lizabet passed the first door. "That was Sir Blane's," she said, her voice hushed as if she thought someone would overhear.

"And that was Broderick's, the late lord's eldest son," she continued as they passed another. "I suppose you heard what happened to him? Killed by a woman! Sir Roland's wife's cousin. I can hardly imagine it."

"A woman?" Celeste repeated, unable to hide her surprise.

Gerrard's older brother had been a big man and a bully, fierce and cruel. To think that any woman had been able to—"

"Aye, it's true. He was about to kill the man Lady Mavis's cousin loved, and Lady Thomasina killed Broderick instead."

Sister Sylvester once said that a loved one in trouble could give a person great and unforeseen strength. It seemed that she was right. "From what I remember of Broderick, I find it difficult to be sorry, however he met his end."

Lizabet slid Celeste a questioning glance. "You know the family?"

"In a way. I'm Audrey D'Orleau's sister."

The young woman came to a startled halt. "I—I'm sorry, Sister!" she stammered.

She didn't wait for Celeste to respond, but quickly continued on their way.

"This chamber is Gerrard's when he sleeps here," she said, hurrying past another door, "and this is Sir Roland's." Lizabet opened the last door in the corridor and stood aside to let Celeste enter.

The room was a far cry from the way she'd imagined

any chamber of Roland's. She'd been expecting bare walls and few amenities, something Spartan in keeping with his cold, stern demeanor. Instead, there were tapestries on the wall, linen shutters as well as wooden ones on the window to keep out the cold, a dressing table and two brightly painted wooden chests for clothing. Against the far wall was the biggest bed Celeste had ever seen, made up with thick blankets and a silken coverlet. The bed curtains were a bright blue damask and there was even a carpet on the floor.

She immediately conjured a vision of a couple in that luxurious bed, a well-built man with shoulder-length hair making love to some faceless naked woman with long, curling brown tresses.

But what price did a woman pay for such luxury?

"Aye, it's big," Lizabet said with a smile when she saw where Celeste was looking. "Lady Mavis—Sir Roland's wife, that is—she asked for a new one the day she got here. Could have heard a cow cough a mile away when she said his bed wasn't big enough."

The maidservant blushed and lowered her eyes. "Sorry, Sister. I didn't mean to offend."

"It's all right," Celeste assured her, turning away to hide her own embarrassed blushes.

"Anything you need, Sister? Other than some warm water to wash?"

"No, that will be enough. Thank you."

"Then I'll be back soon with the water and some fresh linen," Lizabet said, leaving the room.

Celeste immediately removed her cap, veil and constricting wimple. She was relieved to be rid of them and glad to be alone, away from curious people and their stares and whispers, as well as Gerrard and the memories he brought back.

She unpinned her braid and ran her fingers through the thick, waving brown curls. As she did, she wondered what Gerrard would think if he could see her hair. More than once the mother superior had threatened to cut it off. More than once Celeste had avoided that.

It wasn't that she cherished the long locks so much. Her hair had been a sort of battleground, and every time she kept her curls, she felt the mother superior had lost a battle, although the war wouldn't be won until she was allowed to take her final vows.

Sighing, Celeste looked down at her hands and thought of all the times she'd tried, usually without success, to braid her sister's shining hair.

These were the same hands that Audrey had held tight when their father raged at their unhappy mother, proof that marriage was no sanctuary. The same hands that had scrubbed and cleaned and been clasped in prayer when Celeste displeased the mother superior at the convent, which was almost every day.

The same hands that she hoped would be carrying a cask of gold and jewels when she returned to Saint Agatha's, if what her father had said was true and he had hidden treasure in the house. She would present the cask to the bishop and tell him it was for the church on the condition that the mother superior be sent to a convent as far away from Saint Agatha's as possible. Then life at Saint Agatha's would be perfect. She would be safe and at peace, out of the world that had so much conflict and misery.

First, though, Celeste had to find her father's hidden hoard, and soon, in case the mother superior came looking for her.

Not that she regretted running away. She'd had no choice about that, for the mother superior never should have forbidden her to come back after her sister had died. Celeste was only sorry she'd stolen Sister Sylvester's habit, even though that, too, had been necessary, for safety on the road. As for claiming to be a nun, that was for safety, too.

Especially when she saw the look in Gerrard of Dunborough's eyes. She didn't want to be the object of any man's lust.

And certainly not his.

Norbert regarded his son with scornful disbelief as they stood in his shop, surrounded by candles of various sizes.

"Your eyesight must be going, boy," the well-dressed chandler sneered. "Gerrard and a nun? I'd as soon believe you could make a decent wick."

"I saw her myself," Lewis insisted, his tall, thin frame slightly hunched as if to protect himself from a blow. "They were coming from Audrey D'Orleau's house. Maybe she's her sister come to look for the treasure."

Norbert gave his pockmarked son a sour look. "There's no treasure in that house and you're a fool if you think so. And if that *is* Audrey's sister, she's probably come to sell the house and all the furnishings and maybe her sister's clothes, too. After all, a nun won't have any use for them."

Norbert stroked his beardless chin. "Put up the shutters. It's nearly time to close up for the day, anyway."

Lewis stared at him, dumbfounded, and wasn't fast enough to avoid the slap that stung his cheek.

"What are you gawking at, boy?" his father demanded.

"You've never closed the shop early before."

"I am today." His father licked his palm and smoothed down what remained of his hair, then straightened the leather belt around his narrow waist and long, dark green tunic. "I'm going to the castle to find out if that woman is Audrey's sister, and if she is, to offer my condolences."

"But you said Audrey was no better than a whore who got what she deserved."

Scowling, his father raised his arm and Lewis immediately moved out of reach. "Don't you dare repeat anything I said about Audrey D'Orleau to anybody," Norbert warned, "or you'll feel the back of my hand."

"I won't say a word," his son promised. "I wonder what Ewald will do when he hears about her."

Norbert's eyes widened. If he hadn't considered that, Lewis thought, his father was the fool, not him.

"It would be like that lout to try to see her first," Norbert muttered, although he was clearly preparing to do the same thing.

"She might be tired after her journey and unwilling to talk about business so soon after she's arrived," Lewis suggested.

Norbert frowned. "You may be right—for once," he grudgingly acknowledged. "Ewald probably won't be so thoughtful. On the other hand, if that *is* Audrey's sister, I wouldn't want him to get the house for a pittance. What does a woman, let alone a nun, know about the value of things? Now get those shutters up. I'm going to the castle."

"Aye, a nun and the prettiest one I ever saw," Lizabet said as she got a ewer for hot water in the kitchen. "And she says she's Audrey D'Orleau's sister!"

Baskets of beans and peas, lentils and leeks, were on low shelves nearby. On higher shelves were the spices, some very expensive indeed, for Sir Blane had liked fine food, at least for himself. Doors led into the larder and the buttery, another to the hall, and there were stairs for the servants to the family chambers.

"Audrey D'Orleau's sister?" Florian, the cook, cried, looking up from the pastry he was rolling on the large, flour-covered table. He was of middle height, not exactly fat but not slim, either, and could have been any age from twenty-five to forty. Tom, the skinny, freckled spit boy, likewise took his attention from the chickens he was turning over the fire in the enormous hearth.

Peg stopped shelling peas into the wooden bowl she had in her lap and rested her forearms on the rim of the bowl, regarding her companions gravely. She was a little older and a little plumper than Lizabet, and a little prettier, too. "Audrey D'Orleau's sister, eh? That would be Celeste. My ma told me she used to follow Audrey about like a puppy, and Gerrard, too, back in the day. Once, when the girls were at the castle—their father was doing some kind of business with old Sir Blane— Gerrard, rascal that he was, cut off Celeste's hair almost to her scalp. Something about a game, I think. Anyway, she had a devil of a fit—knocked him down and broke his collarbone. She got sent to Saint Agatha's after."

"Must have been some fit," Lizabet said. "And if she was a hoyden, well, all I can say is the convent's calmed her down. I can't imagine the nun up in Sir Roland's chamber raisin' her voice, let alone attacking someone."

"If she's Audrey's sister," Florian pointed out, wiping his forehead with a floury hand, "why didn't she come here sooner? It's been weeks since her sister died. Sir Roland sent word after, didn't he?"

"Aye," Peg said. "He sent a priest and Arnhelm went with him as escort." She lowered her voice as if about to reveal something shocking. "Arnhelm told me the mother superior at Saint Agatha's was the most hard, mean-spirited harridan he'd ever met. When he said why he'd come, she looked at him as if he'd come to sell a loaf of bread, and stale at that." Peg shook her head and leaned back. "Made Sir Roland look soft, Arnhelm said."

"God have mercy!" Florian murmured, aghast, while Lizabet's eyes filled with tears.

"A sister murdered, and to have to hear it from a woman like that!" she exclaimed.

"Aye," Peg agreed. "I wouldn't be surprised if it's the mother superior's fault Celeste took so long to get here. Probably had to say prayers for days."

"Tom!" Florian cried. "The chickens!"

The spit boy hurried back to his duty, the chickens only slightly charred.

"We had all best get back to work," the cook added.

Peg returned to shelling the peas and, with a heart full of sympathy, Lizabet took the hot water back to Sir Roland's chamber.

Celeste realized something had changed the moment Lizabet returned. She was like a candle that had been snuffed, and Celeste could guess why.

She didn't want to talk about Audrey, but she had other questions, ones she hoped Lizabet could answer. "I grew up in Dunborough, but I don't think we've ever met. Are you from here, too?" she asked as Lizabet poured warm water from the ewer into the basin on the washstand.

"Aye. My father's a woodcutter. I came to work in the castle after Sir Blane and Broderick died. Peg and me both. My father wouldn't let us come before that because of them, although we could have used the wages."

"Yet he had no such reservations about Sir Roland and Gerrard?"

Lizabet shook her head. "Not once Sir Roland was named the lord. My father was sure he'd see that the servants were safe. And ever since Sir Roland got wounded, Gerrard's been like a new man. It's as if he's seen the error of his ways. O'course, it could be Sir Roland's wife helped him see that. She wouldn't put up with any nonsense from Gerrard, that's for certain."

"Were you here when Sir Roland came home with his bride?"

"Indeed I was, Sister. We were all that surprised, I must say! Rumor was Sir Roland was going to DeLac to end any talk of an alliance with the lord there, and then he comes home with the man's daughter as his bride. Verdan—he come with her from DeLac, one of the escort—he said they was all surprised Lady Mavis agreed to the match and didn't run off. Spirited, she is, Sister. And beautiful, so maybe no wonder Sir Roland wanted her."

"I remember Sir Roland as a boy, and he didn't seem the sort of fellow to make a very pleasant husband. If it was a contracted marriage, perhaps his wife felt she had no choice. Indeed, I can find it in my heart to pity her."

Lizabet's eyes widened. "Oh, there's no need for that, Sister! It might have been arranged at the start, but it was a love match, too, for all that. She looks at him like he's the most wonderful man in the world and he looks at her like she's an angel come to earth. She's expecting already."

That might not be a surprise to Lizabet, but it seemed miraculous to Celeste.

"Verdan says…" Lizabet flushed and looked at her toes. "I'm sorry, Sister, I forgot you were a nun."

"Can't you pretend I'm not? And it's not as if I haven't heard things in the convent from the other women. Some of them are widows."

The maidservant looked around furtively, as if about to divulge a state secret. "Verdan says they go at it like rabbits, even in the woods one time where anybody might have seen them."

Now it was Celeste's turn to blush, and blush she did as she envisioned not Roland, but Gerrard, making love with a woman in the woods to assuage their carnal desires. Yet when desire died, what was left?

Celeste decided she'd asked enough questions. "I'm rather tired, Lizabet, and fear I'll be very poor company tonight. I'd rather take my meal here. Please convey my regrets to Gerrard."

Lizabet bit her lip and her brows contracted.

"If you'd rather not tell Gerrard—"

"No, no, it's no trouble, Sister," Lizabet replied, although her attitude implied otherwise.

Celeste gave the nervous maidservant a reassuring smile. "I shall tell him myself. Is he still in the hall?"

"I think he's in the outer ward with some of the men, Sister."

"Then I shall go to him there."

Chapter Three

Stripped to the waist and crouching, Gerrard circled his opponent. Gerrard was fast and clever, while Verdan, likewise wearing only breeches and boots despite the chilly air, was big and slow and sometimes clumsy. Nevertheless, Gerrard knew it would be a mistake to think Verdan was too slow to beat him or too stupid to guess his next move.

Other soldiers had formed a ring around the wrestlers, shouting encouragement and advice to both. Gerrard could also hear the wagers being made, albeit in quieter tones, especially from those who were betting against him.

"Now then, Verdan," he said, not taking his eyes from the man's bearded face, "it's time we put an end to this, don't you think? Concede and we can all go have an ale."

"Aye, give up!" one of the younger, thinner soldiers called out, stamping his feet. "I'm getting bloody cold!"

"Ah, shut yer gob," another, with darker hair and clean-shaven, retorted. "Verdan can take him. Show him, Verdan!"

"A southern man beat a Yorkshireman born and

bred?" a third demanded, scowling as he crossed thick
and powerful arms. "Not likely!"

"He's got half a head on Gerrard."

"Half a brain, too. Come on, Gerrard, take him
down!"

"Show 'im what a good soldier's made of, Verdan!"

"Show 'im what a Yorkshireman's made of!"

Gerrard suddenly feinted left, then dived right, grabbing Verdan around the legs and pulling him down. In
the next instant, more cheers went up as Gerrard flipped
the big man onto his stomach and sat on his back. Verdan flailed about, trying to grab him, but Gerrard got
his arms under his opponent's and his hands clasped
behind Verdan's neck. The bigger man was helpless.

"I had somethin' in me eye!" Verdan declared, spit-
ting out bits of grass as he continued to shift from side
to side as well as up and down, trying to buck Gerrard off.

"Come, man, you've lost," Gerrard said. "Admit it
and let's go get some ale. I think we've both worked up
a mighty thirst. And since you're no doubt exhausted,
I'll excuse you from guard duty tonight."

"Well, since you put it that way..." Verdan stopped
moving and let Gerrard climb off him.

Grinning, Gerrard reached down to help the soldier
to his feet. Bets were paid off, some grudgingly, while
the two combatants wiped the perspiration from their
faces, put on their shirts and tunics, Gerrard's of wool
and Verdan's of boiled leather. Before the contest, Gerrard had taken a loose bit of thread from the hem of his
tunic and tied back his hair to keep it off his face, and
he didn't bother to undo it. "As for the rest of you men, I
expect to find all your weapons clean and sharp tomorrow," he said. "And nobody the worse for drink, myself

included," he added ruefully, earning chuckles from the men, who began to move toward the castle gate.

He clapped a hand on Verdan's broad shoulder. "So, your mother still won't come to Yorkshire?"

"Not yet. But Arnhelm and me have hope," Verdan replied, grinning and revealing unexpectedly good teeth.

Out of the corner of his eye, Gerrard noticed the thin chandler scurrying toward them, his woolen tunic flapping about his ankles, his silk-lined cloak fluttering behind him.

"Sweet Mother Mary, what the devil is he doing here?" he muttered under his breath before he addressed Verdan again. "You go ahead. The chandler must have business to discuss."

Although what that could possibly be, Gerrard had no idea. He hoped it wouldn't take long, either. He had never liked the greedy little man who had browbeaten his late wife and treated his son like a lackey.

"Greetings, Norbert," he said as the panting chandler reached him. "What brings you to the castle?"

"I've come to give my condolences to Audrey's sister. I heard that she had come."

Gerrard frowned. "Yes, she has, and you wish to speak with Sister Augustine?" he asked as Norbert shifted from foot to foot like a horse nervously awaiting the start of a race.

The last thing Celeste—or anyone—needed was to talk to this fellow, about anything.

"If that's what Audrey D'Orleau's sister is called now, yes," the chandler replied with a hint of defiance.

That was not something to encourage Gerrard to grant his request. "Sister Augustine is resting and cannot be disturbed."

Norbert frowned and looked far from pleased. His state of mind, however, was not Gerrard's concern.

"Perhaps you'll be good enough to tell her I was here," Norbert said.

"Perhaps," Gerrard replied with a smile that was not meant to be pleasant.

"Now see here, Gerrard—" Norbert began. He fell silent when he saw the look in Gerrard's eyes. "Oh, very well!"

The chandler turned on his heel and started back to the inner gate just as it opened to admit another man, this one also richly dressed, but plump and darkly bearded. His tunic was shorter and more embellished, with an embroidered hem and neck. His boots were of fine leather, as were his bossed belt and gauntlet gloves.

Ewald. Of course. The dealer in hides and tallow was as broad and boisterous as Norbert was thin and wheedling, but equally as greedy. The two were like vultures come hurrying to the battlefield, and Celeste a corpse.

"Good day, Gerrard! And you, too, Norbert!" Ewald declared. "Why am I not surprised that you're here already, Norbert? That nosy son of yours should be a spy for the king."

"I doubt *you've* come to pass the time of day," Norbert retorted. "You want to see her, too, don't you?"

Ewald's cheeks flushed. "Well…" he began, drawing the word out as he rocked back and forth on his heels, his thumbs tucked in his wide leather belt beneath his protruding belly, "as a matter of fact, I do. To give her my sympathy on her sister's death. A bad business, that, a very bad business."

Business had nothing to do with it, Gerrard thought sourly. Warped and thwarted love did. "Unfortunately,

Sister Augustine is resting and cannot be disturbed," he said firmly.

Norbert, not surprisingly, continued to scowl, while Ewald, equally not surprisingly, smiled like a man who'd won a bet.

"Tomorrow will do just as well," the tanner jovially replied. "Tell her I was here, if you will, and I'll be delighted to speak with her at a time of her convenience. I'll offer her a very good price for the house."

"I will do no such thing," Gerrard said. "You will wait to discuss business with her when she comes to you, and not before. Now I give you good day, gentlemen."

With a look of sly triumph, Norbert nodded and started toward the gate. Only slightly subdued, Ewald bowed and followed.

Carrion crows, the pair of them, and Gerrard would be damned before he'd tell Celeste that they'd been there. He wasn't their messenger and she didn't need to be bothered, he thought as he walked back to the gate.

He came to a startled halt. Celeste—Sister Augustine— was gliding toward him across the grass, the ends of her veil lifting in the breeze. Even in a nun's habit, she looked like royalty, poised and proud and beautiful.

"I thought you were resting," he said, baffled by her presence and wondering if he should have let Norbert and Ewald meet her.

"I *am* rather weary," she replied, her lips set in a thin line, "so if it's possible, I'd prefer to have the evening meal in Roland's chamber. Alone."

He was glad he'd sent the chandler and the tanner away, yet couldn't help feeling somewhat dismayed by her manner and that she apparently didn't want to dine with him, either. Still, that might be for the best. She aroused old memories and some of them were best forgotten.And if she hated him, he could hardly blame her. It was his fault she'd been sent to Saint Agatha's.

"Since you're a guest, you're free to do as you like," he said. "I'll have the meal and some wine sent up to the chamber in due course."

She nodded and her lips curved up into a little smile. A very little smile. "Thank you, Gerrard."

After that, she walked gracefully away, leaving him to ponder what she would think of him if she ever found out *all* that had happened while she was in the convent.

Later that night, Gerrard sat alone on the dais in the great hall of Dunborough. The evening meal had been served, and most of the soldiers not on guard duty had already returned to the barracks or bedded down on pallets in the hall, along with the ever-present hounds. A few of the household servants were still awake and talking quietly in a corner. The female servants had their own quarters above the kitchen, while the rest either slept in the kitchen or in the loft above the stalls where the grooms and stable boys also bedded down.

Gerrard glanced at the stairs leading to the family chambers. What would Celeste think if she knew about his dealings with her sister? And the offer Roland had made to him?

He had planned to use Audrey's wealth for his own ends and had even been prepared to marry her to get it, although that hadn't been his idea. It had been Audrey's suggestion that he bribe the king to give him Dunborough and a title. When he and Audrey wed, she would have had what she desired most—a powerful and titled husband—and he would have had his heart's desire, the estate of Dunborough and the power to rule it.

Now Audrey was dead and Roland had another estate,

thanks to his marriage, so he had offered Dunborough to Gerrard, pending the king's approval.

Although Roland was no doubt sincere, Gerrard still couldn't quite believe that he would willingly give up the estate they both had craved for so long, especially after his father's will revealed Roland was indeed the elder twin and given the way Gerrard had treated Roland all these years. But he had.

It was tempting to accept Roland's offer, even though that would mean being beholden to his brother for the rest of his life. And when he remembered that he'd been willing to use Audrey D'Orleau and her wealth to get what he wanted, he felt so ashamed, it seemed better to leave Dunborough and never return.

Yet to give up the chance of being the lord of Dunborough! He had yearned for that for as long as he could remember.

Gerrard abruptly rose and started for the door, grabbing his cloak from a peg before he went out. It did no good to sit and brood. That was the sort of thing Roland would do. Better to be doing something—anything—than mope.

He'd go to the tavern in the village. It was always lively, even at this time of night. There were other places a man could find companionship of a different sort, but he'd given that up along with too much ale.

Gerrard stepped into the yard. A quick glance confirmed that the watchmen were on the wall walk and two guards stood at the gate.

A cold Yorkshire wind sent clouds scudding across the half-moon and he sniffed the air, wondering if it would snow before morning. Hard to say.

How much he hated winter and the cold that forced him to spend too much time indoors! He felt imprisoned when the weather was too bad to ride. Perhaps that was what being in a convent was like, and not only in the winter. Considering that and celibacy, he knew he could never stay in such a place. He would flee at the first opportunity.

A movement near the large oak beside the inner wall caught his eye. Someone clad in a long dark cloak was moving in the shadows near the kitchen.

"You there, what are you doing?" he demanded as he hurried forward.

Celeste—Sister Augustine—stepped out of the shadows. At the same time, one of the soldiers appeared on the wall walk above and the guards at the gate charged toward her.

"All's well," Gerrard called to them. "You can go back to your posts."

They obeyed and he turned to face Celeste, trying not to notice her large eyes or full lips. "You had better stay inside at night. My men are all trained archers. You might have been mistaken for an intruder and shot."

"Fortunately, I was not."

Her voice was as placid as her expression. Where *had* that lively, daring girl gone? He would have wagered much that even the nuns couldn't stifle her vivacity, although apparently they had.

"Is anything the matter?" he asked. "Is there something you require?"

Dolt! If she wanted something, she would go to the hall and summon a servant, not wander about the yard like a lost soul.

"The chamber is very comfortable, thank you," she replied. "I simply couldn't sleep. And you?"

"I often check to make sure the watch is awake," he lied. He never did that. He didn't have to. His father had severely punished any man caught sleeping at his post, and it was still too soon after his father's death for the men to realize neither he nor Roland would ever be as cruel.

Celeste nodded at the oak tree. "That's the tree we climbed that All Hallow's Eve, isn't it?"

The memory rose up as vividly as if it had been yesterday. He and Roland had gotten out of the castle by climbing the oak, then slipping out a postern gate, one All Hallow's Eve. They'd wanted to go to the village to see the bonfire. Audrey and Celeste were already there when they arrived. Audrey claimed she didn't believe they'd done anything so bold as climb over the castle wall like thieves. Sir Blane must have let them come.

Determined to prove her wrong, Gerrard had suggested that she return with them the same way and spend the night in the hayloft. Roland had been against the idea from the first. It would be too dangerous. She surely couldn't climb as well and they'd all be caught and punished.

Audrey had laughed at Roland, and Gerrard and she had called him a grumpy old woman and a host of other unflattering names until he gave in.

Celeste had begged to go along and finally they had let her. She had kept up with them, and never made a whimper, even after they were caught, as Roland had predicted. Audrey and Celeste had been escorted home, for their father was too wealthy to offend, while the twins had been beaten and forced to stand until dawn.

"I was so afraid I'd fall," Celeste murmured, moving back into the shadows.

"You never gave any sign you were afraid," Gerrard replied, following her. "I thought you were very brave."

She laughed softly, a sound that roused more memories. Of chasing her through the forest, but never quite catching her. The admiring look in her eyes when he told a funny story. The time he'd suggested they play a kissing game and she had laughed and blushed and run away.

He wanted to kiss her now.

She is a nun, he reminded himself, *even if she's also a beautiful woman.* "I was afraid, too," he confessed.

Glistening in the moonlight, her large eyes widened with a look of wonderment. "I didn't think you were afraid of anything."

She is a nun. "I was afraid of many things, my father most of all."

"So was I."

"Everyone was frightened of him."

"I meant my own. He used to fly into terrible tempers. Audrey and I would hide, and she would tell me stories to make me feel better."

"I never knew that." Even as a girl, Audrey had seemed too cold and calculating to offer a younger sister comfort.

"I realize she had her faults, but I loved her very much," Celeste whispered, her voice full of sorrow.

Nun or not, there seemed but one thing to do. Gerrard put his arms around her and pulled her into his embrace.

He meant only to offer comfort, yet heat coursed through his body as her breasts pressed against his chest. He thought of her full lips so close to his own. All he need do was put a knuckle beneath her chin and tilt her head up to kiss her.

They were in shadow. No light shone from the narrow windows nearby. No one could see them.

She is a nun! She is a nun!

"I'm sorry I broke your collarbone that day, Gerrard," she said softly.

"I'm sorry I cut off your hair," he replied just as quietly.

If he were wise, he would move away. Leave her. Go to the farthest corner of the castle. Or the village.

He wasn't wise.

Chapter Four

Celeste knew what Gerrard was going to do before he did it. What he shouldn't do, especially if he thought she was a nun.

She also knew what she ought to do. Stop him. Move away. Leave. Go back to her chamber.

She didn't. She couldn't. For too long she had dreamed of being in Gerrard's arms. For too many years he'd been her idea of a hero, the ideal man. Of all the worldly longings she'd sought to stifle in the convent, the most difficult was the dream of being held in Gerrard's arms with his lips upon hers.

So when he kissed her as she'd always imagined, she could not resist. She couldn't protest, for his kiss was even more wonderful and exciting than her most vivid dreams, and some of them had been very vivid indeed.

His embrace tightened about her and her body seemed to become like liquid wax in his arms, without bones or muscles or sinews. Her only strength seemed to be in her hands as she clutched his shoulders to keep from falling, and to continue kissing him.

Her desire increased, heating her blood and sending it throbbing through her body. This was the sort of passionate encounter some of the girls had talked of. Being with the men they loved, and how they'd felt in their arms.

They hadn't described the yearning building within her, the need for something more than lips on lips, or that a man might slide his hand along her arm and down her side, letting it rest on her hip before he began to slowly glide his palm up toward her breast.

When Gerrard cupped her there, she opened her lips to gasp, and his tongue slid into her mouth—a shocking, unexpected act she had never heard of or imagined.

Surprise and shame hit her like twin blows of a hammer.

Horrified by her own weakness, she put her hands on his chest and shoved him away. She knew too well what men were like, how violent and angry they could get, yet it seemed she'd forgoteen everything for a moment's fleeting pleasure. "Stop! How could you?"

His brow furrowed, Gerrard spread his arms wide as he moved back. "I only meant to—"

"What?" she demanded, hiding her regret and remorse behind anger of her own. "Seduce me?"

His expression hardened and his lips became a grim, hard line, like Roland's. Like Broderick's and, yes, like their father's. "No, that was not my intention."

"I am a nun!"

"I forgot."

"Forgot?" she repeated incredulously, as if she'd never heard anything so ridiculous.

"That's the truth, whether you believe it or not," he defensively replied. "And it wasn't my idea to move farther back beneath the tree. It was you who led us here."

"I thought..." What had she been thinking? She had no explanation. Nevertheless, she gave him one.

"I thought it would be more sheltered from the wind and so easier to talk. And that was no excuse to kiss me."

"I may have begun the kiss, but you were just as eager once I did."

"I was not!" she protested, although that was a lie. A terrible, shameful lie. "You caught me off guard."

He made a sweeping bow and his expression became a sort of mocking grin. She'd seen that look on his face before, but never had it been directed at her.

She didn't want to see it now, even if she had been in the wrong to accuse him so unjustly, and even if it was better than his anger.

"I beg your forgiveness, Sister Augustine," he said, his voice smooth and full of derision. "I promise I'll never surprise you again. Now I give you good night and I hope you'll have very pleasant dreams."

In spite of his sardonic attitude, she saw something else in his eyes that filled her with dismay and regret and shame. She had hurt him. He'd been hurt many times in the past by his father and his brothers and now she had hurt him, too.

Gerrard turned on his heel and started across the yard toward the gate, chin up, back straight, like a conquering hero.

A hero she had wounded.

Another sin to beg forgiveness for, like letting him kiss and caress her.

No, the greater sin was his, she told herself as she hurried back to Roland's chamber. Gerrard had kissed her first. That was the truth, whatever else had happened.

They were never going to kiss again. She would see to that.

They must never kiss again. She was going to be a nun. She wanted that more than anything in this world or the next. Then she would be protected, secure and close to God. She would be free of worldly cares and concerns and no longer troubled by the desires of the flesh. She would be away from violence and hatred and quarrels, men and women arguing far into the night regardless of the children who could hear, trembling and clutching each other for comfort in the dark.

She would be safe and maybe even happy, and if she had to give up certain longings and desires, it would surely be worth it.

The two guards at the inner gate snapped to attention as Gerrard approached. The garrison commander frowned when he saw that one of the guards was Verdan.

"What are you doing here?" he demanded. "I gave you leave from duty."

"Well, sir, it's like this," Verdan replied, shifting his spear from one hand to the other. "The roster was all made up and one of the lads has a sweetheart in the village and he was plannin' to see her, and he'd have to take my place, so—"

"Oh, very well. Spare me your explanation. I, too, am going to the village and I likely won't be back until morning. And the next time you're excused from duty, Verdan, stay excused. I won't make such an offer a third time."

"Yes, sir," the soldier gruffly replied as young Hedley opened the smaller wicket gate.

After Gerrard had passed through and Hedley closed the gate, Verdan regarded his fellow soldier with dismay. "I didn't think he'd be cross because I was on duty. And where's he goin' this time o' night? You don't think he's goin' back to his old ways, do ya?"

"I hope not," Hedley glumly replied. "Maybe Sister

Augustine was trying to talk him into staying in the castle."

"What?"

"He was talking to the nun who came today, there by the tree."

"Never!" Verdan exclaimed, although Hedley was famous for his eyesight. He could hit an apple with an arrow from fifty yards.

"Aye, he was. At least he met her there," Hedley said. "Then they moved under the tree. I couldn't see them after that."

"Maybe you're right, and she got wind he was goin' to the village and tried to put a stop to it. He wouldn't like that. No wonder he looked so peeved."

"Aye," Hedley agreed, leaning on his spear. "I could have sworn it was Sir Roland standing here."

"Reckon there's anything we ought to do?"

"Like what? We can't stop Gerrard if he takes a notion to go to the village at night. He's the garrison commander. And he might only have said he was going to the village and won't be back till morning to see if we're slack on the watch, and he'll circle round and check again. He's a clever one, after all, and takes his duties serious."

Verdan hitched up his sword belt. "Aye, that's true enough. Still, we'd best keep our eyes open. I like Gerrard, but our first duty's to Sir Roland. He's the lord of Dunborough, and he ought to know if his brother's a sot or up to no good, no matter how much we hope he ain't."

The proprietor of the Cock's Crow smiled broadly as Gerrard entered the smoky confines of the tavern. "Greetings, Gerrard! It's been a while since you've darkened our door."

"A mug of ale," Gerrard said as he sat at a table in a far corner of the taproom, which smelled not only of smoke from the fire in the hearth, but also ale and beef stew, herb-strewn rushes on the floor and the bodies of hardworking men taking their ease after a day of toil.

"Aye, sir, aye!" Matheus replied. He hurried to bring it, setting it down and standing back. "Anything else you want?"

"A bed for the night—and just a bed," Gerrard added when he saw Matheus's expression. There had been times a woman had joined him there, but not tonight and not for days. Not since he'd returned from DeLac after Roland had been attacked.

"Of course, sir! And more ale when that one's finished?"

"Perhaps."

Ignoring the curious looks from the other customers, Gerrard took a swallow of the excellent ale, then wrapped his hands around the cup. He would have this one drink. It wouldn't be wise to get drunk, not with Celeste—Sister Augustine—no doubt ready to denounce him for a drunkard as well as a libertine.

Even though she'd returned his kiss with equal passion, he still felt like the most disgusting reprobate in the kingdom—deservedly so. Only weeks ago he had been what gossip and rumor claimed he was: a rogue and a wastrel, carrying on with no concern for whom he hurt or why, seeking to annoy Roland, assuage his own desires and assert some independence.

He'd chosen for his friends young men with little to recommend them except their agreement that he deserved to be lord of Dunborough more than his brother.

Gerrard had paid for his pleasure, cheated at games

of sport and toyed with women's hearts, although he truly hadn't meant for Esmerelda to get hurt.

Ever since the attack on Roland, though, he'd kept away from taverns, gambling dens and unwholesome women. He'd busied himself with training the men and the business of the estate, as much as he was able. He'd sought to lead a better, more respectable life and thought he'd been succeeding.

Until today. Until tonight, when his desire had compelled him to take a nun into his arms.

Perhaps he truly was his father's son.

No, he was not. If his father had wanted Celeste, he would have taken her, no matter what she said or did, and even if she'd fought him tooth and nail.

Gerrard ran his hand through his hair. God help him, why had he kissed her?

The first answers came to him in Roland's censorious voice. *Because you wanted to and didn't care about the consequences. Because she's pretty and you have a weakness for pretty girls.*

Yet in his heart he knew there was more to it than that. Standing so close to her in the dark, he had felt as he had when they were younger, when he was afraid of his father and brothers and she had regarded him with awe and admiration, as if he could do anything. Be anything.

And then what had he done? He'd lost his temper over some stupid game, held her down and cut off her lovely, curling hair.

His feelings had overruled his head tonight, too. Was he never going to be master of himself? Why could he not foresee the consequences of his actions, especially the ones that would cause hurt and pain and anger?

He would. He must.

He drained his ale and took himself to bed.

* * *

Just past dawn the next morning, Celeste walked across the courtyard toward the gate. The weak November sun did little to warm the air and frost was heavy on the ground, but at least it wasn't snowing.

Mercifully, and perhaps in answer to her prayers, Gerrard hadn't been in the hall this morning, nor had any of the servants acted as if there had been any talk of improper behavior on her part.

For a long time last night she'd prayed for forgiveness for her lust, and the strength to resist the temptation Gerrard embodied. In future, she vowed, she'd have as little to do with him as possible. If Roland returned soon, she might never have to speak to Gerrard again.

Which was what she wanted, just as she needed… wanted…to be safe and secure in the religious life.

Nevertheless, and despite what had happened between them, she couldn't help wishing that the tales told about Gerrard weren't true. That he wasn't a drunkard and lust-filled libertine. That he was a better man than his father and older brother, and more like the hero of a ballad than the wastrel gossip and rumor said he was.

That she was right to still have hope that Esmerelda had unjustly blamed him for what had happened to her. Even if she never saw him again, she wanted to think of him as a good man.

As Celeste got closer to the gate, she couldn't be sure if the guards were the same men who'd been on duty last night. In case they were and had seen that shameful embrace, she would do her very best imitation of the always serene Sister Sylvester. That way they might have doubts about who had been with Gerrard under the tree.

"Good day," she said with a pleasant smile when she reached them. "Please open the gate."

The two men exchanged wary glances.

"Is there some reason you should not?" she sweetly inquired.

"Not at all, Sister," the older, bearded one replied, moving to open the wicket gate for her.

With a nod of thanks she lifted her skirts to pass over the threshold—and nearly bumped into Gerrard.

He fell back a step and his surprise soon gave way to that slightly mocking grin. "Where might you be going this fine morning, Sister Augustine?"

He didn't look the worse for drink, but that didn't mean he wasn't. She had learned from her father that a man could be far from sober and still look it.

Perhaps he'd been in his cups last night when he'd kissed her. She hadn't considered that.

Even if he had been, that didn't excuse him. Indeed, if anything, it magnified his offense.

"Since I am a guest, I don't believe I need answer that question," she replied.

"No, you don't," he agreed with exaggerated courtesy as he stepped aside. "After you, Sister."

"Good day, Gerrard," she replied, walking briskly past him. She did not look back to see what, if anything, he did as she continued toward the village and her family's home.

She passed a group of old men gathered by the smithy and several servants already gossiping by the well. More than one gave her a quizzical look, and one of the women immediately covered her mouth and turned aside to whisper to another. About her? About Audrey? About their father and his mistreatment of their mother, or had those tales of quarrels, harsh words and bruises been forgotten long ago?

As Celeste quickened her pace, a youth of about sixteen, with sandy hair and a pockmarked face, paused while removing the shutters of a shop. He gave her a shy smile and nodded a hello, reminding her that not everyone in Dunborough was regarding her with curiosity.

A baby cried from within a nearby house and a woman began a lullaby, soft and low and tender. Again she felt that yearning ache, and she pictured herself by a glowing hearth with a dark-haired baby at her breast.

But the image quickly faded, for she had already decided what her fate would be.

Reaching the house, she slipped the key into the sturdy lock, silently blessing Audrey for making sure she had a key, and for telling her to hide it. Otherwise, she would have turned it over to the mother superior, who would surely have taken as long to "find" it as she had to send word to Ireland that Celeste should return to the convent. There was news of her family, the message had said, giving no hint of what Celeste was going to hear when she arrived back from her pilgrimage, which had been more of an exile.

Celeste pushed open the heavy door and stepped into the empty house. As she had told Gerrard, she didn't fear ghosts, but there were unwelcome memories and, worst of all, no Audrey there to greet her and remind her of the few happy times they'd shared.

She hurried past the main chamber with that horrible stain, trying not to envision what had happened there or imagine a man capable of such jealous rage that he could brutally attack a woman he claimed to love.

In the kitchen at the back of the house, a pot with a ladle still in it hung over the cold ashes in the hearth. A basket of laundry, wrinkled and musty, lay on its side beside the worktable, its contents spilled onto the floor. There were spoons and a wooden bowl in the stone sink. The room looked as if it had been suddenly, abruptly abandoned, as it probably had.

She went to the larder, noting that the door stood slightly open. That was not so surprising if the servants had fled quickly. Inside, a few mice had been at work, tearing open a sack of lentils and another of peas to get at the contents, although the destruction was less than might have been expected. Fortunately, there were plenty of other stores that were untouched, enough to last her for several days.

Her eyes narrowed as she ventured farther into the storeroom. The contents on the shelves were as neat and tidy as Audrey would have wanted, but there was only the slightest coating of dust on the shelves. To be sure, the nearly closed door might explain that, but perhaps somebody else had been there looking for—

Two eyes gleamed in the dark.

She gave a little shriek and jumped back, her heart racing until she realized it was a cat. A big orange cat. The animal studied her solemnly, then jumped down and walked out of the larder, bushy tail swishing, as if this was his house and she an unwelcome intruder.

His presence likely explained the lack of dust, given the size of his tail.

"Have you been keeping the mice at bay, too?" she asked, reaching down to stroke it.

The cat ran under the worktable, then crouched and stared at her again.

"Very well, I'll leave you alone," she said, before she went to the servants' stairs that led up to the second floor, where the bedchambers were.

She peered into the one she had shared with Audrey. The shutters were closed and the room dim. Nevertheless, she could see well enough to tell that the two cots were still there, albeit without any bedding. Otherwise, the space was empty.

Audrey must have taken her parents' bedchamber for her own.

It, too, was dark, the shutters closed. Celeste could make out the bed, though, and the shape of other furnishings. She felt the softness of a carpet beneath her feet as she went to the window and opened both the cloth and wooden shutters. Cold air streamed into the room, as well as light, so she hurried to close the cloth shutters over the opening before she turned back.

Yes, the bed was the same; the opulent silken hangings and bedding, however, were not. A large and colorful tapestry depicting a colorful garden hung on the wall opposite. A bronze brazier with a full bowl of coal stood near the dressing table.

She spotted a flint and steel on the table and, taking some straw from the mattress beneath the feather bed, kindled a fire. Grateful for the warmth, she also lit what was left of a candle on the dressing table, noting the fine sandalwood combs, the carved box of hairpins, the brush and, most expensive of all, a mirror.

She couldn't resist looking at her reflection, so she did—and gasped. Why, she looked like Audrey! Although God didn't care what she looked like, and neither should she, Celeste couldn't subdue a little thrill to discover that she resembled the sister everyone called a beauty more than she remembered.

Trying to dismiss such vain thoughts, she began to examine the contents of the largest wooden chest. It was full of clothes—costly gowns and fine linen shifts, silken stockings, veils and beaded caps. These things must have cost a great deal of money...

Audrey must have found their father's treasure! How else would she have been able to afford all these clothes and run the household, too?

How much was left and where was it? There had to be a considerable amount still. Many times their father had bragged to their mother that he was rich as Croesus and if she left him, she would never see a penny of his wealth.

Rummaging again in the chest, Celeste found a carved wooden box and opened it to find a host of jewelry—rings and necklaces, as well as broaches and pins that glittered red and green and blue and white among their golden settings.

Trembling with excitement, she took the box to the window, setting it on the sill. The value of these things would surely be enough to bribe...encourage...the bishop to send the mother superior away from Saint Agatha's, perhaps even to the far reaches of Scotland.

Celeste drew out a ruby necklace and held it up to the window to examine it closely.

Her stomach knotted.

The one lesson their father had purposefully taught them was how to tell the difference between real gems and fake, "so you won't be cheated by charlatans, even if you're only women and all women are mostly fools."

The rubies were paste and a swift examination proved the other jewels were false, too, as well as the gold that bound them.

These couldn't be part of the wealth her father had hidden.

Another moment's reflection gave her some relief. Of course Audrey wouldn't keep real jewels in so obvious a hiding place, even if she had a fierce Scot to guard the house. Any thief who managed to get in and over-power him would look in the chests. Audrey must have found a better hiding spot.

A loud series of knocks rattled the door at the front of the house.

She went to the window and opened the cloth shut-ters to look into the yard, trying to see who it might be. Unfortunately, she couldn't. However, there was no white horse or group of soldiers outside her gates, so it couldn't be Gerrard, not that there was any reason for him to come here. As for anyone else, she was in no mood to entertain inquisitive visitors.

Perhaps if she stayed upstairs and didn't answer, whoever it was would go away.

The knocking commenced again, just as loud and persistent. If it *was* Gerrard, he was stubborn enough to knock for a very long time, especially if he was sure she was there.

Her lips pursed, Celeste adjusted her veil and wimple and went to deal with whoever was pounding so insis-tently on her door.

Chapter Five

It was not Gerrard. A thin man wearing a dark brown cloak over a fawn-colored tunic cinched with a tooled leather belt stood on the threshold. There was something about his narrow face, pale blue eyes and long nose that nudged the edge of her memory, but she couldn't come up with a name.

"Good day, Celeste! Or I suppose I should say, Sister! Welcome back to Dunborough." A sorrowful frown came to the man's homely face. "Although naturally we're all upset at the reason why. Your dear sister will be much missed."

His name came to her. "Norbert, isn't it?"

"Indeed, indeed!" he cried with delight. "To think that you remember me!"

He wouldn't have been so pleased if he knew that she remembered him as a skinny young man several years older than Roland and Gerrard, a nasty fellow Audrey called "Nosy Norbert." Since he was the first of the villagers to come to call, she suspected that name would still apply.

"How delightful to have you back home in Dunborough!" he exclaimed as he stepped over the threshold, although she hadn't invited him to enter. He half turned and made a swift, impatient gesture for someone on the other side of the door to enter, too.

The slender, pockmarked youth who'd been taking down the shutters of the shop sidled into the house, his head bowed, his cheeks aflame with a blush. His cloak was of a lesser quality than the older man's and frayed about the edges. His short tunic exposed lean legs and knobby knees, and his boots looked old enough to be castoffs.

"This is my son, Lewis," Norbert said. She recalled that Norbert's father had been a chandler and the shop that the young man had been opening had been full of candles. Clearly Norbert had become a candle maker, too.

"I'm pleased to meet you, Lewis," she replied, hoping to dispel some of the lad's obvious embarrassment.

Lewis raised his head and bright blue eyes met hers. His gaze was unexpectedly intense before he looked down again and mumbled, "Good day, Sister."

Disconcerted by the boldness of that swift glance so at odds with the rest of his demeanor, she turned toward his father.

"Forgive him, Sister," Norbert said, regarding his son with displeasure. "He's a shy lad. Takes after his late mother that way."

That glance had been anything but shy. Nevertheless, Celeste let the remark pass. "It's a pleasure to meet a modest young man. So many are not these days."

"That is sadly true," Norbert agreed. He came farther into the house. "I hope, Sister, that you have not had any impertinence from that young rogue in the castle."

She certainly wasn't going to tell Norbert about her dealings with Gerrard. "If you mean the garrison commander," she replied, "he has been courteous and accommodating."

Most of the time.

"I'm glad to hear it, Sister, very glad!" Norbert cried. "When I heard you'd spent the night there, I confess I feared…"

He fell awkwardly silent, and she wasn't about to ease his discomfort.

"If you'll excuse me, I have business to attend to," she said. "I thank you for coming, Norbert, and I'm happy to have made your acquaintance, Lewis."

"Anything I can do to help, you have only to ask," Norbert replied. "I was a good friend of your sister's. A very good friend."

Celeste doubted that, given what Audrey used to call him.

"Ah, Norbert! Trust you to be first to pay a call on a lovely lady!" a voice boomed from the doorway.

A middle-aged man dressed in a fur-lined red cloak and long black tunic strode into the house. He had a belt of silver links around his broad middle, and his hair was cut in the Norman fashion.

It was not a flattering style for a man with such full cheeks, and his eyes above his wide nose were beady and rather too shrewd.

Nevertheless, she smiled in return. "Greetings, sir."

"You must forgive me for not waiting to be introduced properly," he declared. "I came as soon as I heard you'd returned to the house." His gaze darted to Norbert, who did not hide a scowl. "I wanted to express my condolences. I cared very much for your sister."

"Thank you…?"

"Ewald!" he bellowed. "Ewald of York, and Dunborough, too."

"He deals in hides and tallow," Norbert clarified, his tone implying that Ewald's profession merited disdain.

"Indeed I do! Best hides, best tanning, best tallow, although this fellow won't agree."

"Most expensive tallow," Norbert retorted, "and not worth the cost."

Ewald's eyes narrowed until they were mere slits. "Plenty of folk in York disagree, but then, they make better candles."

Celeste noted Lewis edging his way toward the door and didn't blame him. "Please, gentlemen, I must ask you both to excuse me. I have much to do."

"No doubt, no doubt!" Ewald agreed, giving her a sympathetic smile, though his tone was no milder. "I suppose you'll be wanting to sell the house quickly and get back to the convent?"

"I shall be wanting to sell the house, yes."

"I'm your man for that!"

Norbert stepped in front of him. "If you wish to sell the house, Sister, I wouldn't deal with this fellow."

"Who should she deal with? You?" Ewald demanded as he elbowed Norbert aside.

"Better me than you," Norbert retorted, shoving him in return.

Ewald tried to ignore him. "About this house, though, Sister, should you wish to sell it, I shall be more than happy to—"

"His offer will be far too low," Norbert interjected.

His thick fingers balling into fists, Ewald glared at the chandler. "Shut your mouth, you—"

"Gentlemen!" Celeste hurried to interrupt before they came to blows. "I am not yet ready to discuss the sale of this house."

Ewald loudly cleared his throat and straightened his

belt. "Of course. You need to take an inventory of the furniture and other goods first. I understand. Take as long as you like."

"How magnanimous!" Norbert sneered, fairly trembling with rage. "She has no need to deal with you at all, you…you scoundrel!"

"And I suppose you came here because of your vast sorrow over Audrey D'Orleau's death? I've heard you denouncing her more than once in the Cock's Crow because she owed you money."

"I'm not the only one complaining about that. You yourself have sat in the tavern bemoaning how much she owed to you."

Celeste regarded them both with stunned disbelief before she managed to speak. "What are you saying? Did Audrey owe you money?"

How could that possibly be true, with all the fine and costly garments upstairs?

The men blushed and neither one would meet her gaze.

"Did Audrey owe you money?" she repeated.

"As a matter of fact, Sister," Ewald began, after darting another angry look at Norbert, "she did. I'm sorry to say there are likely a few other merchants who will be looking to you to pay her debts. But the house alone—"

"If Audrey was in debt, I will repay all that she owed," Celeste interrupted. "Any debts she left will be honored once I sell the house." *Or find our father's wealth.* "Now if you'll *please* excuse me, I *do* have things to do."

Mercifully, or perhaps because he understood her tone of voice, Ewald gave a brisk nod and headed out the door. "Good day, Sister."

Norbert looked as if he was about to refuse. Once

Ewald had gone, however, he likewise nodded and with a hasty "Good day" mercifully took his leave.

Flushing as red as a holly berry, Lewis was the last to go. "I'm sorry, Sister," he said quietly, his expression one of genuine sympathy, "but I'm afraid it's true about your sister. She left many debts."

Sorrow and dismay washed over Celeste and she leaned against the wall.

"Can I get you anything?" the youth asked anxiously. "Some wine perhaps?"

"Lewis!" his father shouted from outside.

"No, no, I'm all right," she assured the kindhearted young man, even though she'd been shaken to the core. "You should go."

Lewis gave her a last pitying look, then hurried away, softly closing the door behind him.

"Oh, Audrey," Celeste murmured as she slowly made her way to the kitchen, "what did you do?"

Some time later, Celeste was in the storeroom looking for any signs of a hiding place when she heard a tentative knock on the kitchen door. She hurried from the room, grabbed the veil and wimple lying on the kitchen table and swiftly put them on. "One moment!"

Going to the door, she tucked in any stray wisps of hair that might have escaped, then pushed down the rolled-up sleeves of her tunic. "Who is it?" she asked, dreading another creditor.

People had been coming to the house ever since Norbert and Ewald had left, making it difficult for her to search, and adding to her worries. Apparently Audrey owed money to the butcher, the shoemaker, the smith for repairs to a kettle and some pots, the alewife, the wine merchant and the miller. Indeed, Celeste was beginning to think there was no tradesman in Dunborough to whom she did *not* owe money.

"It's me, Sister. Lizabet, from the hall."

Celeste let out her breath slowly and opened the door, to find the young woman standing on the threshold. Instead of a cloak, she wore a large and colorful shawl and a kerchief over her dark hair. Her gown was of thick wool and she had an apron over that.

Despite her heavy clothing, her nose was red with cold and she had her hands tucked in her shawl to warm them.

"Please, come inside," Celeste said at once.

"No, thank you, Sister," Lizabet replied, her teeth starting to chatter. "I can't stay. I came to tell you that it's nearly time for the evening meal."

Celeste's brows contracted. If it was a busy time at the castle, why had she...?

"It's nearly time for the evening meal," Lizabet repeated more firmly, as if she thought Celeste hadn't heard her. "You're a guest of Dunborough."

With sudden understanding, Celeste replied, "Only for last night. I should have made it clear that I had no intention of imposing on Gerrard's hospitality for any longer than that."

The maidservant frowned with concern, or possibly dismay.

Celeste gave the young woman her most pleasant, placid smile. "Please convey my thanks to Gerrard for the invitation, as well as my assurances that I'm quite content to remain in my family's house while I'm here."

"If you say so, Sister," she hesitantly replied.

"I do. Now you'd best be off before you catch a chill."

Lizabet did as she was told and, thinking Gerrard would likely be as glad of her absence as she was relieved not to see him again, Celeste went back to searching the larder for any sign of money hidden there.

Albeit with a heavy sigh.

The sun was setting when Gerrard and his men returned from their patrol. There was no reason for them to go so far that frigid day except that Gerrard wasn't eager to return to Dunborough.

This time, though, it wasn't his irate, cruel father he was reluctant to see. It was a nun.

He handed the reins of his horse to a stable boy and went to the hall. A few of the hounds trotted toward him, eager for a pat and a good word. The trestle tables had been set up for the evening meal and the servants and soldiers not on duty or seeing to the horses and other tasks were already assembled.

Gerrard removed his cloak and hung it on a peg beside the door, then scanned the hall.

He scanned it again, thinking he must be mistaken.

He was not.

Celeste—Sister Augustine—was not there.

Gerrard sighed with relief, then frowned. It would look bad to the soldiers and servants if she kept to her room a second night, and rumors would start circulating in the castle and probably the village, too, that she refused to have anything to do with him.

That could very well be true. Nevertheless, it would likely start other rumors, none of them good, at least where he was concerned.

Or perhaps there was another reason for her absence. Maybe she was sick, exhausted from her journey.

"Lizabet!" he called, summoning the maidservant standing with the others at the entrance to the kitchen.

"Where is Sister Augustine?" he asked when she reached him. "Is she unwell?"

The servant shook her head. "No, sir. She's at the house…her family's house," she added when Gerrard's frown deepened.

"Did no one send word that it was time for the evening meal?"

"Yes, sir, I went myself, but she said she wasn't coming back. She said she'd rather stay in her own house."

"By *herself*?"

Wringing her hands, Lizabet looked as if she was about to cry.

Gerrard instantly regretted his harsh tone. The blame was not hers, after all.

"It's not your fault," he assured her. "She's always been stubborn."

That was true. Even when she was a child, it had been nearly impossible to make Celeste change her mind. Nevertheless, he wasn't about to allow her to put herself in danger by staying in that house alone at night. Too many people believed there was a fortune hidden somewhere inside.

"Serve the meal," he ordered, putting his cloak on again. "I'll be back soon with Sister Augustine."

Whether she wants to come or not.

With a sigh, Celeste sank onto the bed in the upper chamber lit by a flickering oil lamp. She hadn't found anything in this room, either. She'd checked all the chests and boxes for hidden compartments and even looked in the rafters overhead. When she'd taken time to make a stew, she'd searched on and under the shelves in the larder again, sneezing from the dust, while the ginger cat stared at her as only a cat can.

She was beginning to believe Audrey hadn't found their father's hidden hoard. Surely if she had, she wouldn't have been indebted, unless she'd spent the entire fortune on fine clothes and furnishings. Audrey had often said a woman had to look wealthy to attract a wealthy husband.

Celeste gazed again at the beautiful embroidered gown of scarlet silk that lay on top of the large open chest. It was, without doubt, the loveliest gown she had ever seen, and likely cost more than many a man earned in a year.

But even so, and despite the other costly garments, Audrey couldn't have spent *all* their father's wealth on clothing. From what he had said, the treasure would have paid for a hundred costly garments and more besides.

It was, unfortunately, more likely that Audrey *hadn't* found the cache and that's why she was indebted. Their father wouldn't have made it easy to find his treasure, not for anyone. Celeste hoped that she could find it, and that when she did, there would be enough to pay all Audrey's debts. Whatever remained, together with the sale of the house, as well as Audrey's gowns and jewelry, she would give to the church, as she had intended.

It had to be so. She couldn't wait forever to take her final vows and begin a life of calm and quiet service. As long as the mother superior who detested her was in charge of Saint Agatha's, Celeste might never see that day.

Removing her veil, cap and wimple, she shook out her hair. It would be cut again the day she took those vows, but she wouldn't regret it. She'd lost her hair once before and that had taken her to the peace of the convent.

She wondered what Gerrard would say if she told

him she was actually grateful for what he'd done, then dismissed the notion. She didn't want to speak to him at all.

She went to Audrey's dressing table to get the comb, then paused and reached for the brush. As she ran it over her scalp, she sighed with pleasure at the sensation.

It had to be nearly as sinful as that kiss, she realized, putting the brush down quickly. She grabbed the comb and worked it through her thick and curling hair.

The beautifully embroidered red gown caught her eye again. Audrey must have looked so regal in it, to no avail now.

Poor Audrey. So ambitious, so determined to be rich and titled, even if that meant a loveless marriage. All marriages were no better than a bargain made in the market, she would say, and she intended to get the most for what she had to offer. She had felt that way ever since a rich woman had called her a common brat for getting mud on her gown. Celeste would never forget Audrey's angry, humiliated tears, or her defiance and determination as she vowed "to marry well, or never!"

With another sigh Celeste put the comb beside the looking glass and began to undress. She took off the scapula and then her plain leather belt so that the tunic gathered at her neck hung straight to the floor. After removing her tunic, she untied the rough linen underskirt and stepped out of it. Wearing only her shift, she was ready to sleep, once she'd said her prayers.

Before she knelt at the side of the bed, she glanced again at the embroidered gown. When she returned to the convent, she would likely never see such a garment again. She would certainly never have the chance to wear a gown like that, or even try one on.

She was alone. No one except God would see if she

tried it on for a few moments. Surely He would forgive her this little indulgence. After all, it would be just this once.

She went to the chest and ran her hand over the lovely, soft silk fabric, noting the details of the embroidery, certain Audrey herself had done it. She was very skilled at needlework and could have earned a living at it, if she hadn't considered that beneath her.

"Me? Work like any peasant?" Audrey had demanded when Celeste suggested it. "Never! I am made for finer things!"

Such as this gown, and a rich husband. Not for Audrey the austere but peaceful life of a convent, where everyone wore the same plain garments every day. Celeste wished that might have been possible, but she knew her sister too well to hope that it could ever have been so.

She picked up the gown and quickly stepped into it before she changed her mind. She pulled it up and reached back to tie and knot the laces.

It fit surprisingly well.

Smiling, she tried a curtsy, as if she were being presented to the king.

She spotted a white silken veil, a wisp of a thing very different from the heavier linen one she had taken from the convent. There were lovely bronze hairpins on the dressing table, too.

With the speed of long practice, she braided her hair and fixed it around her head before attaching the silken veil. She twirled around, letting the full skirts blossom out while the veil fluttered about her cheeks like a butterfly's wings.

What was that?

She stumbled to a halt and listened. Something had made a noise below.

Or someone?

Gerrard had said there might be thieves who'd heard about her father's money.

And she was all alone.

Chapter Six

Swallowing hard, Celeste told herself it might simply be a mouse or a rat or the ginger cat.

But she couldn't remember if she'd locked the doors. She never had to do that at the convent. Maybe she'd forgotten.

Perhaps it was another tradesman come to ask for payment. At this hour, though? Not likely!

What was she going to do? She could go below and see if it was vermin or the cat, or stay up here and hope whoever—or whatever—it was remained below.

Footsteps! Footsteps coming up the stairs!

Her heart racing, she hurried to the large chest and pushed it against the thick wooden door. She ran back across the room and grabbed another, smaller chest and put it on top of the larger one. Panting, she picked up the stool by the dressing table, holding it at the ready.

"Celeste? Are you there, Celeste?"

Her arms shaking, her heart still beating like a galloping horse, she put down the stool. "What do you want, Gerrard?"

"Lizabet tells me you plan to stay here by yourself,

and that I cannot permit," he answered through the closed door.

He'd sounded anxious before. Now he seemed annoyed.

Gathering up her skirts, Celeste moved closer. "I'm quite all right."

"I insist," he returned, his voice more impatient. "I will not have your safety jeopardized while I am in command of Dunborough."

"And *I* insist that I'm quite all right." She didn't want to go back to the castle, where he would be. She didn't want to risk a repetition of the previous night's... encounter.

"Open the door or I'll break it in!"

"You wouldn't!"

The door shook as if someone had struck it with a battering ram or a shoulder, knocking the topmost chest to the floor. The lid broke and the bottom shattered, spilling veils and pieces of cheap jewelry onto the floor.

"There was no need for that!" she cried with frustration.

"Open the door!"

He would break it down, of that she was certain, so she shoved the chest out of the way. "You've bent the latch," she charged. "Now I *can't* open it."

"Then stand back," he ordered, clearly not a whit sorry for the damage he had caused.

In another moment, the door burst open and Gerrard stumbled over the threshold.

"It would serve you right if you landed on your head," she muttered as she began to gather up the veils and other items from the broken chest, putting them on the dressing table. She rose and faced him. "Look what you did."

His face red, his mouth a thin line, Gerrard glared at her before his eyes widened. "Well, well, well," he murmured. His lips curved up and his expression became admiring. "Not quite what I was expecting to see."

She'd forgotten she was wearing Audrey's gown and silken veil. She rushed to the bed and snatched up her heavy black tunic, holding it against her as if she were naked underneath. "There was no need for you to barge in like a…like a barbarian!"

His grin disappeared into gravity. "What would you have done if I were?" he asked, crossing his arms and leaning his weight on one leg.

What could she reply to that? That she would have hit him with a stool? "I managed to travel all the way from Saint Agatha's without incident."

"By some miracle."

"I made the entire journey without any trouble at all."

Or any sign of pursuit, likely because the mother superior was more relieved by her absence than concerned about her well-being. "Not *every* man is a lustful scoundrel."

"And not every nun a saint," he replied. "You're lucky you didn't walk right into the hands of thieves. Or been robbed here already. You hadn't even locked the door."

"I will remember after this, of that you may be sure. I have no wish to have half-drunk miscreants breaking down doors and ruining latches."

"I am not half-drunk. I haven't been drunk since Roland was attacked. Unfortunately, *you've* apparently lost what sense you were born with. If I had been an outlaw, you would be as dead as…" He paused, frowning.

She could guess what he'd been about to say. She would be as dead as Audrey. Although the comparison had been made in the heat of the moment, it pained her nonetheless.

He must have realized the effect of those harsh words, for when he spoke again, his voice was calmer and more compassionate. "Come, Celeste... Sister, we're going back to the castle."

His compassion was welcome. Nevertheless, she wasn't going to return with him. "I thank you for your concern. However, I'm sure I'll be safe here, so I see no need to leave."

He frowned, grim as Roland. Then he smiled in a way that made her even more aware that he was a young and handsome man. "I have other, more enjoyable methods of persuading women, if you would prefer me to use them."

God help her! He was temptation made flesh and she must keep away from him. "I think not."

His smile dissolved. "If you won't come willingly, you'll leave me no alternative except to take you by force."

She took a step back. "That would be the act of a savage."

"Perhaps you'd prefer that the very civilized Roland was here instead of me."

"Perhaps—yes, I would. He would never make such a threat."

Gerrard ignored her criticism. "You said 'perhaps.' That means you still like me best."

"I've never said I liked you best. Ever," she replied, although her throat was suddenly dry and that was another lie. She had liked him better than anyone in Dunborough, except for Audrey.

He took a step closer. "You did once. I was certain

of it then and I'm certain of it now. You still like me, I think."

She moved farther back. "I don't recall that you were ever *quite* so vain."

"Granted, it's been a long time and much has changed," he said, his voice deep and low and soft as butter, "but I like *you*, Celeste, even when you're angry with me."

Warmth flooded through her. The heat of desire. Lust. Sin.

She didn't want that. She didn't want her emotions turned to turmoil. She wanted peace. She wanted the security of a calm and ordered life.

She didn't want *him*, or the passion that his presence promised. She didn't want a life governed by a man's mood. She would have a quiet, safe life in the convent, away from him and other men and the trouble that they caused. That was what she yearned for, no matter what other things she had to sacrifice. "I don't care whether you like me or not," she declared, telling herself that was the truth and not another lie. "I am *not* leaving."

"Oh, yes, you are," he replied in that same low, seductive tone. "You can come quietly and obediently like a good little nun, or I'll carry you."

She must be strong. Her faith, her duty and her self-respect must make her so. "I will not allow you to drag me through the village like some chattel."

"I didn't say I'd drag you. I shall pick you up and carry you, like a bridegroom across the threshold."

She swallowed hard and fought to maintain her composure, such as it was. "I am a bride of Christ and shall never be a man's."

"A pity, that." He made another of those sweeping bows. "Forgive me. I fear that your gown has addled my mind."

The gown! She could easily imagine the rumors and gossip that would follow if anyone saw her in such a garment, rumors that might reach the mother superior's ears. This was what came of succumbing to vanity and worldly desires.

Gerrard's smile became a rascal's mocking grin. "It's lovely and suits you well, but it's not exactly what a nun should be wearing, is it? No doubt you'd like to remove it. I'd be happy to help you."

"I don't doubt you have vast experience assisting women out of their clothes," she replied, trying to maintain her self-control. "I suspect you have considerably less helping them get into them, so I shall manage on my own, thank you. You may go back to the castle."

He turned into the stern, stubborn Gerrard again. "Not without you."

It was obvious he wasn't going to let her stay, no matter what she said. She must concede, at least this once, although not without some concessions on his part, too. "If I do go with you now, you must allow me to come back here during the day."

"As you wish. I'll send a servant and guards with you."

"Surely I don't need protection during the day," she protested.

"Celeste… Sister," he replied, his voice rougher, "I will not debate with you any longer. My patience is at an end, and I swear by all that's holy, if you say another word, I'm going to throw you over my shoulder and carry you out of here."

Clutching her tunic tighter, she shook her head. "You wouldn't dare!"

In two purposeful strides he closed on her and did as he'd threatened, swinging her up onto his shoulder, nearly knocking the wind from her lungs. Her head was level with his waist, her legs dangled down his back, and the tunic was a crumpled heap on the floor.

"Stop, you beast! Cur!" she cried, pounding him with her fists.

He might as well have been made of wood for all the effect her efforts had as he left the chamber and carried her down the stairs.

"Stop! You can't— Stop!" she panted, growing more desperate.

At the front entrance to the house, he finally halted and swung her down. It took her a moment to find her balance, but as soon as she did, she shoved him backward. "How dare you! I am no slave, no prize of war! I am a bride of—"

"Don't say it!" he commanded, his words iron as he held up his hand to silence her.

"I *will* speak! I will tell you exactly—"

"What sort of man I am?" he charged as he pulled her to him, his intense gaze searching her face. "A rogue, a barbarian, a lazy lout, while you are a holy, sacred, untouchable bride of Christ? I may not be a holy man, or even a good one, but here you're not a bride of Christ. Not in that gown. Not with me. Not after that kiss in the courtyard."

Celeste wrenched herself free and fled into the main room. She grabbed the bronze candleholder and raised it like a cudgel. "Stay away from me, Gerrard!" she cried as he appeared in the doorway.

"Don't be a fool, Celeste. Put that down and—"

"Don't say another word!" she ordered. "I will *not* go back to the castle with you, tonight or at any time. You *are* a rogue and lustful scoundrel! I could not rest easy knowing a man like you was anywhere nearby. I will gladly risk thieves and brigands rather than fall prey to your lust."

"So you'd prefer to hazard murder?"

Years ago she had watched his father walk through the village with the coldest, hardest expression she had ever thought to see on a man's face, until today. Until now.

But she would feel no remorse, no regret for her impetuous words. Gerrard was not the boy she remembered, or the man she'd hoped he'd be.

"I'll take that chance," she replied, fighting to keep her voice level and her face free of emotion. "If you're at all sincere in your concern for my safety in this house, you can send guards."

He crossed his arms as if trying to contain his anger. "Have it your way, Sister. I am the evil, lustful son of Sir Blane of Dunborough and you are the holy virgin of Saint Agatha's." His lip curled with scorn. "Who dresses like a courtesan and kisses like a—"

"Get out!" she cried, before he could finish. Before he could insult her more.

"Gladly!" He turned to go, then looked back at her over his shoulder. "Don't forget to lock the door after me, though. I wouldn't want you to blame me if you're robbed. Or worse."

With that, he went out, slamming the door behind him.

Celeste dropped the candleholder and hurried to turn the lock, then gathered up her skirts and ran back to the bedchamber. She tore off the veil, struggled out of the gown, went down on her knees, clasped her hands together and began to pray.

She had been a fool, like the most vain and silly of women, to put on that gown.

She was going to be a nun.

She had to be a nun if she was going to have a life of peace and contentment. She had heard the stories of girls whose lives had been destroyed by lustful, selfish men, such as Esmerelda.

And her own poor mother.

"You there!"

Verdan and Lizabet sprang apart as Gerrard marched toward them.

"Sir?" Verdan said, obviously girding himself for a reprimand.

Disgruntled though he was, Gerrard wasn't angry at the soldier, who was not on duty, or the maidservant with him. If anyone deserved to be chastised, it was he. He shouldn't have gone to fetch Celeste himself. He should have sent a whole patrol. Then she *might* have been more willing.

Except then those men would also have seen her in that astonishing gown. It had fit her perfectly and emphasized her narrow waist and full breasts, exposing just enough of her cleavage to make him want to see more.

He shouldn't think about that gown.

"Find the sergeant at arms," he ordered Verdan, "and tell Ralph I want two men sent to guard the D'Orleau house, one at the front, one at the back, every night until I say otherwise."

"Aye, sir!"

Gerrard looked at Lizabet, who drew back as if she feared he was going to strike her. He had never in his life hit a woman. However, given his family's reputation, he shouldn't be surprised that a woman would fear him when he was angry.

It was bad enough that Celeste, and apparently everyone else, believed he was a sinful satyr unable to control his lust. It was worse, though, that anyone would believe he was capable of cruelty, like his father.

He forced himself to speak with calm deliberation. "Since Sister Augustine still doesn't wish to return, you'll go to her in the morning and stay until the evening meal, doing laundry or cooking or whatever is required. You will do so for the few days that she's here, or until you're ordered not to."

Lizabet relaxed a little, and only then did he realize she and Verdan were holding hands.

"Why haven't you two married yet?" Gerrard asked, attempting to sound jovial. "Roland's given his permission."

"We'd like to, sir," Verdan replied, and he grew more at ease. "It's just that Ma ain't keen to come to Yorkshire."

Gerrard was well aware of a parent's influence, for good or ill. "Let's hope she changes her mind soon. Now go and do as you've been ordered," he said, then continued toward the hall, the wind whipping his cloak around him like an angry cloud.

"S'truth!" Verdan muttered. "What got into him? He was like a bear with a thorn in its paw."

"Aye, he was angry, but not at us, thank God," Lizabet said, patting her beloved's arm. "It's probably Sister Augustine that's got him upset, and it wouldn't be the first time." She leaned in and gave Verdan a kiss. "After you've seen Ralph, I'll tell you all about Sister Augustine and Gerrard."

Chapter Seven

Later that night, Verdan stared openmouthed at Lizabet, who was sitting on his lap near the kitchen hearth. The other servants had all retired, so they had the chamber, lit only by the glowing embers, to themselves. "She never!"

"Aye, she did," Lizabet confirmed. "Broke it so bad he couldn't hold a sword or shield or even a spoon for weeks. That's when she got sent to Saint Agatha's."

"From what I hear about old Sir Blane," Verdan mused aloud, "could have been worse than that for her."

"It wasn't him that sent her there. It was her own father—and he was some piece of work, too. Sly and greedy, and beat his wife, or so they say."

"It might have been a mercy that she got sent away."

"Maybe, but some of them convents are like prisons," Lizabet concluded with a shiver.

Verdan's embrace tightened. "That's something you need never worry about, my love."

"Believe me, I'm glad of it!" She gave him a peck on the cheek. "Very glad."

Instead of returning her kiss and more, Verdan's arms loosened about her and he gazed at the fire. "Sister Augustine didn't look to hold a grudge when she arrived."

"Nor today, neither," Lizabet agreed, "but she was that firm about not coming back to the castle. You don't suppose something happened between 'em to upset her?"

"Might have." Verdan told her what had occurred the night before, and again that morning. "Hedley thinks maybe she was tryin' to stop Gerrard from goin' to the village last night. And then this mornin', she wasn't any too pleased to meet him coming back. Suspicious, she looked, like she suspected he'd been up to no good."

"It could be she heard what he was like before."

"In a convent?"

"Others have gone there from Dunborough and hereabouts, and they'd have stories to tell."

Verdan sighed heavily. "Here I was thinkin' there'd be peaceful times here."

Lizabet stroked his cheek. "It's likely Sister Augustine won't stay for long. And you got me," she reminded him with a sultry smile.

Verdan grinned. "Aye, so I do," he murmured, before he kissed her.

When the first glimmer of dawn appeared on the horizon, Celeste rose, her knees stiff, her body exhausted. She had spent the night in prayer, asking for forgiveness, pleading for rectitude, hoping for peace. She wasn't sure she had received any of those things as she went to open the shutters to the early-morning sun. She almost wished she hadn't come here, but there was the hope of finding the means to be rid of the mother superior to lessen that regret. Besides, she knew her weakness now and could guard against it.

There was a soldier standing by the gate in the front yard. He wore chain mail and a surcoat bearing the crest of Dunborough, a boar being strangled by a snake, and he was leaning on his spear as if he'd been there a long time.

That had to be Gerrard's doing. No one else would have the authority to send a soldier to stand guard over her house.

In spite of all that she had said to him, he had sent men to protect her. Perhaps there really were thieves and outlaws about, and perhaps Gerrard was a better man than she gave him credit for.

Or perhaps he had simply wanted to demonstrate his authority.

It was likely the latter.

She dressed quickly, not looking at the scarlet gown that she'd thrown over the chest, before she went below. She hurried into the main room to pick up the candle-holder she'd dropped, a little embarrassed that she'd brandished it like some kind of crazed harpy, but only a little. After all, Gerrard might have tried to kiss her again.

To her surprise, the bronze holder was farther from the door than she expected. Perhaps she'd imagined that Gerrard was standing so close to her last night.

However far away he'd been, she was sure she'd seen lustful desire flashing in his dark eyes, a need that seemed to call out to—

Someone knocked on the door.

If that was Gerrard, what would she say to him?

Maybe she should pretend she hadn't heard it.

Yet if she didn't answer, he might barge in anyway, as he had last night.

She went to the door and threw it open, startling Lizabet, who nearly dropped the basket she was carrying. "Oh, Sister! You gave me such a turn!"

"I'm sorry. Good morning, Lizabet. May I help you?"

"It's me been sent to help you, Sister. Gerrard says I'm to do the laundry and meals and anything else you need for the few days that you're here."

How was Celeste going to search the house if Lizabet was there? And who was Gerrard to determine how long she would be in Dunborough?

The maidservant gave her a friendly smile. "And he's ordered that there's to be two men every night to guard the house." The young woman clutched her basket tighter. "I must say I'm glad of it, Sister! There was a band of outlaws in the wood this past summer, terrible men the lot of them, and while most of them were caught, we can't be sure they all were and, well, men like that, if they heard about you staying here alone, and with the stories about your father's money, well..."

"Yes, I see." So there might really be thieves in the vicinity.

Guilt and shame arose within Celeste as she remembered the accusations she'd hurled at Gerrard. Unfortunately, the words couldn't be called back.

"I'm grateful that he sent you, Lizabet, and the guards, too," she said as she opened the door to let the servant enter.

As Lizabet went into the D'Orleau house, Gerrard was sitting on the dais in the castle's hall, waiting for the middle-aged sergeant at arms to finish his report about the night's watch. He was also stifling the urge to yawn.

He'd lain awake most of the night tossing and turning, trying not to think about women, or red silk gowns, or soft lips and harsh retorts. He didn't regret sending the guards. He only regretted losing his temper. That was a weakness and something he must learn to control.

"All was quiet here and at the D'Orleau house," the gray-bearded Ralph said, his muscular body stiffly at attention, as if he were facing Gerrard's father.

"Good," Gerrard replied, hoping it wouldn't be much longer before the men realized that he aimed to be a different sort of leader from his father or his older brother, or even Roland, who never seemed to relax around anyone.

"Are the men mustered for patrol?" he asked, getting to his feet. He'd already broken his fast and it was time to be doing something.

"Yes, sir. The weather's looking a bit chancy, though, sir. You might want to hold off a day or so."

Gerrard inclined his head to acknowledge that he'd heard the sergeant at arms's concern, then continued toward the door. If it appeared a storm was brewing, the patrol wouldn't ride out. If it seemed as if rain was merely pending, they would.

He opened the door and saw the ten men assigned to the patrol waiting by their horses. He was about to check the sky when he spotted a soldier being admitted at the gate, leading his horse rather than riding it.

Gerrard turned back to Ralph, who had taken his seat at one of the trestle tables and started to slather some butter on a thick piece of brown bread. "Where's Verdan?"

"Here, sir!" the soldier declared from the door to the kitchen. He had a mouth full of bread and held the heel of a loaf in his hand. There were crumbs in his beard and down the front of his hauberk.

Gerrard decided to be lenient and not comment on the crumbs. "Your brother's come from DeLac."

Wiping his buttery lips with the back of his hand and tossing the loaf to the hounds, the stocky soldier hurried to stand beside Gerrard at the door.

"Just in time to avoid a good soaking," Verdan noted with a laugh as they watched his brother dash across the yard toward the hall, his mail jingling, while rain began to fall.

"No patrol unless the rain stops!" Gerrard called out to the men in the yard, repeating the order to Ralph, behind him. Wet mail and weapons got rusty, but it didn't look to be a heavy or a lasting rain.

"Greetings, sir!" the bearded, wiry Arnhelm said as Gerrard and Verdan moved aside to let him enter. "And you, too, brother." He slapped the pouch at his belt and addressed Gerrard. "I've brought a letter from Sir Roland."

Another one. In spite of his dismay, Gerrard put a smile on his face. "How fares my brother?"

"He's well," Arnhelm replied. "He's still got some pain, but the apothecary says he should be good as new in no time."

"And his wife? Glowing, no doubt."

"Aye, indeed, sir! Beautiful as ever and happy as a lark."

Of course she was. Gerrard had never seen a more happily married woman than Mavis, although only a few short months ago he would have wagered a goodly sum that no woman could ever be happily married to Roland. "Something wrong with your horse?"

"Aye, sire, had a pebble in the hoof. Seems to be coming along, though."

Arnhelm reached into the pouch on his belt and pulled out a parchment sealed with wax and the imprint of Roland's ring, the ring that had been their father's and all the lords of Dunborough back to the Conqueror's day. He handed it to Gerrard.

"This time I, um, I'm to stay until you've got an answer to send him," Arnhelm said, his face reddening.

That was something new, although perhaps to be expected. Roland had been waiting days to learn his decision about the estate.

Nevertheless, Gerrard acted as if this order didn't disturb him in the slightest. "Not much of a hardship for you to wait a day or two, eh?"

Arnhelm tried to look as if he didn't understand what Gerrard was referring to. His efforts were all for naught when Peg appeared at the entrance to the kitchen, the smile on her face making her look five years younger and even more attractive.

It was no secret that Arnhelm had asked Roland for permission to marry Peg at the same time Verdan had sought Lizabet's hand.

Gerrard tucked the letter into his belt. "Now be off with you, man!" he genially ordered. "You, too, Verdan."

As the brothers hurried away, Gerrard called for Ralph to join him. They would go to the armory and see how many new swords might be needed. Or lances or pikes or arrows. Roland's letter and his answer could wait until later.

Or possibly tomorrow. Or the day after.

A short time later, Arnhelm and Verdan settled themselves comfortably in an out-of-the-way corner of the kitchen. Arnhelm had a little smile on his face as he watched Peg bustle about among the other servants busy at their various tasks. She, in turn, occasionally cast a blatantly fraudulent look of annoyance his way. Otherwise, Arnhelm and Verdan might have been alone in a cell in the dungeon for all the attention anyone paid them.

"Ma's well, then?" Verdan asked, leaning back against the wall.

"Fine as ever," Arnhelm answered, his smile dwindling. "Still won't come to Yorkshire, though."

Verdan frowned. "She ain't even met the girls!"

"Aye, and that's got me thinking. Maybe when I go back, you should come with me—all three of you. Once Ma meets 'em, she'll love 'em, and I'm sure she'll leave DeLac."

"Gerrard'll have to agree to the journey," Verdan said grimly.

Arnhelm gave his brother a puzzled look. "Why wouldn't he?"

"'Cause he's been like a bear with a toothache since Sister Augustine came."

"Who's she?"

"Audrey D'Orleau's sister, that's who."

"Didn't know she had one."

"No more did I, but so she does. Or did. Anyway, Sister Augustine's come here to deal with the house and furnishings and such, and accordin' to Lizabet, she and Gerrard hate each other." He briefly told his brother about the cut hair and broken collarbone.

Arnhelm whistled. "That explains it, then."

"What?"

"Why Sir Roland's been lookin' so worried. I thought he was anxious to get an answer to the letters he's been sendin' Gerrard, but maybe he's heard she's come and he's afraid of what's goin' to happen between 'em."

Verdan snorted a laugh. "What? Come to blows? Gerrard might not be the most chivalrous man in England, yet I've never heard he's ever hit a woman."

"It's not that I'm thinkin' about. Gerrard's handsome

and charmin', too, and has a way with women. And she's a woman."

Verdan rapidly shook his head. "No. Not them two. He was pretty angry when she wouldn't come back to the castle."

Arnhelm frowned. "What happened?"

Verdan shrugged. "I dunno, but he was madder'n a wet hen, and she won't come back."

"Have they ever been alone together?"

"What, like in the solar or somewhere?"

"Aye. Where they could have had a quarrel without anybody else hearin'."

Scratching his beard, Verdan mused a moment. "That first night they were in the courtyard together, over by the big tree."

"Doin' what?"

"Talkin', far as I could see."

"What about?"

"I wasn't listenin', nor near enough to hear, and they wasn't shoutin'. They was way over by the kitchen, where it was pretty dark."

Arnhelm raised a brow. "They were talkin' together in the dark where no one else could hear?"

"It was night," Verdan replied, "so o'course it was dark."

"And that's all they did, just talk?"

"What else? She's a nun, for God's sake!"

Arnhelm crossed his arms. "Wouldn't be the first time anger turned into something else just as strong. One kind of powerful feelin' leads to another, I always say."

"You do not!"

"Maybe I don't, but it's true enough for all that."

"Since when are you an expert?"

Arnhelm gave his brother the sort of condescending look an older sibling gives a younger one. "Doesn't take an expert to figure out a man like Gerrard can get just about anything he wants from a woman."

Verdan regarded his older brother with equal condescension. "You ain't met Sister Augustine."

Chapter Eight

Two days later, the early-morning sun was barely lighting the horizon as Celeste raised her head from the pillow of her arms. Sometime after midnight, she'd rested her forehead on the table in the kitchen and fallen asleep.

She'd spent most of the previous evening examining various bits of parchment she'd found in a wooden box in her old bedchamber. Letters, receipts, bills of lading, bills of sale, lists, figures and notations were now in various piles on the table. She'd also found a few pennies in the box beneath the papers. That was a pleasant surprise. She could use the money in the market.

As for the documents, they had been jumbled together without any apparent rhyme or reason, as if Audrey had simply thrown them into the box. Celeste had tried to make sense of them, sorting them into piles, and hoping that one might be a clue about the location of her father's money.

She'd found nothing of any use in that regard. All her efforts seemed to show was that Audrey had indeed spent freely on credit, and with apparently no attempts to repay her debts.

Rubbing her neck, Celeste rotated her head, trying to work out a dull ache. Noticing a shaft of light across the flagstone floor, she went to the window and discovered a narrow gap between the shutters, which were held closed by a hook and eye. The wood must have shrunk over the years, leaving a space. She likely hadn't noticed it before because she hadn't been in the kitchen when the sun rose.

A thief could slip a knife through that gap and raise the hook and thus open the shutters.

Yet she'd never seen it before and Lizabet hadn't mentioned it. Maybe the maidservant hadn't seen it, either, because as the sun moved, that gap would be in shadow. Celeste doubted it would be any more visible outside, even if she had a candle lit. Nevertheless, it was troubling and made her more grateful for the guards. When she sold the house, she would tell the new owner to obtain a more secure fastener.

She heard a cat's meow and went to the door. Joseph, as she'd decided to name the ginger cat because of his bright coat, was waiting outside. She let him in and closed the door, then began to gather up the papers and put them back into the box.

She would take them to her room and try to get a little more sleep before Lizabet arrived.

"Watch what you're doing, you oaf!" Norbert cried as the wax dripped from the form onto the table beneath. "I can't afford to have beeswax wasted!"

Lewis quickly scraped up the overflow and put it back into the small cauldron of melted wax that sat in a holder over a low flame on the worktable.

"What's the matter with you, anyway?" his father demanded, swatting him on the back of the head. "You

can't put it back! It's dirty. Now the whole lot's ruined."
He grabbed the hot container, gasped and let it fall.

"Idiot!" he shouted, as if it was his son's fault he'd
burned himself, and raised his hand again.

Trying to avoid another blow, Lewis jumped up from
his stool, knocking it over and into his father's way, so
that the older man nearly tripped.

Clutching his burning fingers, Norbert shouted, "Get
out!"

Lewis didn't hesitate to obey. He ran out of the work-
room and into the alley, then slipped into the tavern. It
was busy and crowded on market day, and nobody noticed him in a dark corner.

He sat and leaned his head back and closed his eyes.
God, he was tired! It was no wonder he'd made that
mistake in the shop. Nevertheless, he wasn't about to
tell his father he'd spent most of the past night up in the
garret watching the D'Orleau house, wondering what
Sister Augustine was doing and why there'd been a
light in the kitchen.

At least she hadn't been with Gerrard. Lewis was
sure about that, or he would have seen him. He wished
Gerrard would catch a chill and die. Or better yet, some
lingering, wasting, disfiguring disease. It would serve
that arrogant lout right. Unfortunately, the men who
most deserved to be punished for their sins all too often
weren't. It had been Gerrard's equally sinful friends
who'd died. To be sure, they'd gone outside the law
after Roland had sent them from Dunborough, but still,
it wasn't fair. Men like Gerrard never suffered enough.

"What'll you have, Lewis? Buttermilk?"

He opened his eyes to find Matheus smirking at him.
"Nothing from you," he retorted, getting to his feet.

He'd find another place to keep warm, such as the empty stable in the D'Orleau yard. That way, he'd be near Sister Augustine, too.

"Well, now, Sister, see something you like?" the butcher asked. His lips were smiling, but not his eyes. No doubt he was thinking of the five marks Audrey owed him, and wondering if and when he might be repaid.

Giving the big man in a bloody apron a pleasant smile to hide the shame she felt, Celeste reached into her cuff and pulled out her nearly empty purse. "I need a bit of meat for a stew, if you please."

The butcher nodded and bundled a few pieces of the cheapest cut in a cabbage leaf, handing it over to her after she gave him the price he asked for. "So you're not leaving for a bit, eh, Sister?"

"Not until the house is sold and all of Audrey's debts are paid," she assured him before she left his shop, not lingering in case she saw a skeptical expression on his face.

She went past the well and the women gathered there. She smiled at them, too, and they nodded a greeting in return. Despite their apparent friendliness, she was sure she would be the subject of their conversation when they began talking again. Being the sister of a murdered woman would be more than enough to kindle a lot of gossip and speculation.

It would be worse if she wasn't garbed in the habit of a nun. She didn't regret taking it, and she suspected the mother superior probably considered the loss of a habit a small price to pay for being rid of a troublesome novice whom no amount of punishment would render completely obedient.

"Alms, good Sister, alms!"

Celeste halted abruptly. She hadn't noticed the old woman sitting on the ground inside the entrance to an alley. If she had, she'd more than likely have thought it was a bundle of rags, not a person. The woman was small in stature and her face barely visible beneath the cloth wrapped around her head.

A filthy, bony hand appeared. "Alms?" the beggar repeated in a weak, quavering voice.

Celeste took out her leather drawstring purse. She hadn't much money left, but she would give something to the poor soul to buy a bit of bread.

She fished out a ha'penny and, bending down, put it in the outstretched palm.

"Bless you, Sister, bless you!" the old woman murmured, drawing her hand back.

Celeste got a good look at the old woman's filthy face and nearly dropped her purse. "Eua?"

Clutching the coin, Gerrard's old nurse scuttled back against the wall like a crab. "No, no, I ain't!"

"You are!" Celeste cried, moving toward the woman who had been like a mother to Gerrard. "What happened? How have you come to this?"

"Go 'way!" she cried. "You ain't seen me!"

Celeste reached down to take Eua's arm and help her to her feet. The stench was nearly overpowering. Even so, she couldn't leave her there like that.

With unexpected strength Eua tried to push her away. "Don't tell nobody you seen me! Don't tell *him*!"

Celeste didn't have to ask who she meant. "You must let me get you some food."

And a bath. And clean clothes.

"No, no, let me go!" Eua cried frantically, hobbling into the street just as Gerrard and his men rode through the market.

"Look out there!" Gerrard cried, reining in abruptly.

As his horse neighed in protest and the rest of the patrol behind him brought their mounts to a halt, Eua screeched and fell to her knees. She threw her hands over her head and started to sob, her whole body shaking.

Celeste knelt beside the distraught old woman, trying to see if she was hurt or ill or simply frightened.

"Don't tell him who I am!" Eua wailed, writhing as if someone had set her on fire.

"S'blood!" Gerrard cried in disbelief as he dismounted. "Eua?"

The old woman covered her face and twisted away. "No, no, I ain't, I ain't!"

Gerrard didn't move. "Get up, Eua."

"No, no!"

"You must. You shouldn't have come back here."

"Why shouldn't she be here?" Celeste asked, appalled by his harsh tone. "This is her home."

"She has forfeited that right."

Celeste regarded him with bafflement. "What has she done that you should say that? This woman was like a mother to you."

"This woman enabled the former steward of Dunborough to steal from the estate while he blamed me for the loss."

That gave Celeste a moment's pause. Stealing was a very serious offense. But the woman was still in dire need, whatever she had done. "Even so, for mercy's sake—"

"Verdan!" Gerrard called out.

A soldier rode forward.

"Take charge of the patrol."

"Aye!" Verdan raised his hand and led the group of mounted men past them.

With more gentleness than she expected, and no hint that he found Eua repulsive, Gerrard reached down to help the sobbing old woman to her feet.

"For mercy's sake and Sister Augustine's, you can stay one night in the castle," he said to the trembling Eua, "but then you must be on your way."

"Gerrard, surely—" Celeste started to protest.

The look he gave her silenced her, at least on that one point. But she had something else to say to him and might never have another chance. "Thank you for the guards, Gerrard, and Lizabet, too. I feel safer for their presence."

His eyes lit up in a way that made her blush, and his lips curved in a grin that wasn't mocking or insolent. It was as if time had not wrought so very great a change, and he was again the Gerrard she'd admired so long ago.

Until he muttered a quiet curse, for Eua was sidling down the alley away from them. He darted after her and once more gently gripped her arm. "Come along, Eua, and be a good woman, as I was your good boy once. You can have something to eat and a warm bed for the night."

She made no further protest.

"Good day, Sister," Gerrard said with great politeness before they started toward the castle.

"Good day, Gerrard," she murmured as she watched him lead the old woman and his snow-white horse away.

Leaving her to wonder what else had changed while she was far from home.

"Oh, that's lovely, that is!" Lizabet said when Celeste returned with the meat for the stew. "Ben must like you."

Celeste doubted that very much, yet didn't say so.

"Have you ever heard tell of a servant called Eua at the castle?" she asked while Lizabet fetched a bowl and some flour.

Lizabet started to cut the meat into smaller pieces. "She was here when Lady Mavis come, but not for long."

"Lady Mavis sent her away?"

"Aye. She didn't have much choice, really. Eua was disrespectful and made it no secret that she thought Gerrard ought to have Dunborough, not Roland, no matter who was born first or what their father wanted. We was all glad to see the back of Eua. What a tongue that woman had!

"And then it turns out she was helping Dalfrid—he was the steward—to steal. Gerrard found her in York with Dalfrid and his mistress and realized what she'd done."

"So he brought her back here to face justice?"

"Lord love you, no," Lizabet said as she put some fat into one of the pots and swung it over the fire. When it began to sizzle, she dropped the flour-coated meat into it. "He let her stay in York with the mistress."

"I met her in the village today. She's in a wretched state, starving and in rags."

Lizabet didn't look particularly sympathetic. "Why she'd come back here, I don't know. Maybe Dalfrid's leman got tired of her nasty tongue, too."

"I thought she might have come back to seek help from Gerrard. She was always good to him and he was generous to her."

"Until that Dalfrid made out it was Gerrard costing the estate, when it was him stealing, and Eua knew it. Dalfrid paid her to keep quiet."

No wonder Gerrard had been so stiff and cold toward

Eua. How it must have hurt him to find out the woman he loved like a mother was willing to betray him for money. Yet he had offered Eua food and shelter. "He's letting her stay the night in the castle."

Stirring the beef, Lizabet didn't appear surprised. "All the beggars that come to the village can stay a night in the castle stables, but only one, and they get a loaf of bread to take with them when they go."

Sir Blane or Broderick would never have done that. "Sir Roland has a generous nature."

"Oh, that isn't his doing," Lizabet said, adding water to the pot. "It's Gerrard's. Some say he's trying to atone for all the sins he's committed."

Joseph came out of the shadows in the corner and pushed his head against Celeste's leg. She picked up the cat and stroked his back and listened to his purring.

If Gerrard was trying to atone, she thought, he was starting well.

She hoped she would be successful at atonement when her time came, for it surely must.

As the patrol continued on its way, Verdan addressed his brother. "Told you Sister Augustine was something, didn't I? Did you hear how she spoke to Gerrard?"

"Aye," Arnhelm replied. He mused for a moment, his hips swaying with his horse's ambling walk. "She don't seem much like a nun."

"Too pretty, aye."

"Not just that. I thought nuns were supposed to be meek and mild."

"Aye, there's that."

"Reckon Gerrard'll be glad when she's gone. No man likes to be dressed down by a woman, and in the market, too."

Arnhelm grinned. "You mind the time Ma chased you all around the green when you'd stepped on the sheets she'd laid out on the verge to dry?"

"If Gerrard feels half as shamed as I did that day," Verdan said with certainty, "he'll be having a celebration when she's gone."

Florian, the cook, looked decidedly less than pleased to have Eua back in his kitchen. No doubt he would have been just as unhappy about it even if she didn't smell and likely harbor fleas. Peg glanced at the former servant with a combination of disgust and dismay, and Tom the spit boy stared as if she were a witch come to gobble him up for dinner.

"Thank you, Gerrard," Eua mumbled as he handed her a loaf of bread. "You always were a good boy."

A good boy she had never really loved, he thought, trying to keep his expression stoic.

"You can stay one night, Eua," he reminded her, setting down a wooden bowl of stew.

Celeste no doubt thought him cruel, but she didn't know what Eua had done. The harm she'd caused, the way she'd hurt him, and not only when the truth about Dalfrid had been revealed.

Gerrard would never forget the day he'd realized that Eua's affection was his so long as he paid for it with compliments and little gifts. He had been six years old when she'd threatened to tell his father that he'd chased the chickens until one dropped dead. He'd begged her not to and she had stood there hard as stone until he'd promised to give her a copper-and-enamel bracelet that had been his mother's. He'd found it in the grass in the garden, glistening near a rock, and she had discovered it in his little box of treasures. Most were worthless to anyone save him: an interesting stone, a bit of colored glass, the shed skin of a snake, a brass buckle. Nothing except the bracelet had any value.

From that day on, he was aware he had to buy the love he craved.

Eua took a bite from the loaf, then reached out and grasped his hand in her cold, dirty ones. "Thank you, my precious boy."

He didn't want her thanks. He wanted her gone, the same way he'd thought he'd wanted Celeste gone, until she'd looked at him with sincere gratitude and thanked him for his help.

She was not a woman he should have anything to do with. She wanted the church, not a man.

"One night," he repeated firmly, heading for the door. "One night in the stable, Eua, and then you must go."

Chapter Nine

The next day the garrison commander of Dunborough stood at the window high in the castle keep, in an upper room his father and brothers used as a solar, and where the records of the estate were kept. From here, he could see over the roofs of the village, all the way to the big house of the D'Orleaus—or he could have if it wasn't raining, a cold, chill rain that felt like needles on the skin.

So here he was, shut up in the solar like a prisoner, trying to start a letter to his brother.

As well as finally decide what he would do about Roland's offer.

There were other obstacles besides his own reluctance to be beholden to his brother. King John would have to agree, for one thing. Roland was confident the king would be quick to approve the gift, for it would mean less land and power in one man's hands.

But how could Gerrard govern a place where his reputation was against him? Where he was still viewed as a wastrel, a sot and a gamester? To be sure, the soldiers liked him—he seemed like one of them and, indeed, felt that way most of the time.

Commanding soldiers was different from running an estate, though, as these few weeks had made clear. Perhaps it would be better to be a simple soldier and start afresh somewhere else, to make his own way in the world and be beholden to no one.

With a sigh, he went back to the table where he'd set out a pot of ink covered with waxed cloth and a piece of clean parchment in preparation for composing an answer to Roland's letter. Gerrard selected three quills and picked up the small knife to strip off the lower feathers and sharpen the point of the shaft. Once that was done, he sat down and studied again the message he'd received from his brother.

As always, the written letters often looked backward and in the wrong order, as if someone was writing in code, and it took him a long time to decipher every word. Only once had he ventured to tell anyone about his difficulties reading. Roland had regarded him as if he were completely stupid, and so, Gerrard reckoned, he must be when it came to reading—and writing, which was worse.

Thank God he was good at other things, such as getting people to like him.

In that he was alone among his family. Broderick had wanted everyone to fear him, as had their father. Roland didn't seem to care what people thought about him. Only Gerrard wanted everybody to like him, and it pained him when they didn't.

He studied the scroll again and the words slowly started to make sense. Roland began with a greeting and the assumption that all was well at Dunborough, despite whatever doubts he might secretly harbor.

Gerrard couldn't fault Roland if he did have doubts.

He was too well aware that his cautious brother had taken a leap of faith leaving him in command.

Even a month ago, no one, including himself, would have anticipated that. He, like most of the inhabitants of the estate, had expected Roland to send him away.

Instead, Roland had decided to go to DeLac to tell Lord Simon there would be no alliance between them, either by marriage or by treaty, and had left Gerrard temporarily in command.

Nobody had been more surprised than he when Roland returned with DeLac's daughter as his bride, and no one was more surprised than he that Mavis genuinely loved and admired Roland and condemned him—Gerrard—for acting like a spoiled brat.

He would never forget how she'd upbraided him and pointed out that his insolent treatment of his brother undermined people's respect for both of them. Her words had stung more when he'd realized she was right.

Then he'd found out about Dalfrid, and Roland had been attacked by Duncan MacHeath and nearly died.

Gerrard ran his hand through his hair. If he accepted Roland's offer, perhaps he could learn to rule in time. Maybe he could become patient and thoughtful and grow to understand all the financial business attendant on that task, or else find a clerk to help him.

Freedom from his reputation and any expectations had its own appeal, though. He could leave behind his past and all the bitter pain and unhappy memories, as well. There weren't many good ones here.

There would be even fewer when Celeste returned to the convent.

What the devil did she have to do with his decision? Nothing. Absolutely nothing.

Stay and be beholden, or go and be free, yet without lands and title. How could he decide?

He couldn't. Not today.

He looked out the window and realized the rain had stopped. Water dripped from the roof and the ground would be soaked, but Roland could wait another day or two. Arnhelm would undoubtedly be happy to stay in Dunborough awhile longer and he had better things to do.

Or if not better, at least more entertaining.

Celeste put the salted cod she had purchased from the fishmonger into her basket and, making her way around a puddle, hurried past the chandler's shop. She didn't want to see Norbert, or for him to see her. He'd come to the house once already to ask when she was going to sell it and—

"Sister Augustine!"

Too late.

She turned toward the chandler. "Good day, Norbert. It turned into a fine day, did it not? And warm for November."

"We won't have many good days left for traveling."

The man likely couldn't be subtle if he was offered the king of England's crown to be so. "No, I daresay you're right," she replied, keeping a placid smile on her face.

"What are you up to now, Norbert?" Ewald boomed from behind her. "Harassing the good sister, I don't doubt!"

"I'm doing nothing of the kind. We're talking about the weather," Norbert retorted, his narrow face looking longer with his frown.

"It'll be cold and snowing before much longer. And

wet. All the signs point to a wet winter. The roads'll be a muddy mess."

Apparently Ewald was no more subtle than his enemy.

"I hope to be on my way in a few days," Celeste said, trying not to sigh with impatience, weariness and dismay.

She didn't need them to remind her that she would have to sell the house soon if she was to leave Dunborough before the harsh winter weather arrived. She would have sold the house, paid the debts and been gone already if she'd found her father's hidden wealth.

Unfortunately for them all, she had not, and she was beginning to fear she never would. She was also beginning to doubt that it had ever existed. It might have been a lie her father had told to torment their unhappy mother.

Celeste had started to wonder if she should accept that she would never find the treasure. She'd spent so much of her nights searching fruitlessly, she was near exhaustion.

At least nobody from the convent had come looking for her.

"As I've said, I'll make you a good offer." Ewald spoke so loudly, half the people in the market turned to look at them.

"I'll make a better one," Norbert declared, "and I won't rush you from the premises. You can leave whenever it suits you."

"You make it sound as if I'll throw her out the door," Ewald grumbled.

"Won't you?"

"Sweet Jesu, no, you little—"

"Please don't squabble," Celeste pleaded, her patience

nearly at an end. "I will sell when *I* am ready, and not before."

She hurried past them, although not fast enough that she didn't hear them continue to argue and call each other names. She'd had her fill of childish quarrels when she was young, and at least Gerrard and Roland had *been* children then.

Norbert and Ewald could wait some time longer, she decided. She wouldn't give up yet. She would look for another week, and if she hadn't found the treasure by then, she'd sell the house, pay what debts she could and seek another convent to take her in.

"Here, Sister, let me help you!"

With a start, she realized Lewis was at her elbow.

Although she didn't require any assistance, the youth appeared so eager, she didn't have the heart to send him on his way.

Instead, she let him take the basket containing butter, dried apples and the salted cod. "Thank you."

"I'm sorry about my father," he said, falling into step beside her. "He shouldn't keep bothering you about the house."

"It does have to be sold."

"But not *right* away," Lewis replied. "It must be difficult for you, having to sort through everything."

"Yes, it is."

"I'm sure you'll get a good price when you do decide to sell. I overheard you dealing with the fishmonger. You drive a harder bargain than my father! I daresay you could hold your own even in London."

Celeste gave the young man a smile, although his compliment conjured unhappy memories. "I learned to bargain at my father's knee."

She'd also heard the whispered insults and curses

when the bargaining was over and her parsimonious father not in the room.

She caught sight of Gerrard striding through the market and instinctively ducked into the nearest doorway. She was still ashamed and embarrassed by how she'd acted the day she'd encountered Eua, and didn't want to meet him.

She was surprised that he was alone, for he so rarely was.

Clearly, he enjoyed the company of the soldiers of the garrison and was comfortable among them in a way Broderick and Roland never were. He was not an aloof lordling to them, but a respected leader and good comrade—a rare combination.

"I don't like him, either," Lewis muttered, frowning as Gerrard passed by. "He rides as if he's the lord, although he's only the garrison commander. He wouldn't even be that if he hadn't found out about Dalfrid and brought him back for trial."

Dalfrid—the steward Eua had been in league with.

"He was the steward of Dunborough and Gerrard discovered he'd been stealing to keep a mistress in York."

Obviously Lewis didn't think she'd heard about that. "Lizabet told me something about it," Celeste said. "I'm surprised anyone would try to steal from Dunborough. Sir Blane would have had him put to death at once on suspicion alone."

"Not Roland."

Neither had Gerrard, despite his impetuous temper.

"Dalfrid's been taken to York for his trial. It shouldn't be long now."

Once Gerrard had disappeared among the crowd, Celeste started toward her house again. "You said it was Gerrard who discovered the man was stealing?"

"Merely by chance," Lewis replied with a hint of defiant scorn. "He'd gone to York after another argument with Roland, swearing he would never come back. He was in a tavern when he overheard some men talking about Dalfrid, and figured out something wasn't right.

"Of course it would be in a tavern," Lewis noted with more disdain. "The men he called friends!" he added when Celeste didn't reply. "Rogues and wastrels and gamesters the lot of them. The last of his cronies were the worst, though."

"His brother wouldn't have been pleased that he had such companions."

Indeed, she could think of fewer things that would drive the dour, dutiful Roland to distraction, which might very well have been Gerrard's plan at the time.

"Roland sent them away and they turned outlaw."

"Is that why Gerrard rides out on patrol every day?"

Lewis shrugged. "The outlaws in the band his friends joined are all dead or scattered. Gerrard just likes to ride around on his fine white horse, lording it over everyone, while Roland's at his wife's estate. Roland and his wife seem quite happy together, no thanks to Gerrard. He made trouble for them from the moment she arrived."

Celeste's heart sank a little. Unfortunately, she could see Gerrard being envious of his brother's marriage to a nobleman's daughter and knew that he would take no pains to hide it.

"He didn't dare try to seduce her, though, much as he might have wanted to. Roland would have killed him."

Celeste felt a chill that was not from the breeze. Yes, Roland would probably have attacked Gerrard if his brother had tried such a thing. Nevertheless, she wanted to believe it was something other than fear that had prevented Gerrard from any attempt at seduction.

"He'd finally met a woman who didn't like him," Lewis added with a snide little laugh. "Lady Mavis saw him for the scoundrel he is, no matter how much he tries to pretend he's changed since Roland got hurt and let him stay on as commander of the garrison.

"Gerrard doesn't only drink and gamble," Lewis continued. He lowered his voice. "There's a place in the village, down an alley, with women who—"

"I don't need to hear all of Gerrard's vices."

Celeste had heard more than enough already. Fortunately, they had reached the gate to her yard.

"I'm sorry if I upset you, Sister."

She was sorry she'd let it show. "It's always disturbing to learn of men's sins," she said by way of explanation. She took back the basket and gave Lewis another smile. "Thank you again."

"Is there anything else I can do for you, Sister?" the young man asked fervently. "Anything at all?"

"As a matter of fact, there is one thing."

The youth's face lit up. "Yes?"

"There are several gowns that belonged to my sister that should be sold. Can you think of anyone who—"

"Absolutely, Sister! Bartholemew and Marmaduke. They sell fabric. Some of it comes from London."

"Would it be too much trouble for you to ask them to visit me today, unless they're otherwise engaged?"

"I'll fetch them at once!"

"Only if it's convenient!" she called as the young man dashed back toward town.

He's an excitable lad, she thought as she walked into the house. Enthusiastic, kindhearted, yet also capable of derision and anger. In that, he wasn't so different from

the youthful Gerrard, who had once had such promise
and now…?

And now she must try to see Gerrard as he truly was,
not as she wished him to be.

Chapter Ten

"Sorry to disturb you, Sister," Lizabet called from the bottom of the ladder to the garret. "Marmaduke and Bartholemew are here."

Surrounded by old wooden packing boxes and dusty furniture, Celeste sneezed, then rose from her knees and brushed off her hands. "I'm coming."

She went to the ladder and carefully began to descend. "There are a few pieces of furniture up there," she said to the maidservant when she reached the bottom. "Once they're cleaned, I should be able to sell them. Otherwise, it's mostly dust and cobwebs."

And no sign that anybody had been up there in years.

With a nod Lizabet returned to the kitchen and Celeste went to meet the men to whom Audrey probably owed the most, if her wardrobe was any measure.

The two were waiting in the main room. The stain was now covered by the carpet that had been in Audrey's bedchamber, and the remaining furniture had been put back in its rightful place. The needlepoint had been packed away in a leather pouch for Celeste to take with her, and the stand dismantled. The candleholder had been moved to the center of the table, probably when Lizabet polished it.

One of the men was tall and thin, the other short and plumper. Both were very well dressed, the tall one in a long tunic of soft blue wool with a wide leather belt around his slender waist. The other had on a short yellow tunic over green breeches and was holding the most amazing yellow-and-green-striped cap she had ever seen. The colors were so bright it almost hurt her eyes to look at them.

"Good afternoon, Sister," the short one began. "I'm Bartholemew and this is Marmaduke. We would have come to express our condolences for the loss of your dear sister sooner, but we thought you might need some more time to…time to…"

"Grieve," Marmaduke supplied.

"Yes, grieve," Bartholemew continued. "However, Lewis gave us to understand you wished to see us right away."

Their willingness to wait until she summoned them, as well as their genuinely sorrowful and respectful demeanors—so different from most of the tradesmen she'd already met—made her like them instantly.

"We didn't really get the chance to know your sister well," Bartholemew admitted, twisting the cap in his hands. "Still, I'd like to think we were her friends. Isn't that so, Marmaduke?"

"Indeed! She had many friends, and admirers, too. Such a lovely woman! And she always dressed so well."

"Audrey did like pretty things," Celeste said.

"She certainly did!" Marmaduke confirmed.

A blushing Bartholemew cleared his throat. "Costly things."

Celeste hurried to set them at their ease, at least on

this one point. "I suspect she owed you money for some of her gowns."

"As a matter of fact," Bartholemew began, while Marmaduke looked down at the toes of his polished boots, "there is the small matter of the last three bolts of fabric she had yet to pay for."

"Naturally you must either have the money repaid or the fabric returned," Celeste replied. "Unfortunately, I've found no bolts of fabric, only gowns. I have no need for such finery, so will you take the gowns as payment instead?"

The two men exchanged uneasy glances. "We don't deal in clothing already worn," Marmaduke said after an equally uneasy silence.

"They are hardly worn," she said. "And there are silk veils, too, and scarves. The value of all should be more than enough to cover your loss, I'm sure. Won't you please come upstairs and look at them?"

Again the men exchanged wary looks.

"I must confess to you, gentlemen," Celeste reluctantly continued, "that if they will not satisfy you, you may not get all that you're owed. Audrey had many creditors, and even with the sale of the house, there might not be sufficient—"

"No, no, it isn't that," Bartholemew interrupted.

The two men turned as red as ripe apples before Marmaduke leaned forward and whispered, "I fear it wouldn't be proper, we being men, you see, and you a woman, to go upstairs together."

"I am a nun," she replied with a smile, appreciative of their concern for her reputation, especially when other men were not, and sorry that she had to lie to them. She nodded at the entrance to the kitchen. "There is another woman in the house, so I see no harm."

The two men relaxed. "If you see none, we will be glad to go with you," Bartholemew said.

Together they followed Celeste up the stairs and into the large upper chamber.

Bartholemew immediately rushed toward the bed. "By blessed Saint Dorcas!" he exclaimed, feeling the fabric. "Look at these bed curtains! Venetian silk, as I live and breathe!"

"And look at that tapestry!" Marmaduke cried. "It has to be Italian, too, or maybe French."

"They will have to be sold, as well," Celeste noted as she opened the large chest.

Out of the corner of her eye she saw the men give each other significant looks and guessed the bed curtains and tapestry were as good as sold if they could agree upon a price.

She lifted out the red gown and refused to feel a pang of regret. What use would she ever have for such a garment? And the one time she'd worn it had been a disaster.

"Oh, my!" Bartholemew gasped.

"It's lovely, simply lovely!" Marmaduke declared, hurrying to hold out the full skirt while Bartholemew carefully examined the embroidery. "I've never seen anything so well done," he murmured reverently.

"I think Audrey did it," Celeste said with a hint of pride. "She was good with a needle."

Bartholemew ran a measuring gaze over her. "It would fit *you*, I think."

"Indeed, I believe it would!" Marmaduke cried with sudden excitement. "And the color would suit you perfectly! You would look like a queen, wouldn't she, Bartholemew?"

"I should say so!"

Shaking her head, Celeste stepped back. "I have no wish to look like a queen."

"Ah, yes, forgive me, Sister," a chastised Bartholemew replied.

"I'm not offended," she quickly assured him. "Will you take the clothes in lieu of payment?"

"Although as I said, we don't usually deal in worn gowns," Bartholemew answered, "I believe in this instance we can make an exception. Isn't that so, Marmaduke?"

His companion nodded.

"All these things are worth somewhat more than the debt. If you include the bed curtains and tapestry, we'll give you…" Bartholemew glanced at Marmaduke, then back at her. "Twenty marks, as well."

"That is most generous of you!" she replied with heartfelt gratitude.

"Unfortunately, we didn't come prepared for such a transaction and have a shipment from London to deal with before the day is out," Bartholemew said. "We could return tomorrow."

"There is no great hurry if tomorrow will not do," she replied. "I don't intend to leave until the sale of the house is concluded."

And I've either found my father's money or searched everywhere I can.

"Excellent. We do have a bit of time at the moment to see more of the gowns, Sister, if we may."

"Of course. Please, go ahead."

Sitting on the stool, she watched as the two men removed gowns, shifts, caps and veils from Audrey's chests and boxes. They gave many excited exclamations and were clearly delighted.

Yet these had been her sister's things. Gowns and

caps and veils and scarves Audrey had worn. Lovely things she'd no doubt enjoyed.

If only she could have spent more time with Audrey and gotten to know her better. She remembered Audrey as so much older and more mature, although only a few years had separated them.

The ginger cat padded into the room and wound itself around the stool. A tear fell down Celeste's cheek as she bent to stroke it.

At the same time, she realized Bartholemew and Marmaduke had stopped talking. They were regarding her with sorrow and sympathy once again, and she quickly wiped her cheek.

"We're sorry, Sister, if we've upset you," Bartholemew said quietly. "Under the circumstances, we should have given you more time to consider."

"No, no, it's quite all right," she said, putting on the mask of placid calm she had learned to wear. "It's just difficult thinking about Audrey."

"We quite understand, and if you'd rather we depart—"

"Not yet," she interrupted. She clasped her hands together and regarded them with sincere longing. "I know so little about my sister's life since I went to the convent. I want to think she was happy and admired before she…died."

"She was certainly admired!" Marmaduke exclaimed.

"Indeed! So many admirers! And offers to wed, too, no doubt. I thought Sir Roland would marry her. However, in hindsight, I think it was for the best he didn't. Such a grim fellow, and your sister…well, Gerrard would have been a much better match."

His words were like a cold finger down Celeste's spine. "Did he ask for her hand?"

Batholemew looked stricken, as if he'd said something

rude. "Not that I heard of, and I don't think she would have accepted."

"Nor I," Marmaduke agreed. "Your sister was an, ahem, ambitious woman."

It was true Gerrard had no wealth or title, and Audrey had wanted both. Even if she had felt something for Gerrard, she would never have married him.

As for what Gerrard might have felt for Audrey…

It would have come to nothing. Audrey wouldn't have risked any gossip about a liaison with Gerrard lest it hurt her chances to catch a rich and powerful husband.

Celeste gave them both another sad little smile. "I'm aware that my sister wanted to marry well. I admit I'm as surprised as anyone that she hadn't wed already, unless…"

Both men leaned closer.

"Was it common knowledge she was in debt?"

They both reared back. "*We* didn't know," they said in unison, and so firmly she believed them.

They might not be ignorant of other things concerning her sister and her household, though. "Did either of you ever think that Duncan MacHeath might hurt her? Or that she should fear him?"

"No," they replied together.

"He was clearly a rough and rather savage fellow," Bartholemew added, "but we never thought he'd hurt her."

"And he's paying a terrible, everlasting price for his crime, especially if he killed himself," Marmaduke said.

Gerrard hadn't said that MacHeath had ended his own life. "I was told he fell into the river after Roland wounded him."

"Well, he might have," Bartholemew hastily admitted. "Nobody knows what happened to him, not exactly.

He'd been wounded by Sir Roland and they found his body in the river. That's all we know for certain. He *could* have fallen in."

"He didn't seem the remorseful sort," Marmaduke helpfully noted, "but when you think about what he did—"

Bartholemew put his hand on his partner's shoulder and steered him toward the door. "Either way, he drowned," he said with firm dismissal. "Now you really must pardon us. That shipment may be here already. Good day, Sister!"

"If there's anything more we can do, please ask!" Marmaduke called over his shoulder.

When they were gone, Celeste sank onto the bed, wondering what else she hadn't been told. Surely she had a right to know everything about Audrey's death and the fate of the man who'd killed her. That would be only just.

She recalled what she did know about Audrey, Duncan MacHeath and that horrific day.

Audrey had been ambitious, eager for a rich and titled husband. Duncan MacHeath, who was neither, had claimed to love her and had killed her in a fit of jealousy when she rebuffed him. Afterward he'd gone after Roland, thinking he was her lover. He'd nearly killed him, but Roland had wounded the Scot, who had then been found dead in the river.

On the surface, it seemed a simple, horrible tale with a deadly ending, until questions began to surface. Why hadn't Audrey, who'd been dealing with eager, lustful men for years, recognized that MacHeath was a danger? Or as much of one as he proved to be?

What had prompted MacHeath to reveal his feelings

that particular day? Was it possible someone had inadvertently prompted him to confess his love?

Or had someone provoked him?

If Audrey had refused a different man and he was upset by her rejection of his suit, and if this other man had an inkling of MacHeath's feelings, how difficult would it have been to inspire MacHeath to tell Audrey how he felt, guessing the Scot would also be rejected and likely exact a harsh punishment for that rejection? It would have been very convenient for that person if Duncan MacHeath died right after.

Perhaps MacHeath hadn't fallen into the river by accident or taken his own life. Maybe someone had pushed him.

Who in Dunborough knew how the Scot had felt about Audrey? And who else in Dunborough might have wanted Audrey dead?

Celeste went to the window, looking out at the great mass of the castle now dark in the dusk. She couldn't leave Dunborough until she had the answers to these questions, and if that meant talking to Gerrard to get them, she would.

Chapter Eleven

"Bella, beautiful Bella!" Gerrard called out as he staggered into the brothel much later that night. "Where are you, Bella?"

The brothel-keeper hurried to help him over the threshold. Edric didn't want Gerrard to fall or rouse the neighbors. Everyone in Dunborough and for miles around knew of his brothel, and most were willing to turn a blind eye as long as he kept a peaceable establishment.

At least for now. Edric had his doubts that Sir Roland would let his business continue, although soldiers needed such recreation.

There were a few soldiers from the castle there now, and if they were a bit surprised to see Gerrard come staggering in, well, what of it? The man's money was as good as theirs and he wasn't married or betrothed, so it was with a smile that the proprietor closed the door and got Gerrard into a chair.

The very drunk Gerrard. Edric didn't need to smell the ale on him to be sure of that. The slurred words, loud voice and glazed eyes were more than enough.

"Where's Bella?" Gerrard demanded, blinking and giving Edric a sodden grin. He frowned. "Busy?"

"Not too busy for you!" Edric hurried to reply. "Stay here and I'll fetch her."

"Now that's what I like to hear," Gerrard declared to no one in particular. "Respect!"

Bella appeared, pulling her bodice back into place, her face wreathed with smiles, her dark brown hair disheveled. She pushed a lock behind her ear as she hurried toward Gerrard. She was not particularly slender and not as pretty as Celeste, but she was attractive enough in her own way.

"Aha!" he cried, pulling her down onto his lap. "You like me, don't you, Bella?"

"I should say so," she answered, planting a kiss on his lips.

"Missed me?"

"Ain't I just?" She rose and grabbed his hand to lead him to one of the several small rooms where she and the other girls plied their trade.

Gerrard didn't protest. He let her take him to her little chamber. There was a bed, a washstand and not much else. The linens weren't the cleanest, but he could be sure there were no fleas.

He sat heavily on the messy bed and rubbed his temples. "I think I need some wine."

Bella slipped her bodice off her shoulders and sat down beside him. "I think you've had enough for tonight, my honey."

He turned to look at her, his expression unexpectedly serious. "Do you really like me, Bella?"

"O'course I do!"

"If I didn't pay you, would you still like me?"

"O'course! Now what's got into you?" she asked, stroking his cheek. "You ain't usually so serious."

"I fear, Bella my dear, that I've developed a conssh... a consken... I don't feel right about this anymore."

Bella drew back in disbelief. "What?"

Gerrard started to stand, swaying as if he were on the deck of a ship at sea. "She wouldn't like it. Neither would Roland, and neither do I. Not really. It's not the same if you have to pay."

Bella rose, her face red with anger. "What's that you say?"

He patted her cheek. "Sorry, sweet. Those days are done. Now be a lamb and get me some wine, will you?"

"Get it yourself!" Bella said angrily, and she shoved him out the door.

Long after the moon had risen, Verdan yawned as he and his brother left the stables and headed toward the hall. They'd gone to check Arnhelm's horse again, for Arnhelm found it impossible to rest until he'd made sure Oaken was all right. Verdan, who knew more about horses than his brother, had agreed to accompany him.

"Just as well there's no letter for you to take back yet, eh?" Verdan noted as they skirted a large puddle. "Gives Oaken more time to heal." He slid his brother a sly grin. "And you get more time with Peg."

"Aye, that's so," Arnhelm replied, but not with the good humor his brother expected.

"What? There's no trouble between the two o' you, is there?"

"Peg and me? Not a bit!"

"Are you worried Ma won't ever come here?"

"Well, there's that, too."

"What else, then?"

"I can't fathom why Gerrard won't write a letter to

his brother. Seems simple enough for them as knows how to write."

"Gerrard's a busy fellow. Might not have the time."

Arnhelm gave Verdan a puzzled look as they neared the gate. "He's got plenty o' time if he wants it. Seems he'd rather ride out or oversee the trainin'. I can understand that, but not when his brother's waitin' on an answer."

"What's the question?"

"D'ya think I know? Sir Roland ain't about to confide that sort o' thing to me, or anybody else 'cept his wife."

"Well then, maybe it's a question takes a lot o' thinkin' about," Verdan proposed.

At the same time they heard a strange sound on the other side of the castle wall.

"What in God's name is that?" Arnhelm demanded, turning toward the gate.

Verdan squinted as if that would improve his hearing. "Somebody's singing."

"If you could call that singing," Arnhelm muttered while young Hedley, standing guard, moved forward to open the wicket gate.

A man stumbled over the threshold and grabbed Hedley's shoulder for support while loudly and drunkenly warbling, "Oh-h-h, I told her that I loved her and she *spit* right in my face!"

"S'truth, that's Gerrard!" Verdan gasped.

"Drunk as a tinker at a fair," Arnhelm grimly agreed.

The brothers trotted toward the gate while Gerrard continued to hang on to Hedley as if he'd fall without the man's support.

That was likely the case.

"Ah, Arnhelm! And Verdan!" Gerrard cried when he saw them. "Evening, men! I was just saying to eagle-eyed Hedley here that it's a chilly night. Cold enough to freeze your toes to icicles, like Roland when he's angry. And her, too, only she's *worse*."

Arnhelm had no idea to whom he was referring, but he did notice a distinctly unpleasant odor of dung coming from the vicinity of Gerrard's left boot. Trying to ignore it, he ducked under his shoulder to help support him. "Come along, sir. Time for bed."

"Bed?" Gerrard cried, pushing him away, then swaying like a tree in a heavy wind. "Bed? Why, man, it's early! Bed? Not for merry lads like us, eh?" He frowned and peered at Arnhelm and Verdan. "Such good brothers. Friends forever. Not like me and mine."

He grabbed Arnhelm's shoulder. Leaning forward and breathing full in the man's face, he patted Arnhelm's chest. Meanwhile, Arnhelm reared back as far as possible to escape Gerrard's wine-soaked breath.

"And now you've got sweethearts, too!" Gerrard continued, his words slurring. "Lucky chaps! Some of us aren't. Never going to have that kind of luck, either."

After barking a laugh that was not joyful, he started to sing again. "I told her that I loved her and she *spit* right in my face!"

He took a step forward and fell flat on his face.

As if of one mind, Arnhelm and Verdan reached down and hauled the semiconscious man to his feet.

"God's blood, he stinks!" muttered Verdan. "How much wine did he have?"

"Far too much, that's for sure," his brother replied, "and I don't want to know what else he might have got up to."

"I got *nothing* up," Gerrard declared as he twisted away from their grasp and attempted to brush himself off. "No more whores for me, men. Those days are done.

Not that some people will ever believe it, even if they dress in red gowns and act like Delilah."

The brothers exchanged confused looks before they again attempted to take hold of Gerrard.

"Come along, sir, it's late and getting later," Arnhelm cajoled.

"Late? Aye, too late," Gerrard agreed as his legs seemed to lose what strength they possessed and he started to sink to the ground. "Too late to change, no matter how much..."

His voice trailed off as he landed facedown once again, barely missing a puddle.

"Oh, God help us, he's out," Verdan muttered with dismay.

"Might be for the best," Arnhelm grunted as they did their best to lift the deadweight of Gerrard's unconscious body.

They got their shoulders under his arms and half carried, half dragged him to the hall and up to his chamber. After they got him on the bed and pulled off his stinking boots, they looked down at the snoring, mud-splattered young man.

"I really thought he'd changed," Arnhelm said with regret.

"Aye, me, too. Do you think you ought to tell Sir Roland?"

Arnhelm stroked his beard. "I suppose so. If Gerrard's going to drink like this, he's not fit to be the garrison commander."

"Aye," Verdan said with a sigh as they went out and closed the door.

His head aching, his throat dry as a desert, Gerrard cracked open one eyelid to see a shaft of weak sunlight coming through the slightly open shutters. Without moving his head, he looked around.

He was on his own bed in his own chamber and it was morning.

With a low moan, he closed his eyes again. He could remember going to the Cock's Crow and then the brothel, and that Bella had been angry. Everything else was a mystery.

You weak, stupid, disgraceful fool!

He didn't hear those words in Roland's voice. Or Celeste's. His own was bad enough.

As he eased himself upright, he noticed he was fully clothed, except for his boots. They were on the floor on the far side of the chamber. Somebody must have brought him here and taken them off. Otherwise, they'd likely still be on his feet.

Gingerly he got up and went over to the washstand. He lifted the ewer of frigid water to his parched lips and drank before pouring the rest into the basin and rinsing his face.

He leaned on the washstand and wondered who had brought him back and who else might have seen him in that drunken state. Please God not Celeste. She thought little enough of him as it was.

He sniffed. God save him, was that...?

Not his clothes, although they were soiled and muddy. Thank heaven for small mercies.

He looked around and saw his boots and the origin of the odor.

Sweet saints, how drunk *had* he been?

Did it matter? He could already hear the gossip. See the looks on people's faces. Celeste's—Sister Augustine's— too.

Having her here was like having Roland back. Like

his brother, she made him want to drink until he forgot everything that troubled him and didn't feel like a worthless rogue.

No, she made him feel worse. Not only stupid, but unredeemable, too. The virtuous, untouchable Sister Augustine, driving him to drink.

He shook his head. He was past blaming others. It was his weakness, and he alone was to blame. Perhaps it would indeed be better if he left here and began again somewhere else where no one knew him, maybe taking a different name, like Celeste, albeit for a very different reason.

After he changed his tunic and breeches, and found his old boots under the bed, Gerrard decided he would feel better if he had some bread. That usually settled his stomach after a night of carousing. Carousing meant drinking and—

Heaven help him, was there more to regret? He quickly grabbed the purse he carried in his belt and counted the coins.

Thank God most of it was still there—a small triumph, but still a triumph, enough to make him feel not quite so wretched as he went to the hall.

There were a few off-duty soldiers and servants still breaking their fast.

And one habit-clad woman waiting on the dais.

Chapter Twelve

What was Celeste doing here? Oh, sweet Mary, if she had seen him last night…

Gerrard adjusted his tunic, straightened his shoulders and reminded himself Celeste had no authority to upbraid him.

Maybe she had come to say that she was going back to Saint Agatha's. That should be welcome news, and if he thought it wasn't, he must still be the worse for wine.

"Good day, Sister Augustine," he said, attempting to sound cheerful. "What brings you here this morning?"

Her eyes narrowed and she frowned as she studied him. "Are you ill?"

"Not at all," he lied. His head hurt as if a thousand angry little demons were prodding him with spears. "Are you?" he asked, for she was paler than he recalled and there were dark circles under her eyes.

"Merely tired. I didn't sleep well last night."

Oh, sweet Mother Mary! Maybe she *had* seen him.

In spite of his shame and remorse, he smiled as he gestured for her to sit before he sank onto one of the chairs.

Regardless of his invitation, she continued to stand

as stiff as a spear, with her hands in the cuffs of her habit. "I would like to speak with you, Gerrard. Alone."

Alone? That was unexpected.

Aware that there were still servants and soldiers in the hall, he raised a brow, yet kept his voice carefully cool as he replied. "What can we possibly have to discuss that would require privacy?"

"My sister's murder."

Not last night—but this subject was just as unwelcome. "Surely there is nothing more to say about that."

"I believe there is," she replied, still grimly determined, and she had that stubborn look in her eyes. She wasn't going to give up until she got what she wanted.

"We can talk in the solar," he said, rising and starting down the hall.

He didn't look to see if she followed. He didn't have to. The soft swish of her habit gave her away. He wished he'd never seen her in anything else, and certainly not that beautiful gown cut low enough to reveal the swell of her breasts.

She is a nun, so don't even think of her in that gown.

Instead, Gerrard forced himself to ponder what more she might want to know about Audrey's death as he led her from the hall to the yard and around to the outer steps of the keep. It was the oldest part of the castle and couldn't be reached from the newer hall. His father had wanted it that way.

He pushed open the door and went in first, grabbing Roland's letter and shoving it under some other documents on the table.

When she entered, he nonchalantly continued around the table until it was between them. "Now then, I gather something's troubling you about your sister's death?"

This time Celeste did sit down, although she looked

no less resolute. "Not just Audrey's death, but Duncan MacHeath's, as well," she answered. "You told me he fell into the river. Is that what really happened?"

Wondering what she was getting at, Gerrard nodded. "Yes. His footprints were on the riverbank."

"And no one else's?"

Baffled, he replied, "No, why do you ask?"

"It's been suggested to me that he might have killed himself."

"Who the devil told you that?" Gerrard demanded with a frown.

"Is it possible?" she persisted.

Certain he was right, Gerrard shook his head. "No. MacHeath wasn't that sort of fellow."

"I, too, find it difficult to believe even a murderer would risk his immortal soul that way."

Trying not to scowl, for he had no such rosy notions of an evil man's thoughts regarding his immortal soul, Gerrard sat down. "I meant he was not a man to feel regret or remorse."

"Have you ever wondered what made him attack Audrey that particular day?"

That, too, was unexpected—and unwelcome. The less Celeste delved into Audrey's past, the better, even if her questions didn't exactly touch upon his dealings with her sister. "I assumed she told him he stood no chance with her."

"Yet Audrey has had suitors and admirers for years and she was skilled at putting them off without angering them. Surely she would have been able to refuse MacHeath without making him angry enough to kill her."

Gerrard hadn't considered that. "Maybe he did more than ask. If she pushed him away, that might have made him attack her. A man like MacHeath—it would be natural for him to use his fists or weapons."

Celeste leaned forward, her eyes shrewdly bright. "Or perhaps Duncan wasn't the only man who wanted Audrey and who was refused. Perhaps another man was as angry and sought to punish her, but wasn't the sort to resort to physical violence, lest he risk imprisonment and execution. What if this other man realized how MacHeath felt and used the Scot's jealousy and savagery for his own ends? Who knows what such a person might have said to MacHeath, the ideas he could have put into his head? It might not have taken much to goad the Scot into a rage before he spoke to my sister that day."

Gerrard regarded Celeste incredulously. "You mean someone *used* Duncan to kill your sister?"

"Yes."

He rose abruptly. "God's blood, Celeste! Do you really believe any man could be so sly and underhanded?"

"Can't you?" she asked as she, too, got to her feet and looked at him as if he were a child who failed to comprehend an easy lesson. "Are you truly that innocent?"

"I haven't been considered innocent in a very long time."

"Naive, then, if you don't realize that some people are capable of any manner of bad things to get what they want, including revenge, especially if they can cast the blame on someone else."

As he had sometimes cast it on Roland, Gerrard thought.

He wondered if she meant to make that comparison. Or was it purely by chance?

"What kind of convent is Saint Agatha's, anyway,"

he asked warily, "that you would come up with such an idea?"

"One like any other," she replied, "where women are shut up together with few things to take their minds from slights, no matter how petty. Where they have plenty of time to brood and scheme."

"Sweet merciful Mary! As bad as that?"

"There are only a few among the sisters and novices who are like that. A good mother superior soon discovers who they are and deals with them, either by showing them the error of their ways or sending them to another convent if need be. Or, if they are truly unable to find peace, back to their families with the suggestion that the holy life does not suit them.

"Now, as to my sister's suitors," she continued, "did you hear of anyone arguing or quarreling with her? Or denouncing her in any way?"

"No," Gerrard honestly replied. His men talked and jested about the women with whom they dallied, but Audrey had never been among them.

"No gossip among the soldiers here?"

"Not about your sister."

"There must be others who might have such information. Her maidservant, perhaps, or the village priest."

"Martha hasn't been…well…since it happened. She found your sister's body."

Celeste's expression softened as she crossed herself and murmured, "Poor woman."

In the next moment, however, that determined, resolute look returned. "What about the priest?"

"Audrey was no nun."

Unlike Celeste, Audrey was a worldly woman, willing to use whatever means a beautiful one possessed to get what she wanted.

"No, but he would not be a suitor, either," Celeste replied, "so she might have felt free to speak to him about any difficulties."

Gerrard frowned. He didn't think talking to Father Denzail would do any good. Celeste might find out things about her sister that would be unpleasant to hear. "Are you sure you want to do this? Duncan MacHeath confessed his guilt to Roland and then died. Does it really matter how his death came about?"

"I need to know if there was more to my sister's death than one angry, jealous man," she said firmly. "And shouldn't you find out if there's someone in Dunborough who would compel another to murder? Who can say what other things a man like that might be capable of?"

If such a fellow existed, which Gerrard truly doubted. Nevertheless, he was also certain that Celeste would not give up until she'd spoken to the priest and Martha, so it would be useless to argue any more.

It would be best if he went with her, too, especially to see Audrey's maidservant. He could well believe Celeste would go there by herself, regardless of the distance, and he didn't want her traveling alone.

"Very well," he said. "First we'll go to see Father Denzail, then I'll take you to Martha."

Mass had already started by the time Celeste and Gerrard reached the church. Celeste quickly knelt with the villagers and, as the ceremony progressed, tried not to look at Gerrard. He stood leaning against a pillar, his expression unreadable, his arms crossed and his brows lowered. Like the rest of his family, he apparently had no use for the church. It was unfortunate he had never had the chance to learn the comfort it could bring and the different kind of family it could provide.

Unfortunately, Father Denzail wasn't likely to encourage him to want to learn those lessons. The priest was about forty-five, she thought, his hair more gray than brown. He was shorter than Gerrard, as were most men, and his shoulders slightly rounded, as if he'd spent days hunched over a desk in a scriptorium copying manuscripts. Perhaps he had and so was more used to dealing with quill, ink and parchment than inspiring his flock.

After the mass had concluded and the people were filing out, Celeste continued to kneel in prayer. She would not draw any more attention to herself by acknowledging Gerrard. That they had arrived together was enough to get tongues wagging.

But when it looked as if the priest was going to leave, she rose and called out to him. "Father!"

Father Denzail put on a welcoming smile. In spite of that, she could tell he wasn't pleased even before he darted a swift and wary sideways glance at Gerrard.

"I'm sorry to detain you, Father," she said. "I'm Sister Augustine, Audrey D'Orleau's sister."

"Ah, yes. I heard you had arrived," he answered. "I've been expecting you at mass long before now."

Celeste clasped her hands and, regarding him woefully, wondered if it was a greater sin to lie to a priest. However, she wasn't going to admit that guilt for feigning holy sisterhood had kept her away. "I've been overwhelmed with the need to prepare the house for sale, and sorrow for my sister, too."

The little man's visage softened. "I've offered many prayers for your poor sister and masses have been said."

"Thank you, Father. I wanted to ask you now, though, if Audrey ever spoke to you of any fears she harbored."

"I wish she *had* been afraid," he mournfully replied. "I wish she'd feared for her immortal soul."

His expression decidedly unfriendly, Gerrard pushed himself from the pillar and strolled closer. "I've heard you often went to visit Audrey. I wonder why."

The priest straightened his narrow, rounded shoulders. "I was trying to make her see the error of her ways and bring her closer to God."

"God, or yourself?"

"Gerrard!" Celeste gasped.

He raised a brow at her and said, "You want the truth, don't you?"

"Perhaps Father Denzail and I should speak alone," she replied, not pleased by Gerrard's hostile manner. That was hardly going to encourage the priest to provide information. "Come, Father, let us go to the sacristy. We can talk privately there."

"There's no need, Sister," he replied, licking his lips and nervously fingering his crucifix. "I have nothing to say that this man need not hear. Yes, I visited your sister. I tried to get her to lead a more sedate and serious life. Regrettably, she paid me no heed. In spite of her defiance, I have done all I can to ensure that she finds her way to heaven. Eventually."

"You never noticed anything amiss between her and Duncan MacHeath?"

"No, although I suggested such a barbarian was not a fit servant for her." There was a hint of anger in the little man's voice as he added, "She laughed at me when I tried to warn her."

"At least you tried," Celeste said placatingly. "No one else did."

"I confess I had no idea you were such a perceptive man," Gerrard remarked, "provided you did indeed dare to say such a thing to Audrey, which I doubt."

There was no need for him to be so insolent. Yet before Celeste could speak, Father Denzail displayed more backbone than she expected. "And I fear no amount of praying will save your tarnished soul, Gerrard!"

The priest started to leave and Celeste quickly put her hand on his arm to detain him. "Please, Father, I'm trying to learn more about my sister and her life. Did you hear of any quarrels she had with other men?"

"My concern was with your sister's immortal soul, not rumors and gossip," he snapped.

Gerrard's next remark didn't ease the tension in the church. "If you weren't listening to rumors and gossip, how did you guess her immortal soul was in danger?"

Celeste shot him another condemning glance, then took the priest's arm and led him a little farther away. "Speaking of immortal souls, Father, do you think it's possible that Duncan MacHeath took his own life?"

The priest stared at her with surprise. "The man was clearly in league with the devil, but I never…" He frowned. "I suppose he might, since his soul was already lost, like some others I could name," he said, glaring at Gerrard. "That's all I have to say about your sister or that Scot." He pointed at Gerrard. "As for you, you young rogue, you are indeed your father's son!"

With that parting shot, the priest scurried away like a squirrel and disappeared through the sacristy door.

To be sure, Gerrard hadn't behaved well, either with courtesy or respect, yet to compare him—or anyone—to the vicious Sir Blane was a terrible insult. Gerrard had a long way to go before he could ever be as evil as his father.

"He shouldn't have insulted you that way," Celeste said, hoping to take away some of the sting of that remark. "I'm sure it was only Father Denzail's pride talking. You *were* rude to him and you upset him with your implication that his visits to Audrey had a lustful motive."

Gerrard's cold, dark eyes could have been Roland's gazing back at her. "I *don't* believe his motives were completely pure. A priest can lie and you weren't here. He spent time with your sister to the neglect of others who could have used his ministrations."

"Just as I'm sure it's possible that Father Denzail was trying to help her."

The corners of Gerrard's mouth rose in that mocking grin. "So speaks a woman who's lived in a convent for ten years. How many men did you meet there? One or two?"

"Many priests came to visit over the years, enough for me to learn how to tell which ones were lustful, which ones were truly holy and which ones were trying to be virtuous."

Her companion crossed his arms, leaned his weight on one leg and raised a questioning brow. "Based on this vast experience, where would you place Father Denzail?"

Gerrard's condescending attitude began to try her patience, as well as his denigration of the clergyman. "He may not be completely virtuous, but he's not a lecher. Even if the man did lust after Audrey, it would torment him and drive him to fasting and prayer and perhaps a pilgrimage. His pain would go inward, not outward toward another."

Gerrard shifted and his expression lost its insolence. "You seem very certain."

"I think we can both agree that I would have a better understanding of priests than you."

"I think I have a better understanding of men in general."

"I would agree you likely understand men ruled by their passions better than I."

"You speak as if passion's a bad thing."

"How can it *not* be," she replied, "when it leads to sin? Look what it drove Duncan MacHeath to do. Look what men governed by their lust for money and power have done in their quest for gain. The lives greed has destroyed. The pain they inflict on their families and all who know them."

"Like my father. And like yours."

She hadn't meant to refer to anyone in particular. Nevertheless, he was right. "Yes, like our fathers."

"Yet not all desire is evil," Gerrard replied. "A lust for a better life can be a good thing. Where would we be if all men lacked ambition or a desire to improve their lives or to make their tasks easier?"

He moved closer. "It isn't passion that's evil, Celeste," he said, his voice low and husky. "Neither is desire. It's a part of love."

Her heartbeat throbbed in her ears. Her body warmed and excitement surged through her, accompanied by dread. He was too close, his lips mere inches from hers, his dark-eyed gaze seeming to see into her soul.

Her innermost thoughts. Her dreams. Her desires.

She took a step back. "You said you would take me to speak to Audrey's maidservant."

"Today?"

"Yes, today!"

Whatever Celeste had seen in Gerrard's eyes moments before, it was gone now.

"Your wish is my command, Sister," he said lightly as he bowed. "Wait here while I fetch some horses."

"Is it so far away that we need to ride?"

"If we're to get there and back before the sun sets today."

"Bring them to my house, please. I should finish packing Audrey's gowns. Bartholemew and Marmaduke have bought them from me. *All* of them," she couldn't stop herself from adding.

"Rather a pity, that," Gerrard replied, his tone bland and nonchalant as he left her in the empty, chilly church.

Chapter Thirteen

Sir Melvin threw on his cloak and hurried out into the yard to greet the visitor who had arrived in a heavy wooden carriage. "A fine lady!" the stable boy had said, and one look at the tall, regal woman disembarking from the carriage didn't contradict that description.

Except for one thing.

The woman's black clothing, dark veil and golden crucifix visible in a small gap between the edges of her cloak lined with red fox fur meant she was a nun.

Her imperious gaze and slightly sneering lips warned that she was no ordinary nun, and given her age, as evidenced by the wrinkles at her eyes and the sides of her mouth, he suspected she must be of high office.

"Greetings!" he declared. "Welcome to my estate. Please, enjoy the hospitality of my hall."

In spite of his friendly invitation, the woman regarded him as she might a toad. "I am the mother superior of Saint Agatha's."

She paused as if expecting a response. All Sir Melvin could think to say was, "Is that so?"

The woman frowned. "Yes, it is so."

"Won't you come inside?" Sir Melvin asked. His cloak was not so fine and he was starting to shiver.

She inclined her head and swept past him, leaving him to trot after her like an obedient puppy.

Once in the hall, Sir Melvin waylaid the first servant he saw and urgently whispered, "Tell my wife we have a reverend mother in the hall, and have someone bring wine. The good wine. And some bread if it's ready. Maybe some cheese, too. Or apples. Both!" he added, before ridding himself of his cloak.

The mother superior still wore hers. Indeed, she'd wrapped it around herself as if to protect herself from contagion.

Rubbing his hands together and feeling a bit more sure of himself in his own hall, Sir Melvin approached her with his usual pleasant smile. "May I take your cloak?"

"Not yet," she replied.

"Won't you sit?" he asked with somewhat less good humor, gesturing at the finest chair they owned, drawn up near the fire in the central hearth.

She did and then regarded him with the coldest, blackest eyes he had ever seen. "My servants and I require quarters for the night."

"Indeed? Yes, of course you're welcome to stay here. I'm sure my wife and I will be only too—"

"I also require information. I understand a woman in a nun's habit recently stayed here. She was on her way to Dunborough, I believe."

"I, um, that is…" Sir Melvin was not a man for subterfuge, for he was honest to the marrow of his bones. Nevertheless, he was not keen to answer, although he was fairly certain he knew to whom this haughty woman was referring. "We often give shelter to people going to and from Dunborough. We had the honor of extending our hospitality to the new lord and his charming bride recently. Sir Roland—perhaps you've heard of him? His wife is a lovely woman, lovely! So charming and beautiful! And sweet! Really, he's a very fortunate man."

"I have not stopped here to discuss the merits of Sir Roland or his wife," the mother superior returned. "I wish to know if you did indeed give shelter to a thief pretending to be a nun."

He'd been thinking the young beauty had been a runaway, and now more than ever he could sympathize with anyone who sought to get away from this horrid woman. A thief, though. That was different.

Yet he still found himself reluctant to answer.

The mother superior rose. "If you did and refuse to tell me, the flames of hell await you."

"You must forgive my husband, as I'm sure God will," Lady Viola said as she joined them. "He has a soft heart for all in need."

Sir Melvin had rarely been so relieved to see his wife, especially when she came face-to-face and nose to nose with their imperious visitor. If anybody could stare down a harpy, it was his Viola.

"What exactly did the girl steal?" she asked.

"That is hardly any business of yours," the mother superior replied. "Theft is theft, and a sin. She must be found and punished."

"Well, then it's unfortunate that we don't know where she went," Viola calmly replied.

Sir Melvin nearly choked.

"She said she was going to Dunborough, but I doubt a fleeing thief would go where she claimed. That would be foolish, wouldn't it?" Viola continued. "And that young woman was no fool.

"She also claimed to be Audrey D'Orleau's sister. I suppose she must have been lying about that, too. If she were really Audrey's sister, she would have traveled to Dunborough as soon as she got word of her sister's death, not weeks after—unless, of course, something or someone had prevented her from learning of her sister's demise."

The mother superior's face was so red, Sir Melvin wanted to applaud. If anyone deserved a set-down, it was surely this horrible woman, who'd no doubt kept the news of her sister's death from that sweet and beautiful young woman.

The mother superior gathered her cloak about her. "Now that I have the information I sought, I shall be on my way."

"Oh? You won't stay the night?" Viola coolly inquired, because hospitality demanded it.

"I most certainly will not!" the mother superior huffed before she marched from the hall. Once she reached the yard, they could hear her calling for her wagon to be made ready *at once*!

One of the maidservants appeared with a tray bearing wine and bread and apples. Sir Melvin reached for a goblet and took a fortifying drink. "God help me, I'm glad she's gone!"

"God help Sister Augustine, or whatever her name really is," Viola replied as she joined him at the hearth and took a piece of bread.

"Perhaps we should send word to Dunborough. A swift rider could get there today. Traveling in that wagon, that woman will take another day at least."

"I daresay our visitor is aware that the mother superior will come after her, or send someone else to find her. I suspect she's already gone."

"You're right as always, my dear."

"I think a letter to the bishop in charge of Saint Agatha's might be in order. There's no excuse for keeping the knowledge of a family member's death a secret. Nor do I imagine that mother superior is a tender guardian of novices in her care."

"A fine idea, my dear," Sir Melvin said, patting his beloved wife's hand.

A slight clearing of a throat made Celeste look up. She was packing away the last of Audrey's gowns, the one of red silk, as well as the tapestry and bed curtains, in the large chest. Once that was done, they would be ready to be taken away, and she would never see them again.

"Lewis is below," Lizabet said from the doorway, "and wishes to speak with you."

Not Gerrard, then, Celeste thought as she closed the lid of the chest. She'd been wondering how long it took to get from the church to the castle stables and have two horses saddled. Longer than she'd assumed, apparently.

Unless something had happened at the castle to prevent Gerrard from returning with the horses. Maybe he had decided not to take her to the maidservant after all, or that it was a useless endeavor. Perhaps he thought there wasn't time to get there and return before the sun set. If so, the least he could do was send word.

"These chests and boxes are ready for Bartholemew and Marmaduke," Celeste said, straightening, "should they come by later to collect them."

"Won't you be here, Sister?"

"Perhaps not. Gerrard and I were planning to see Martha."

Lizabet's eyes widened, as if going to see Audrey's former maidservant was a shocking thing to do.

"Is there some reason I should not?" Celeste inquired.

"I guess it won't do any harm," Lizabet replied, "but the poor woman's not been right since your sister died. She won't come back to Dunborough for love nor money."

Celeste was relieved to hear that Lizabet's hesitation was due to concern for the maidservant and not anything to do with Gerrard.

"I'll be gentle with her," Celeste assured Lizabet.

"Is there anything else I should do, Sister?"

"Tidy a bit, if you would, and then start a pottage for later. I'm not sure when we'll be back," Celeste replied before she left the room and went to see what had brought Lewis there.

"Good day to you, Sister!" he cried, taking a few steps toward her and smiling shyly. He had a long, thin bundle wrapped in cloth in his hand and he thrust it toward her. "I brought you some candles."

"How kind!"

She began to unwrap the bundle. "Oh, Lewis, these are too fine to give to me!" she exclaimed when she discovered five well-made beeswax candles.

They were the best candles money could buy, too expensive for her to accept, even if they would burn brighter than a rushlight and aid her searching at night in the short time she had left.

The lad both blushed and beamed with delight. "Not at all, Sister."

"Please give your father my thanks, too," she added, certain such a fine gift had to come from both, and suspecting that Norbert sought to gain her favor by giving her a present.

To her surprise, Lewis frowned and did not look pleased. "They're from me, Sister. My father wouldn't give anything so nice to anyone."

She wasn't quite sure how to respond, except to say, "Then thank *you*, Lewis."

He looked around the room. "Are you going to sell the furniture, too?"

"Yes. I have to pay Audrey's debts, including what she owed to your father, and I won't need furniture when I leave."

"You're really going back to the convent, then?"

"Yes."

Although not Saint Agatha's, if she couldn't find her father's hidden cache, but he didn't need to know that.

The young man's gaze grew more intense. "My father wanted to marry your sister. He was angry when she refused him. After she died, he said he wasn't surprised she was murdered. She had it coming for playing with men's hearts. He said there wasn't a man she met she didn't try to seduce, including Father Denzail."

This was exactly what Celeste had suspected, that Duncan MacHeath wasn't the only man in Dunborough with a grudge against her sister. He simply could have been the only one to take violent action. And it seemed Gerrard might have been right about Father Denzail.

"*I'd* never say anything like that, or believe it, either," Lewis went on.

To give herself time to think, Celeste set one of the candles in the candleholder and put it in the center of the table.

"Ewald wanted to marry her, too, but she said no to him, as well. There were others who asked for her hand, men not worthy enough to touch the hem of her gown."

Celeste was about to ask him who those men were when an irate Norbert appeared in the doorway.

"Lewis!" he snapped. "What are you doing here?"

The young man jumped as if an arrow had pierced his chest.

Celeste moved to intercept his father, the man who had apparently said such cruel things about Audrey, but who was all sweetness and light to her. "He brought me a gift."

Norbert's gaze darted to the candles on the table and the one in the stand. "You gave her—" He took a deep breath, yet despite his efforts to calm down, his flushed face betrayed the extent of his rage, reminding her of the potential for a father's or a husband's tyranny.

"I'm most grateful," Celeste said, trying to pacify him. "Those I don't use I shall take back to the convent as a gift to the order."

"Please do," Norbert said with a weak smile and angry eyes. "Come along, Lewis. We'd best get back to the shop."

"One moment," she said. "You never told me how much money Audrey owed you."

"Ten marks, or thereabouts," Norbert replied. "Of course, should you sell me the house…"

Never. Never would she sell that man this house. "I don't have the money yet, but I shall before I leave Dunborough."

Without a word, an obviously embarrassed Lewis sidled to the door and went out, while Norbert nodded and bade her good day. Then he, too, left her house.

She felt like scrubbing the floor where he had been standing.

That he had dared to think that Audrey should marry him! The only chance he would ever have had with her was if he were a king, and probably not even then, no matter how ambitious Audrey was. Were all men vain and selfish? It seemed so. She would be glad to return to the serenity of a daily life of prayer, contemplation and service in the convent.

A sharp cry of pain came from the yard.

Gathering up her skirts, Celeste ran outside, to find Norbert, his fist upraised, standing over Lewis. The youth was huddled on the ground, his arm thrown over his head to protect it from his father's blows.

"Stop!" she cried, running toward them.

His face nearly purple with rage, Norbert lowered his arm. "I shouldn't have to hare after my son," he said defensively, "and he shouldn't take things without asking. He didn't have permission to leave the shop, either. It's a busy day and he should be there."

"If the day is so busy, shouldn't *you* be there?" Celeste demanded as she helped the young man to his feet, disgusted by the violence men could be capable of. Yes, she would be happy to go back to the convent, regardless of any sacrifice that entailed.

By now, Lizabet had come from the house, Celeste's cloak over her arm. A family on their way to market stopped and stared, and others traveling to and from the town slowed to watch the confrontation in the yard.

Celeste ignored the onlookers and focused on Norbert. "Since Lewis gave me the candles without your knowledge or approval, I will gladly return them, or pay you for them when I make good on Audrey's debts."

Norbert glanced at the growing, curious crowd and became contrite. "No, no, Sister, that won't be necessary. You may keep them, as my gift to you."

"And Lewis's," she added before addressing the young

man himself. "Although in future, Lewis, I suggest you ask permission."

"I did," the lad unexpectedly declared, "and the miserly old skinflint said no."

"Why you—" his father cried, raising his hand again.

Celeste swiftly moved to block the blow. It landed hard on her shoulder, sending her down on one knee.

At the same time, Gerrard's voice rang out across the yard. "Raise your hand to her again and, by God, I'll cut it off!"

Chapter Fourteen

His broadsword slapping against his thigh, Gerrard came striding across the yard toward them. The chandler, looking as if he might be sick and with good cause, backed away, for Gerrard was clearly, frighteningly outraged. Lewis staggered to his feet but didn't seek to interfere, not did any of the onlookers.

Scowling, Gerrard pulled his sword from its sheath and placed the tip against the trembling chandler's chest. "Now then, Norbert," he said, his voice hard and remorseless, "what gives you the right to strike this woman?"

"I didn't mean to hit her," the chandler sniveled as he held his arms wide in surrender. "She got in the way."

"Because he was going to hit his son again and that I will not permit," Celeste explained, coming closer. She was angry at Norbert, yet sought to keep her tone moderate, lest her words enflame Gerrard's temper more.

"He stole from my shop!" Norbert cried, looking desperately to the curious spectators for support. "If a father can't discipline his own son—"

Not a single person came to his defense, nor did anyone regard him with empathy. Some began to go on their way, others stayed behind, clearly curious to see what would happen next. Norbert fell silent when he got no sympathy from anyone and saw the stern expression on Gerrard's face. Perhaps the chandler hadn't heard of Sir Blane's methods of disciplining his sons. If he had not, Celeste had, and it was no wonder Gerrard sought to intervene when Norbert struck his son.

Swallowing hard, the trembling Norbert raised his hands higher in supplication. "I was angry and the lad needs to learn he can't simply take things from the shop."

Gerrard slowly lowered his sword, but didn't sheathe it. "Shall I have him thrown in the dungeon and brought before the king's justice?" he asked with cold deliberation.

Lewis turned as pale as snow.

"Gerrard, please," she said, putting her hand on his arm, hoping he didn't mean what he said.

He turned to regard her as if she were some lowly minion who dared to speak, not the woman he had embraced with passion. Or a nun.

His dark brows lowered, his lips a hard, thin line, Gerrard said, "If Norbert wishes to teach his son a lesson, how better than to show him the lawful consequences of theft?"

"I'm willing to pay for the candles," she replied.

Still Gerrard's expression did not change nor did he even seem to notice her hand upon his arm.

"I'm certain he's learned and you can be merciful," she pleaded, clutching him a little tighter, feeling the strength in his tense muscles.

Gerrard didn't answer her. Instead, he addressed Lewis. "Have you learned it's wrong to steal?"

"Yes!" the young man cried, falling on his knees and nearly in tears. "I have! I promise you I have!"

"And you, Norbert?" Gerrard demanded, glaring at the man. "Have you learned that you must never again strike a woman so long as you live in Dunborough?"

The chandler rapidly nodded his head and took a few steps back. "Yes!"

"Good," Gerrard grimly replied, "because if you do, you will find yourself in the dungeon of Dunborough."

Norbert looked as if he was about to swoon.

Celeste let go of Gerrard's arm. "And if he strikes his son?" she asked.

Gerrard's face still wore that same pitiless expression. "His son is his property until he comes of age."

"Surely you, of all people—"

He held up his hand to silence her, and when he spoke, his steady scrutiny was on the pale young man. "Of course, should Lewis decide to leave his father's house and seek employment elsewhere, there is no law to force him to stay." His voice grew a little more compassionate and his expression less stern, like the Gerrard she wanted him to be. "The commander of a castle might be glad to have such a man in his service."

Looking as if he'd been handed the keys to the kingdom, Lewis scrambled to his feet. Celeste felt as if her childhood hero had indeed returned, even if he was now more like his brother than the boy she remembered.

"I'd gladly be a soldier in your garrison, sir!" Lewis excitedly exclaimed.

Gerrard ran a measuring gaze over him and finally sheathed his sword. "Can you read and write?"

"Y-yes, sir."

"Good. I have more need of a clerk than another soldier."

Although his disappointment was obvious, Lewis nodded. "I'll be happy to serve you any way I can."

Norbert, however cowed, and perhaps because he was now several feet away, could not remain silent. "What am I to do without my son to help me?"

"That is not my concern," Gerrard replied, his voice and visage ice-like once again. "I suggest you return to your shop and sell some more candles in case you find you need to a hire an assistant." He raised his voice so that the remaining onlookers could hear. "Should I learn of any mistreatment of women or children in the village of Dunborough, that man will have to answer to me."

Norbert looked as if he wanted to curse. However, he said nothing as he left the yard, pushing his way through the people still gathered at the gate.

Gerrard's shoulders relaxed. "Go to the kitchen in the castle, Lewis," he said, his voice calmer yet still firm, "and find Peg. Tell her you need a place to sleep and a cot for the night. And know you this—if you ever dare to steal from me, you will regret it."

The young man flushed and nodded. "I won't!"

"Then you may go."

"Yes, sir. Thank you, sir." Lewis turned to Celeste and smiled with more genuine happiness. "Thank you, Sister. If you hadn't come when you did—"

"There's no need to thank me," she demurred, very aware of the powerful warrior standing nearby who had shown himself to be merciful and just. Even so, she was aware of the rage he'd displayed and knew the way a man could oppress his household.

"But I do thank you!" Lewis exclaimed. "I…"

He fell silent and blushed a deeper shade of red before hurrying off toward the castle through the now rapidly diminishing crowd.

"The rest of you should be about your business," Gerrard declared, and the remaining bystanders dispersed, enabling her to see Gerrard's snow-white horse tied to a post farther along the fence, with a light brown saddle horse beside it. For her, no doubt.

"Is there time to visit Martha today?" she asked warily.

"Yes, if you still wish it," he replied, his expression revealing nothing of his innermost thoughts.

She wasn't keen to get up on a horse and the day had already had its share of excitement, but she supposed the sooner she saw the maidservant, the sooner she might have the answers she wanted. "I do."

Gerrard nodded and marched toward the gate while Lizabet hurried to put a cloak around Celeste's shoulders. That done, Celeste had to trot after him, for he didn't slacken his pace or wait for her.

"This is Daisy, your sister's horse," he said matter-of-factly when she joined him and as if nothing of any import had just happened. He patted the neck of the saddle horse standing placidly beside Gerrard's prancing white beast. "I thought you would like her best."

Daisy appeared gentle enough, especially compared to Gerrard's horse, yet Celeste had rarely ridden. Those few times she had didn't instill a feeling of confidence in her now. Nevertheless, mount and ride Daisy she must.

"Do you need help?"

"Yes, I do," she replied, even though that meant Gerrard would have to touch her. She was discovering that any time she touched him, or he touched her, her heart began to race and something surely sinful began to unfurl within her. She must control her wanton feelings, for she was afraid she wouldn't be able to get into the saddle without his assistance.

Fortunately, he didn't actually touch her. He stood beside the mare and clasped his hands together to make a step for her. Then, as she gripped the saddle board, he hoisted her into the air. She learned it wasn't a simple matter to get her leg over the back of the horse.

Nevertheless, she did it and, once seated, drew in a deep, tremulous breath.

"I take it you haven't done much riding," he said, stroking the mare's neck. Again, she could tell nothing of what he was really thinking, much to her dismay. "Have no fear. Daisy is a very quiet, calm horse."

"I'm relieved to hear it," she replied, trying to sound and appear just as calm and composed as he. "Shall we?"

She lifted the reins and as Daisy started forward at a walk, Gerrard mounted his stallion and came to ride beside her.

The last time she'd been on this road, she'd been going to Dunborough and sitting in the back of a cart belonging to a farmer. Certain features of the landscape had been familiar—the low rise to her right, the forest of pine to her left, the scent rich in the air, the little brook nearby and the path that led to it. She'd been anxious and cold, but more upset about Audrey's death and wondering what she would find at Dunborough than concerned about her own comfort.

In spite of herself she'd also been thinking about Gerrard. If he was still there. If he was the generous, kindhearted, merry fellow she remembered, or the lascivious, selfish scoundrel Esmerelda had denounced. And if he was as good-looking as she recalled.

Celeste glanced at the man riding beside her. If anything, he was better looking than she'd imagined. Nor could she help noticing how his hips moved forward and back with his horse's motion, the rocking movements bringing other worldly things to mind.

That they should not.

Had she not just witnessed an example of the kind of distress an angry man could cause? It would be better to be in a convent than subjected to a man's rule.

They both knew what it was like to have a cruel parent. She at least had had Audrey, and he had had Roland, even if the brothers quarreled. Lewis had no one. "It's kind of you to give Lewis a place in your household."

This time when Gerrard answered, she could tell he was still angry. "I have no love for men who beat their sons, and Norbert's an ugly little squint."

Celeste considered telling Gerrard what she'd learned about Norbert's opinion of Audrey, then decided against it. She didn't want to rouse Gerrard's temper any more today. "Still, it was generous of you, and I *will* thank you."

"I'm not so generous as you seem to think. I need a clerk."

"Be that as it may, you saved him." As perhaps they'd both wished for a protector when they were little. "I'm sure he's truly grateful, as am I."

That brought a brief smile to Gerrard's face. "Then I'm even more glad that I did it."

She, too, smiled, feeling more at ease in his company. Too much at ease, perhaps, when she recalled the reason for their journey. She shouldn't be lighthearted when they were going to seek answers about her sister's death.

"Do you ever miss those days when we were children?" he abruptly asked.

"Sometimes," she confessed, wondering if Gerrard was also remembering playing in these woods. She and Audrey had often sought refuge here, and she had enjoyed it even more when Gerrard joined them. "I miss Audrey very much. I suppose you might think that strange, when I've been away for so many years, but as long as I could think of her here, I didn't feel so alone."

He nodded and looked thoughtful. "Even when I believed I hated Roland, I would have mourned him deeply if anything had happened to him."

"You are truly friends now?"

"More friend than foe," he replied, "or he wouldn't have named me garrison commander or offered me—"

She wondered why he'd stopped so abruptly until he turned to her and said, "He's offered me Dunborough."

Chapter Fifteen

Celeste was so taken aback, she pulled too hard on the reins, making Daisy whinny.

"Careful, there!" Gerrard cautioned, reaching out to hold the mare's bridle. "Daisy's gentle, but she can be skittish."

Celeste was glad for his controlling hand. She had come near to falling, both with surprise and the action of the mare.

"Did I hear you aright?" she asked. "Roland has offered you Dunborough?"

Gerrard nodded. "Yes. He has the estate of DeLac, thanks to his wife, so he's willing to give me Dunborough. The king will have to approve, but Roland thinks John will be only too eager to ensure that my brother has less land and power."

From what she'd heard about the king, she found that easier to believe than that Roland would willingly give up his right to their family's estate.

Gerrard regarded her with grave solemnity. "It's quite true, I assure you."

Finally she believed him, and joy replaced her doubt.

"So you will have your heart's desire at last, Gerrard! I'm happy for you."

"I haven't yet decided whether I'll accept Roland's offer or not."

She reined in again and, when he likewise halted Snow, regarded him with incredulity. "Why not?"

"It would mean being beholden to my brother for the rest of my life."

"Your *pride* stands in the way?"

His expression hardened once again. "My pride, as you call it, is one of the few things I have I can call my own."

"But... Dunborough, Gerrard!"

"Yes, Dunborough," he muttered, urging his horse forward again. "And all that goes with it."

They rode past a few more trees and large stones and paths leading from the road that she recognized. The pine trees ended and soon the moor would stretch out before them.

"I take it, then, you won't quarrel with your brother anymore," she ventured at last.

He sighed and then, to her surprise, he chuckled, a low, deep, soft sound as attractive as his voice. "I expect we'll always quarrel about something. Goading Roland is the only way to get him to speak his mind. Otherwise, he's like a statue, as you may recall."

She did remember Roland's reticence, and Gerrard's answer would explain a great many of their quarrels. Nevertheless... "Surely there's another way to get him to express his opinion."

"If there is another way to make him reveal what he's truly thinking, I have yet to find it."

"You will one day, I'm sure of it."

"You sound as if you care."

"I do. I want you—and Roland—to be happy and live in peace with one another."

He slid her a sidelong glance. "Roland is very happy. His wife has made him so."

"Then perhaps when you are wed…"

She fell silent and stared straight ahead. She didn't want to think of Gerrard married, with a wife to love.

"I'll be happy?" he finished for her. "As happy as you'll be in the convent?"

"I shall be very happy there," she said firmly.

Because she would, once the mother superior was gone, she told herself.

Nevertheless, a change of subject seemed in order. "Is it much farther to Martha's?"

"Just around the next bend."

They rode in silence, each wrapped in their own thoughts, until they came upon a fenced yard with a wide gate surrounding a small, squat stone cottage with a slate roof. A bench was by the door and a few chickens scratched in the dirt near a small coop.

"This is the place," Gerrard said. Frowning, he hesitated a moment, then added, "I should warn you that Martha tends to get rather overwrought."

"Perhaps, then, it would be best if I spoke to her alone," Celeste suggested.

Gerrard's frown deepened. "I'm not sure that would be wise. She can also get quite…fierce."

"You think she might try to hurt me?" Celeste asked, her eyes widening.

"Who can say what a woman in that state will do?" he mused with a shrug of his broad shoulders.

"Very well," Celeste replied, nodding. "We'll speak to her together."

Gerrard dismounted and looped Snow's reins over the gatepost.

Celeste stayed where she was. The last time she'd ridden a horse, she'd been a child, and her father had lifted her to the ground.

Gerrard regarded her questioningly. "Have you changed your mind?"

She shook her head. "I'm not sure how to get down."

If Gerrard found that amusing, he mercifully didn't show it. He simply said, "Put your hands on my shoulders and lean toward me as far as you can."

She did and he reached up and grabbed her around the waist. "Now slide off. I'll make sure you land safely."

He held her up as she slipped from the saddle toward him and set her feet upon the ground.

He must be even stronger than she'd suspected.

Her hands were still on his shoulders; his were still around her waist. They were close enough to kiss.

She wanted to kiss him. He looked as if he wanted to kiss her but was awaiting her permission.

"Celeste, I—" he began, his voice soft, almost pleading.

"Gerrard," she whispered. "Please…please don't."

If he kissed her again, she would not be able to resist. And then what? He had asked and promised her nothing.

He stepped back abruptly, his face as red as hers must be if the heat of shame within her was anything to go by.

He opened the gate without so much as a glance at her and immediately a huge and shaggy black dog came racing around from the back of the cottage, barking loudly, its teeth bared as if about to attack.

With a gasp Celeste moved behind Gerrard, who drew his sword.

An elderly man in an old, much-mended woolen tunic and breeches, his boots equally ancient, appeared at the door of the cottage. "Down, Blackie!" he cried, and at once the dog stopped barking and sat on its haunches. "Beg pardon, sir. He's a trifle excitable, is Blackie."

"A quality to be desired in a dog who guards your household," Gerrard replied, sheathing his sword. The grim soldier was back, the yearning lover gone, perhaps forever.

As he must be, Celeste thought as they crossed the yard, Celeste on the side of Gerrard farthest from the dog.

"This is Audrey D'Orleau's sis—" Gerrard began.

"Why, it's wee Celeste, isn't it?" the old man interrupted with a wide, toothless smile. "Don't you remember me?"

Of course! He was one of her father's carters who took goods back and forth between Dunborough, York and London. He'd always had some little treat for her when he returned.

"Oh, Jack, it's good to see you!" she cried, hurrying to press a kiss upon his wrinkled cheek.

Audrey's maidservant must be his daughter. Celeste remembered Martha now, a timid, rather plain young woman.

"We'd like to speak to Martha, if we may," Gerrard said from behind her.

Jack rubbed his whiskered chin. "Well, I dunno. This isn't one of her better days."

"We'll try not to upset her," Celeste said.

"And Celeste—Sister Augustine now—has to return to the convent soon."

Gerrard was right, of course, and yet she wished he hadn't said it.

"Very well, then, come in," Jack said, stepping aside to make way for them to enter the dimly lit, one-room cottage.

It was neat and relatively tidy, but their eyes were immediately drawn to the woman hunched over on a stool near the glowing embers in the hearth. Her brown hair was disheveled, her gown loose but clean. Her cheeks were gaunt, too, as if she rarely ate. It was not poverty that was responsible for that state, Celeste realized, for her father was well fed, and there was smoked ham and baskets of beans in the cottage.

"Look here, Martha!" Jack cried with somewhat forced good cheer. "Here's Celeste come to see you all the way from Saint Agatha's. You remember Celeste."

Martha raised her head, a look of happy surprise on her face, until she saw Gerrard. She jumped up, oversetting the stool, and pressed back against the wall as if she'd seen a ghost.

"I think, um, you'd better wait outside, sir," Jack said under his breath.

Gerrard's visage was so stern and unyielding, Celeste feared he was about to protest.

"Please wait outside, Gerrard," she ordered with quiet, but firm, command. Martha was obviously afraid of him, and they'd get no answers from her in that state.

Although he looked far from pleased, Gerrard left the cottage.

"Now then, Martha, it's all right," Jack said, speaking as he would to a nervous horse. "Sit ye down by the fire again. Celeste wants a few words with you, that's all."

He took his daughter's hand and led her back to the stool, where she sat obediently, as if she were a child.

"I'm sorry if we've upset you," Celeste said, keeping her voice low and soothing, remembering how Sister Sylvester had spoken to the girls who'd arrived at the convent in obvious distress "If you like, I could come back another day."

"He said—" Jack began.

She shook her head to silence him. "I have plenty of time."

She knelt beside Martha. "I want to talk to you about my sister. I've been away so long, you see."

She wouldn't broach the subject of Audrey's murder, at least not right away.

Yet that was clearly what was uppermost in Martha's mind as she sat lacing and unlacing her thin, work-worn fingers clasped in her lap. "I knew he wasn't right in the head," she muttered. "I could tell by the way he looked at her. Like a dog begging for a bone."

She leaned forward and covered her face with her hands. "Oh, God help me! There was so much blood! He'd…he'd…"

Celeste put her arms around the distraught woman. Gerrard was right. She shouldn't have come here. Poor Martha was too distressed to answer any questions. "Never mind what he did, what you saw. It's over now, and he's gone forever."

The woman reared back and stared at her. "Is he? Do you think so?" she cried, getting more and more upset. "Or are they just sayin' that? Drowned, they said. Dead in the river. Fell in, said some. Killed himself, said others. Maybe somebody pushed him. How do we know? How can his soul be at rest? What if his spirit comes back?" She jumped up and peered out the window. "What if he comes looking for *me*?"

Jack hurried to pour some wine in a cup. "Here, Martha, take this," he said, putting it to her lips.

She drank as if she'd been lost in the desert for days.

Jack gave Celeste a woeful look over his daughter's shoulder, as if he realized this wasn't the best way to calm her, yet it was the best one he had.

Celeste was sure Sister Sylvester would have some better medicine, and when—if—she returned to Saint Agatha's, she would ask her to send some here.

"Come, Martha, why don't you lie down like a good girl," her father suggested.

"I'll leave you in peace," Celeste said, moving toward the door.

"No!" Martha declared, pushing her father out of the way. "I want you to know, in case...in case I die! Duncan wanted your sister and she never saw it. Never wanted to see it, because she was after richer men, like that Broderick and that Roland and even that Gerrard. But Gerrard never would have married her. He really wanted his brother's wife, same as he wanted everything else Roland had."

Celeste gasped and lifted her hand to her cheek as if the woman had punched her.

Because Martha was right. Gerrard had always wanted everything Roland had and usually found a way to either get it or take it. Why should he not have felt the same about a woman?

She wanted to believe that he'd changed, but maybe she was wrong. Perhaps she'd let her own lust and desire cloud her judgment, as other women had before her.

"So much greed! So much evil!" Martha moaned. "She was a *whore*, your sister, and she died like one!"

"It's all right, Martha," her father murmured as he put his arm around his daughter. "Best you go lie down."

When he looked up again, Celeste was gone.

As Gerrard watched Celeste approach with quick strides, her cloak flaring out behind her and her face pale, he regretted bringing her here. He should have refused. He should have told her Martha was too upset by what had happened to make much sense, or that she had gone away.

And he should never touch Celeste, or even get too close to her. She was simply too tempting, too desirable. Even if she seemed to want him at times, if he took advantage of those moments, he would surely be damned forever, a creature of lust and depravity like his father.

But he could at least try to offer some comfort after what was surely an upsetting talk with Martha.

"Martha's been distraught since your sister died," he said when Celeste reached him.

"With good reason, I should say," she snapped, her lips thin and her whole body tense. Celeste wasn't distraught, she was angry, and she sounded like his father or his brothers when they'd chastised him. "What did Martha say to you?" he demanded.

For a moment he thought she wasn't going to answer. But she did.

She raised her chin and regarded him with defiant disdain. "She said you wanted Roland's wife."

"And you believed her?" he charged. He, too, was angry, although in truth, her accusation cut him to the quick, especially since she so obviously believed it.

If he had any doubts about that, they faded when she added, "You always wanted whatever Roland had."

Gerrard crossed his arms and grimly, firmly, sternly

told her the truth. "Not anymore and never Mavis. I saw at once how it was between them. She cared very much for Roland and he for her. Although I envied him, I would never have tried to take her from him." Gerrard's frown deepened. "You didn't used to believe everything you heard. Have you grown more gullible?"

"I have learned that often there is some truth in a rumor."

"But most times there is not," he retorted. Disgruntled and anxious to be gone, he linked his fingers and bent down to help her into the saddle. Without a word, looking just as peeved as he felt, she grabbed the saddle board and put her foot into his hands, then got onto the horse with a little less effort than before.

Lifting the reins to turn her horse back the way they had come, she punched her heels into Daisy's side with more force than necessary.

Before he could chastise her, the startled animal leaped forward and took off at a gallop.

By the time he was on Snow, Daisy and her rider had plunged into the wood, along a narrow path.

And then he heard a scream.

Chapter Sixteen

Gerrard was urging Snow into a gallop and riding after Celeste before he took another breath. If she'd come to harm…

If she'd been thrown…

If there were bandits in the woods… He'd been sure they'd captured all the outlaws who had once threatened Mavis, or that any who had not been taken had fled, but what if—

There! Celeste was on the ground near a fallen limb, half on her side, leaning on her elbow. Her wimple and veil were askew, her habit muddy. Holding her ankle with her other hand, she was biting her lip as if trying not to cry.

He jumped down from his horse and hurried to her. "Are you hurt?" *Obviously she was.* "Anywhere other than your ankle?"

She shook her head. "I fell onto that elderberry bush," she replied, nodding toward a low shrub that had several broken branches.

"Thank God you didn't land on that," he noted with relief, gesturing at the stump of a small tree that had snapped off, leaving a jagged point.

"Yes, thank God," she said, her words more like a prayer than his had been.

Regardless of the mud, Gerrard knelt in front of her. "I'm going to have to take hold of your ankle. I'll be as gentle as I can."

Her eyes wide, she again shook her head, this time vigorously. "No!"

He sat back on his haunches and regarded her with frustration. "If your ankle's broken, it should be kept as still as possible until we get back to Dunborough. Otherwise, more damage might be done. *Permanent* damage. If it's only a sprain, we'll still have to take care, but it won't be so serious."

"I'm sure it's just a sprain," she primly replied with a lift of her chin, as if he'd suggested something immoral.

"You have experience, then?" he demanded, his brows knit with annoyance. "Or are you a physician?"

Her lips thinned. "Surely if it were broken, I'd know."

She was the most stubborn, infuriating… "You're willing to risk damaging your ankle for life rather than let me touch you?"

"Are *you* a physician, Gerrard?" she returned, eyeing him with scorn despite his efforts to help her. "Or have you spent time assisting in a hospital? From what I've heard, you've been spending your spare time elsewhere."

He was clearly doomed to be dogged by his reputation forever. And whatever Martha had said had lowered her opinion of him even more. Nevertheless, he was determined to find out the extent of her injury and help her if he could, lest she be crippled forever.

"No, I am not a physician, nor an apothecary, but I *have* seen my share of injuries in training and on the tournament field, at least enough to tell a break from a sprain. And you may set your righteous mind at ease.

I'd as soon risk baiting a bear as take any liberties with you again. Now I *will* examine your ankle."

"Oh, very well," she conceded, looking away, her full lips drawn down into a frown. "You were always stubborn."

"Me?" he retorted. "Who was it insisted upon looking at that bloody badger and then nearly fainted? Who was it kept us so long at the bonfire that we got caught at the changing of the watch because she wanted to keep dancing? Who was so sure she was right about the rules of that game—"

"Who is supposed to be seeing if my ankle's broken?"

With a very great effort he forced himself to be quiet and gently take hold of her foot.

He wouldn't think about anything she said. He wouldn't recall the past, or notice the little brown curl that had escaped from her wimple, or wonder if he'd actually seen her hair wound around her head beneath that flimsy veil when she'd been wearing that red gown. He would concentrate on her ankle and the injury.

He carefully turned her foot from side to side. She gasped a little when he moved it up and down, and winced. If there'd been a break, she would have done considerably more than that. She probably would have slapped him.

"It's not broken," he said, setting her foot carefully on the ground.

"Thank God for that," she said. "How are we going to get back to Dunborough if Daisy doesn't return?"

"We'll both ride Snow."

Celeste wrapped herself more tightly in her cloak and regarded him with cool disdain. "That would not be seemly."

God's blood! There was maidenly modesty and then

there was stubborn foolishness. "It's that or wait until somebody realizes I haven't returned to the castle and sends out a search party. By then it will be dark and much colder and dangerous for those searching for us."

She raised a brow. "Why don't you ride back to the castle and bring some assistance?"

"Because tempting though it may be to leave you here," he said through clenched teeth, his annoyance growing, "it's cold and could be dangerous. If you're so concerned about sharing Snow, you can ride and I'll lead him on foot."

"You let Esmerelda come to the wood alone."

God give him strength! Was he never to be absolved of any wrongdoing over what had happened that night? Was he always going to be cast as the villain, although he hadn't laid a hand on Esmerelda or wanted harm to come to her in any way? "I didn't think she'd come!" he angrily returned. "I thought she'd be too frightened or her father would find out and stop her. If I'd had any notion otherwise, I would have gone to meet her."

"So you might only have seduced her," Celeste noted with displeasure. "A slightly better fate, I grant you, yet your behavior was still less than honorable."

"Esmerelda was a selfish, flighty girl who wanted me much more than I ever wanted her. Wanted more than a kiss, too, although I wasn't willing. So I said I'd meet her in the wood. If she came, I was going to tell her that her quest was hopeless. But I didn't think she'd be there. I cursed myself a thousand times after I learned what happened to her. I wish with all my heart I'd never said I'd meet her. If I could change what befell her, I would in the time it takes a heart to beat. But I can't, and now you seem to think, along with half the village, that I planned to have the poor girl raped. If even you—"

He took a deep, shuddering breath and turned away. "I should refuse Roland's offer and leave Dunborough," he muttered, half under his breath. "If I stay, rumors and gossip are going to haunt me forever."

His words, his tone, the despair in his voice and eyes, the things he'd said, overcame Celeste's distress and dismay. Now she could believe all his denials. He hadn't wanted Roland's wife. He wasn't the roguish, lustful wastrel gossip painted him, or if he had been once, his desire to be a better man was sincere and heartfelt.

He was truly sorry for what had happened to Esmerelda, and while he bore some responsibility for asking her to meet him, the greater blame was with the outlaws who had raped and beaten the unfortunate girl.

If Celeste still harbored any doubts of his sincerity, his muttered vow to leave Dunborough and his disgrace removed the last of them.

And if anything she had said caused him to leave Dunborough, to give up the thing he'd wanted all his life, especially after he'd made peace with his brother, she would regret it all her days.

Keeping her weight off her ankle, she rose to face him, her heart aching to see the pain in his eyes. "Dunborough is your home, and to be the lord there has been your greatest desire. Why not stay and prove to everyone that you're worthy of the gift your brother's offered you?"

He turned away. "Why should I stay where my past follows me around like a dark shadow?" he asked bitterly. "Better to start fresh where nobody knows me or my name. Besides, Dunborough is Roland's, and even if…" He fell silent, then shook his head as if to clear it. "It's better if I go."

As she must. As she should. She had her future planned, and he could not be in it.

He raised his eyes and his gaze searched her face. His yearning, seeking gaze. "And you'll go back to the convent."

"Yes, Gerrard."

He touched her hand.

She clasped his.

He took hold of her other hand. "I'm trying to be a good man, Celeste," he said fervently. "I want to be a good man, someone others can admire and respect."

"Your men esteem you. I've seen it."

"My soldiers, yes, because I'm like them—loud and brash and prone to fighting. Yet there are others," he said softly, drawing her close, his dark eyes full of longing. "Others whose approval and good regard I crave more."

She must not weaken. She must be strong. He was a nobleman; she was going to be a nun. She wanted to be a nun. To be safe, to have a life of peace. Yet it took all her strength to calmly say, "If you continue to behave with honor and chivalry, you'll earn that respect and good regard."

"What if that's not all I want?" he asked, his face close to hers, their bodies almost touching. "My entire life, I've believed Dunborough was all I wanted, all I needed. It would give me everything life has to offer—power, respect, wealth. I know now those aren't enough." His gaze intensified, his voice more yearning. "I want to be loved, Celeste, as Roland is loved. I want to love someone in return. Don't you yearn to be loved, Celeste? Loved and cherished forever?"

She swallowed hard and fought to remember what she wanted, what she was sure she needed. "I want God's love, Gerrard, and peace and security. Life in the convent as a bride of Christ will give me everything I seek."

"What about excitement, Celeste, and passion? Do you truly wish a life free of those things, too? And children. You would give up the hope of children?"

He was reminding her of every doubt that caused her to waver in her decision to pursue the religious life. But he offered nothing in return, except passion and desire.

She pulled away. Turning her back to him, barely noticing the twinge of pain in her ankle, she found the strength to say, "We should return to Dunborough."

It was too late for her to hide her weakness. Gerrard put his hands on her shoulders and turned her to face him. "You want children, don't you, Celeste? What about a husband who loves you? If you were loved— truly loved—that would give you peace and security, wouldn't it? You could have everything you want."

Confused, uncertain, tempted beyond all measure by his heartfelt words, his commanding presence and the yearning look in his eyes, as well as the memory of his arms about her and his lips on hers, she stammered, "Yes... No! I want to go back!"

"To Saint Agatha's, or Dunborough, your home?"

His home, where once upon a time she had dreamed of being his wife, sharing his hall, his chamber, his bed.

A wild, desperate desire welled up within her, one that would no longer be restrained. Her sprain forgotten, she grabbed him by the shoulders and pulled him to her. Her mouth found his and she kissed him with all the passion she'd been trying so hard to deny.

Here in the woods, as primitive as Eden, she gave

herself up to all the feelings he aroused within her. She parted her lips in silent invitation, this time knowing and wanting what he might do as she leaned her body into his. She didn't draw away when his hands roved over her. She stroked and caressed his strong back and shoulders as she had so often imagined.

Here, now, she was not almost a nun. She didn't crave a passionless, peaceful existence. She was a woman alone with the man who had, from the earliest days of her blossoming womanhood, been the object of her romantic dreams, awake and sleeping.

She wanted him so much her knees felt weak, so it was an easy thing for him to guide her back to the wide trunk of a tree. She didn't consider why he did that. She was simply grateful for its rough support.

His hand moved beneath her cloak and scapula, to knead her breast through her tunic and shift. A moan escaped her lips as she held him tighter, and she let his hands go where they would, even to cup her between her legs. Stroking gently at first, Gerrard soon increased his speed and pressure, sending new sensations through her. He kissed her neck, his other hand braced against the tree. Gasping, her eyes closed, she felt the tension grow as he continued to caress her.

Until, like the snapping of a branch, the tautness broke. She clung to his shoulders as if he were a floating spar in a storm-tossed sea, and she pressed her face against his neck while her whole body throbbed.

He continued to hold her gently, yet as the waves receded, she became aware of something else, something that told her she was not the only one aroused, although she had been the only one to journey to release.

And then the realization of her tremendous sin struck her. She had given in to her lust and, worse, encouraged his embrace and all that he had done. Instead of being virtuous, she had been wanton and immoral, and had led him astray, too.

As she moved away from him, full of shame and humbled, the pain in her ankle returned full force, as if her body, as well as her conscience, sought to punish her.

Before she could speak a word or even think of any, he spread his hands. "Celeste, I—"

"Say nothing, Gerrard," she interrupted, her voice low and tremulous. "There is nothing to say except that I regret what happened here. Please take me home."

"What we did is no great sin and shame," he said softly, seriously, his eyes grave, yet yearning. "We are mortal beings, with natural needs and desires. It isn't wrong to give in to those needs and desires if both are willing and free."

She shook her head. "I'm *not* free. I belong to God and the church."

"You can leave it."

She couldn't desert the church and the safe, secure life she'd envisioned for herself. After all, what else was there for her? He'd not said a word about marriage. "And do what? What life will I have if I leave the convent? No, Gerrard, I can't give up the church and all it promises for an uncertain future."

His expression grew hard and distant. "As you say, you are not free, not as long as safety and security is what you most desire."

In the next moment, that mocking grin appeared upon his face and he made one of those sweeping bows. "I beg your forgiveness for this and all my many sins, Sister Augustine."

He pointed at a fallen tree nearby, its trunk about a

foot above the ground. "If you can step up on that, you won't need my help to mount Snow. And I promise you that I won't say another word to you about desire, or anything else."

Nor did he as they made their way back to Dunborough, she on Snow and Gerrard on foot.

Chapter Seventeen

Lizabet hurried to open the kitchen door for Sister Augustine, who stood leaning against the frame.

"Sister, you're hurt!" she cried when Celeste limped inside. "What happened?"

Celeste sank onto the stool near the hearth and, frowning, rubbed her sore limb. "I fell and sprained my ankle."

"Maybe there's some liniment in the larder," the maid-servant suggested.

Celeste let her look, although she was sure none was there. She had searched those shelves so thoroughly she knew every bag, basket, pot, vessel and box by heart.

But she wanted some time to calm herself, to collect her thoughts and decide what to do and when. It was very clear that she couldn't stay in Dunborough or anywhere near Gerrard if she was to have the calm, contented life she'd envisioned for so long.

He was too tempting, too dangerous, and she couldn't control her lustful, wayward passion when she was with him. As for marriage, a home and children, although he'd spoken of them in ways to make her yearn for such a future, he had not so much as hinted that he wanted to marry her. Yet there was no other man she wanted for her husband or the father of her children. She was sure there never would be.

So she would sell the house to Ewald and either pay off all her sister's debts or pay what she could and leave the rest unsettled. If she didn't have enough to bribe the bishop to send the mother superior away, there were other convents. Before she left Dunborough she would write to Roland and tell him her concerns about Duncan MacHeath's death, suggesting he ask more questions about what had happened the day Audrey and her bodyguard had died, particularly of Norbert.

Lizabet returned empty-handed, just as Celeste had expected. "I couldn't find any, Sister."

"Never mind. I'll be all right. I'd like you to go to Norbert and Ewald on your way back to the castle and tell them I've decided to sell the house and all its contents tomorrow. If they want to buy them, they should come after lauds. As soon as the sale's concluded, I shall be returning to Saint Agatha's. Did Bartholemew and Marmaduke—"

"Yes, Sister. They came and took the chests away. You're planning to return to the convent tomorrow? With a sprained ankle?"

"Since Audrey's mare belongs to me now, I can ride."

"Where is Daisy? I didn't see a horse."

"She ran off when I fell, but she'll come back, I'm sure, to the castle if not here. Gerrard brought me home on his horse." Celeste didn't want to tell Lizabet any more about what had happened, so she hurried on. "Please have a groom bring her here tomorrow if she returns to the castle, and tell Gerrard I will have no guards tonight. I would rather be completely alone when I spend my last night in my family's home."

Because this would be her last chance to search. She

didn't want to have to worry that a guard would see the light and wonder what she was about or, worse, come to the door demanding to be told.

"Gerrard won't like that, Sister," Lizabet said warily.

"Whether he likes it or not, it's my wish," Celeste replied, her tone growing harsher as her patience and self-control frayed. "If he does send guards, I shall send them back, however many times I must. Now please go and do as I bid you."

The maidservant's's lip trembled and her limpid gray eyes filled with tears. "And your meal, Sister?" she asked, her voice nearly a whisper.

Celeste was sorry to upset her, yet she wanted so much to be alone. "I can see to that myself."

With a gulp, Lizabet nodded. She took her cloak from the hook near the kitchen door and ran outside.

Celeste started to rise, then sank back down and covered her face with her hands. She was in pain and aching.

But not because of her ankle.

The door to the hall flew open, banging hard against the stone wall as Gerrard strode in. He tore off his cloak and tossed it toward a peg, not bothering to pick it up when it landed on the floor instead.

Peg, Arnhelm and the other servants and soldiers in the hall leaped to their feet, not sure what this sudden fury heralded.

"Wine!" Gerrard called out, sending Peg scurrying to the buttery without so much as a backward glance before he just as abruptly turned on his heel and marched back to the entrance.

"Have the wine brought to the solar," Gerrard ordered.

He opened the door with as much force as before and, without a cloak, stepped out into the cold air.

Arnhelm looked at the soldiers, who were likewise preparing to leave the hall—although to do what, he had no idea. "What's the matter? We're off duty now."

Hedley took him aside while the other men gathered up their helmets and gloves and went to put on their cloaks. "Precautions, that's what," he quietly informed him. "Habit, too, I suppose. When old Sir Blane was in a furious mood, he'd mete out all kinds of punishments for neglect of duty, or anything else that struck his fancy. Best not to be seen."

"That was Gerrard, not his father."

"Nevertheless, precautions," Hedley repeated. "Now I'm off to see that my chain mail's all in order."

Thinking it was better to be safe than sorry, Arnhelm also left the hall.

Was that somebody tapping on the door, or was there a rat somewhere?

Gerrard listened again and decided it was somebody outside the door.

God's blood, why couldn't they leave him alone? They let Roland brood in silence often enough. Did they never think *he* might want to be by himself, to have time to contemplate things he'd done?

Things he was sorry he'd done. Things he would never do again, as well as things he would.

The tapping continued like an annoying drip and he gave up hope that whoever it was would go away. At least he could be sure it wasn't Celeste. She wouldn't have been able to walk here tonight, not with a sore and swollen ankle.

"What is it?" he growled as he opened the door.

Lizabet stood on the threshold, nervously wringing her hands.

"What are you doing here?" She should be with Celeste, especially with her ankle sprained. "Shouldn't you be with Sister Augustine?"

"Sh-she sent me here, sir," the young woman stammered.

"Come in," he replied with glum invitation. Best he should hear what Celeste wanted him to know and get it over with.

He swung the door wider and left it open as Lizabet came into the room. He would rather have a draft than run the risk of tales of impropriety in the solar.

In spite of that precaution, the maidservant sidled into the chamber as if she feared he was going to have her for his evening meal.

"So what message does Sister Augustine send?" he asked, trying to sound less annoyed. After all, it wasn't Lizabet's fault he'd been angry. He shouldn't have entered the hall like one of the Furies, despite how upset he was. Nor should he have left it so abruptly, regardless of the way the soldiers and servants were staring at him.

God's wounds, why couldn't he control his actions and his feelings? Why couldn't he be more a master of himself and his longings? He should have let go of Celeste at once, even if she'd kissed him first, and even if that passionate encounter had been like a dream come true.

"Sister Augustine said to tell you she's selling the house tomorrow and going back to Saint Agatha's and she doesn't want any guards tonight."

"What?"

Lizabet's big eyes filled with tears. "I'm sorry, sir, that's what she said to tell you."

Once again Gerrard cursed himself for an impetuous fool. No wonder Celeste wanted to leave, and soon. He'd made her feel she could be safe only within the confines of the convent. And he could hardly blame her for going when he was thinking of leaving himself. Once she sold the house and contents, there would be no reason for her to stay.

The guards, though…that was another matter. It was still dangerous for her, for any woman, to be in that house alone.

"She also said if you did post guards, she'd send them back, however many times you sent them."

"Then I won't." He knew better than to try to force Celeste to accept the guards. He would find another way to make sure she was safe while she was still in Dunborough.

Lizabet took a deep, quavering breath and straightened her shoulders. "I trust you will, sir, in spite of what she said. She can't know what it's like out in the world."

"Have no fear, Lizabet. I will see that she's kept safe, and I commend you for your concern."

And the nerve to confront him.

The maidservant still looked doubtful, so he decided to risk being more specific. "I will *personally* see that she's not in any danger, although I would rather this didn't become common knowledge."

At last Lizabet's shoulders relaxed and she smiled. "Thank you, sir!"

"Now I suppose you should see what Verdan's up to. Say nothing to him, either. I like the fellow, but I fear he couldn't keep his mouth shut to save his life."

"No, sir," she agreed with a giggle. "Not a drop of guile in him," she added, before she hurried away.

Verdan frowned as he regarded his brother later that night. He'd taken the first opportunity he could to get Arnhelm alone since he'd talked to Lizabet after her return from the D'Orleau house. They stood near the kitchen in the shadow of the inner wall.

"Lizabet said Sister Augustine was different when she got back," he said, trying to keep his voice low. "It was like she'd taken a potion and given up the ghost. She's sellin' the house and everything in it tomorrow and goin' back to Saint Agatha's. She had Lizabet tell Norbert and Ewald to come to see her in the morning."

Arnhelm rubbed his bearded chin. "Aye, something happened, all right. Gerrard came into the hall like a whirlwind and then shut himself up in the solar. Hedley said to get out o' his way, and I did, as fast as I could."

"Any other time I'd say you was after any excuse to see Peg in the kitchen," his brother replied, "but I don't blame you for gettin' out of his way. Lizabet had to go to the solar and tell him that Sister Augustine won't have any guards tonight—her last night in her family's home, she said. He was cross as a trapped boar at first, then changed his mind. Lizabet said not to worry about it, but I don't like it. Maybe we ought to go there and watch from the stable or somewhere."

"Maybe, or maybe Lizabet knows somethin' we don't." Arnhelm took hold of his brother's arm and pulled him deeper into the shadows. "Gerrard and Sister Augustine rode out alone today, didn't they?" he whispered. "No guards at all."

"Lizabet said they went to see Martha, and on the

way back Sister Augustine fell and hurt her ankle. At least that's what she told Lizabet, and she was limpin'. Daisy came back without her, too."

"They were gone a long time," Arnhelm noted significantly, raising his brows.

Verdan's eyes widened. "You don't think they...?" He shook his head. "No, I won't believe it."

"Shhh, you nit!" his brother warned. "I'm not sayin' that they did anythin' they shouldn't. Maybe her horse did throw her. Maybe that's why they took so long, but she's a good-lookin' woman and he's...well, he's Gerrard. Just in case somethin' did happen, though, somethin' that upset her, I think we ought to let Sir Roland know Gerrard might be back to his old ways and Sister Augustine might be returnin' to the convent because of somethin' he done."

Verdan stifled a groan of dismay. "You're not to go back until you've got a message from Gerrard."

"I'll risk it."

"Lady Mavis will be sorry, and Sir Roland, too."

"Not as much as we might be if we keep quiet and they find out another way that something disgraceful's happened."

Arnhelm suddenly reached out and grabbed his brother's arm, pulling him away from the tree toward the kitchen.

"What the—"

"Shhh!" Arnhelm commanded, and he nodded toward the tree. They both watched in stunned surprise as Gerrard swung himself up into the lower branches, light as a cat, then over the wall.

The two men exchanged wide-eyed stares, until Verdan whispered, "You'd best leave at first light."

* * *

Gerrard spent the longest, coldest night of his life huddled in the branches of a large tree outside the fence of the D'Orleau house. From there, though, he could see three sides of the building. There were no windows or other openings on the fourth.

Every so often, he saw the flicker of a candle in one of the windows. Either Celeste had a lot to prepare before she left, or she was spending an equally sleepless night. Maybe her ankle was worse than he'd thought. He should have insisted Lizabet return and remain with her.

Too late now. How would he explain how he'd come by his concern?

As the night wore on, some bushes beneath him stirred. He held his breath, scanning them for what might have caused the noise. It might be house-breakers, or so he thought until the biggest cat he'd ever seen dashed from the bushes to the stable and in through the half-open door.

At last the light went out. Celeste must have finally retired.

Did she ever feel as lonely as he did? he wondered. Would she miss Dunborough at all when she returned to the convent?

Would she miss *him*?

Or had he thoroughly destroyed, once and for all, any affection she might have had for him?

Chapter Eighteen

Gerrard shook Ralph awake at the crack of dawn.

The sergeant at arms was up in an instant and reaching for his sword before Gerrard could say a word. "No need for that!" he quickly told him. "We're not under attack."

Ralph blinked and regarded him warily, as if he wasn't quite sure he could believe the reassurance.

"Get dressed and summon the men to the hall," Gerrard said. "All of them, including the ones on watch."

"Sir?"

"I have an announcement to make."

Only then did Ralph seem to realize that Gerrard was dressed in his mail and surcoat. "You're going somewhere?"

"Yes. Now summon the men."

As Ralph reached for his breeches, Gerrard turned to find Verdan watching him from his cot with wide, amazed eyes. The man looked as tired as he felt, and Gerrard wondered if he might have spent the night elsewhere, too. He would say nothing about that; Verdan's morality, or lack of it, was not his concern. "Since you're already awake, go to the kitchen and tell Florian I want every servant in the hall, as well."

Verdan sat up. "He'll be doing the bread."

"Then he can stay in the kitchen. But I want everyone else there."

"Aye, sir!" Verdan replied. As he, too, rose and reached for his clothes, the other men began to stir.

"Get dressed and stay in the hall, every one of you," Gerrard ordered. "I have something to say and I only want to say it once." He looked around at the sleepy men, some rubbing their eyes, others scratching, a few stretching and more than one yawning. "Where's Arnhelm?"

The half-dressed Verdan cleared his throat and looked down at his feet. "He's seein' to his horse."

"Fetch him and the grooms and stable boys, too."

"Aye, sir," Verdan replied.

By the time Verdan returned from the stable, where Arnhelm was not, most of the soldiers and all the servants except Florian were in the hall, including Lizabet.

"What's happening?" she asked in a whisper, grasping Verdan's hand.

"Gerrard has something he wants to say to everybody," he answered just as quietly.

"About what?"

"Not a notion."

"Where's your brother?"

Verdan didn't reply, except to hush her and nod at Gerrard, who was standing in the center of the dais. The garrison commander of Dunborough wore his chain mail and surcoat, his sword belt and gauntlet gloves, and carried his helmet under his arm. He also looked as if he hadn't slept a wink.

"I have decided to give up command of the garrison and leave Dunborough," Gerrard announced, his expression as grim as his twin brother's could be and maybe even more.

"S'truth," Verdan muttered, and other hushed exclamations filled the hall.

Gerrard waited for the whispers and murmurs to die down before he continued. "I will be going to DeLac today to inform my brother of my decision. Ralph, you will be in command of the garrison until Roland either returns or appoints another."

"Damn," Verdan whispered, sidling toward the kitchen door. "I've got to go, Lizabet. I'll be back—"

"Verdan!"

The soldier turned as still as a stone when Gerrard's voice rang out in the hall, and his face flushed red as poppies.

"Where is Arnhelm?"

Verdan swallowed hard. "H-he's, uh, he's somewhere about, Gerrard. Sir."

"Find him and tell him we'll ride to DeLac together."

"Yes, sir!" Verdan replied. He gave Lizabet a swift farewell glance, then hurried from the hall.

While from the kitchen entrance, a grinning Lewis slipped away.

Celeste rose slowly, her ankle sore and her knees stiff from kneeling on the hard wooden floor of the bedchamber. This time, she hadn't been praying. She'd been knocking on each of the panels that lined the room, thinking there might be a hollow hiding place behind one of them.

All for naught, unfortunately. Her time had run out, for dawn had broken. Today she must sell the house and go. It was leave or endanger her chance for the peaceful security of the religious life, and for a man who would never be hers.

A knocking on the front door interrupted her mournful thoughts.

At least one of the merchants who wanted to purchase the house must have arrived. It couldn't be Gerrard. Things had been so strained when he had left her here that she doubted she would ever see him again.

She limped down the stairs and opened the door, to find both Ewald and Norbert standing on the threshold. Ewald smiled and bade her good morning. Norbert looked like a man about to engage in a battle to the death.

Which he was going to lose. She wasn't going to sell the house to him, no matter how much he offered, not after what he'd said about Audrey. However, she wasn't going to let Ewald be the sole bidder, either.

"Please come in," she said, standing aside to let them pass.

Doing her best not to limp, for she didn't want to answer any questions about her injury, she led them to the main room, where the carpet still covered the floor. The ginger cat, which had been sitting on the windowsill, jumped down and walked sedately from the room as if unimpressed by any of them.

Whistling softly, Ewald wandered toward the window. Norbert stared up at the smoke-darkened beams, probably looking for signs of rot. He appeared tired or unwell, paler than before, a bit blue about the lips and with dark circles under his eyes. Perhaps he was having to do more work, since his son was no longer at his beck and call.

"Won't you please sit down, gentlemen?" Celeste said. "And then we can discuss the price each of you is willing to pay for the house and all the remaining contents."

"The furnishings as well, eh?" Ewald boomed.

"Yes, everything except the few things I'll take with me when I leave."

After that clarification, they sat in the chairs she had arranged near the window, the two men eyeing each other warily while she folded her hands in her lap.

She expected Norbert to make the first offer, so was caught off guard when Ewald did. "I am prepared to pay one hundred marks."

She regarded him serenely and didn't immediately reply.

As she expected, she didn't have to say anything to prompt Norbert into bidding. "I will offer one hundred and twenty."

She thought the house alone was worth well over that. However, she was also fairly certain neither man would accept her estimate of the value of her property because she was a woman. Nevertheless, she furrowed her brow and said, "So little?"

Norbert frowned, while Ewald rubbed his chin. "One hundred and fifty," the latter said at last.

Norbert rose, strode to the wall, then back again. "Sister, I don't know what *some* people have been saying to you, but the house isn't worth as much as you've obviously been led to believe."

Again she waited, and sure enough, Ewald spoke before she had to. "Trust you to try to intimidate a nun into paying less than something's worth," he said. He gave Celeste another smile. "Two hundred is more than fair, Sister, and I hope God will take that into account when I reach the gates of heaven."

"Gates of heaven? You?" the chandler scoffed. "You won't be going there."

She suspected Norbert would be much more likely to find himself in the other place than Ewald, who declared, "At least I'm not trying to gouge a nun out of a fair price."

"Fair price? The furnishings alone are worth—" Norbert caught himself and flushed.

She wasn't going to let him off the branch onto which he'd climbed. "You were about to say?"

He cleared his throat and pointedly ignored his competitor. "The furnishings are lovely."

"My mother's taste was excellent, as was Audrey's, and they paid well for the furniture and other household goods."

"At the time they were newly bought, I'm sure they were worth a great deal," Ewald said.

So not as valuable now, he was implying. On this point Celeste feared both he and Norbert would agree.

Sighing heavily, she wrinkled her brow and bit her lip as if she was trying not to cry. "I had hoped to repay all Audrey's debts after everything was sold, and have some money left for the church, too," she said with a catch in her voice.

Unfortunately, it seemed her words and manner didn't inspire either man to be more generous. After a moment that was far too long, Norbert grudgingly offered, "Two hundred and twenty marks."

"Two fifty," Ewald immediately countered, proving that their mutual animosity was more effective than her attempt to appeal to their sympathy.

"Two sixty," Norbert returned. "And that is far too much."

"You old skinflint!" Ewald exclaimed, glaring at his

rival and apparently forgetting he had ever offered less. "Three hundred."

"You're always claiming to be rich," Norbert retorted. "Obviously you're lying. I wouldn't be surprised to find out you're in debt up to your ears. Three twenty-five."

"Me in debt? Me? That's a dirty lie, you lout." On the edge of his seat, Ewald swiveled toward Celeste. "Four hundred!"

"Who are you calling a lout? Unlike *you*, I come from a respectable family, and one with money, too. Five hundred!"

"Respectable, is it?" Ewald charged. "It's no secret you treated your wife and your son as if they were your slaves. No wonder Sarah died young. You worked her to death!"

Norbert jumped to his feet. "You're bitter because she wanted me, not you! Seven hundred! Match that if you can, you lying, duplicitous dog!"

Glaring, Ewald rose to stand nose to nose with him. "A thousand!"

"I accept!" Celeste cried before Norbert lost his head completely and offered even more. That might make Ewald come to his senses and stop bidding. As it was, a thousand marks was an incredible price.

Staring at his competitor, Norbert opened his mouth and closed it, looking like a landed fish. "You…you… I hope you *die*!" he shouted at last. "I hope you get leprosy!"

With that he turned on his heel and marched out of the room. A moment later they heard the front door slam.

Celeste sat heavily, feeling as if she'd been through a storm at sea.

Ewald, meanwhile, wiped his forehead with his broad

palm. "Forgive me, Sister," he said somewhat shakily. "I lost my temper. I shall go and fetch the money, and have my clerk prepare a bill of sale for you to sign."

"Thank you," she replied.

Still looking rather stunned, Ewald nodded and left her.

Both men were hot-tempered, and perhaps could get angry enough to kill. Ewald, however, seemed more likely to do the deed himself in a fit of ire rather than goad another to do the deed for him. Norbert, though… She could see him using more sly and deceitful means to get what he wanted.

That possibility, among others, would be for Roland to explore. The house was sold and she was going to leave, likely never to return.

"Sister?"

She half turned, to see Lewis in the doorway. "Lewis! How did you—"

"I saw my father coming here and, well, I didn't want him to see me, or to speak to me, either, so I came in through the kitchen."

Wringing his hands, he regarded her anxiously. "You sold the house?"

"Yes. It's time I returned to the convent."

He came closer. "There's no need to rush off. Not now. Gerrard is leaving Dunborough, hopefully forever. He's put Ralph in charge of the garrison and he's going to DeLac to tell Roland. He said so in the hall before I came here."

Celeste stared at Lewis with wonder, trying to comprehend what he was saying. Was it truly possible that Gerrard would leave Dunborough, never to return?

Yesterday, after he had revealed Roland's astonishing offer, he had said he might go, and yet in her heart of hearts she hadn't really believed that he would refuse the chance to rule Dunborough.

Apparently he would.

He had obviously meant what he'd said, that it would be better if he began anew elsewhere, free of reputation and speculation.

She might never know where and she would surely never see him again.

"What's the matter?" Lewis asked, frowning. "I thought you'd be glad he's going. Aren't you pleased he's leaving after the way he treated your sister?"

"What do you mean?" she asked, confused.

"I thought you knew. They were lovers."

Chapter Nineteen

A vision leaped into Celeste's mind, of the wood and Gerrard and…Audrey.

Lewis regarded her with pity. "I thought someone would have told you they were intimate. It was no secret that Gerrard came to visit your sister often, before and after Roland returned with a bride."

Esmerelda and others had said Gerrard was a liar and a rogue, evil and debauched. And Audrey was beautiful. But had he and Audrey been lovers? No, Celeste still couldn't believe it. Even if Gerrard had wanted Audrey—a thought almost too painful to bear—her sister wouldn't have given up her maidenhead without an offer of marriage from a rich and titled man. Gerrard was neither, nor had he had hope for any such achievements until recently.

When had Roland made his offer of the estate to Gerrard? After Audrey's death, or before? If it was before Audrey had been killed, perhaps she had taken him to her bed.

Maybe Gerrard was exactly what rumor and gossip described, after all.

Perhaps she had been wrong to condemn herself

for their lustful encounters. Gerrard could be clever enough, deceitful enough, duplicitous enough, to seduce her in such a way that she didn't realize he was doing so.

Perhaps he was even playing some kind of warped and twisted game with her, or exacting his revenge for the injury she had caused years ago.

She could not, would not, leave here until she had answers to those questions. "Has Gerrard left the castle yet?"

"I don't think so. He'll have to get his baggage—"

She limped toward the door.

Lewis hurried after her. "Where are you going? What's wrong with your leg?"

"A minor injury, and I'm going to the castle. I must and shall speak to Gerrard before he leaves today."

Gerrard sat on the dais finishing his bread and ale. As soon as Arnhelm was found, they would start the journey to DeLac. No doubt the soldier was saying his goodbyes to Peg.

Gerrard rose and was about to go to the kitchen in search of the errant soldier when the door to the hall opened and the last person he expected to see walked in.

Feeling like a trapped beast, he watched Celeste limp toward him.

"Gerrard, I would like to speak with you," she said, coming to a halt in front of the dais, the skirt of her habit swinging and her beautiful face flushed.

His heartbeat quickened. Perhaps she'd heard he was leaving and had come to ask him to stay. Maybe she would tell him she was staying, too.

He hoped so, because he loved her.

Roland's wife had been the first to make him yearn to be a better man, but only Celeste had both touched his heart and excited his desire. He had realized that the day before and done his best to make her want to forgo the life she'd chosen, hoping to eventually persuade her to be his wife. Instead, she had been adamant in her decision.

His wish that she might stay lasted just an instant, for the look in her eyes told him that she was angry and indignant.

It was more likely she'd come to say good riddance, despite her sore ankle, and he was suddenly sorry he hadn't left the day before, if not sooner. Her expression also warned him that she wouldn't leave until she'd said what she wanted to say, and it likely wasn't something he wanted the household to hear. "We can talk in the solar."

"No, I would rather talk here," she replied. "I have questions about Audrey, and you."

Oh, God! He'd dreaded this moment from the day Celeste had arrived. "I would rather answer such questions in private."

"No, Gerrard," she said, staying where she was. "I have been far too ignorant of my sister's life and I will have my questions answered here and now. Were you and Audrey lovers?"

Her boldly stated query resounded through the hall with the clarity of a bell. The soldiers and servants still about swiftly departed and even the dogs made themselves scarce, until the two of them were, in fact, alone.

It was small comfort, yet better than having an audience.

"No, we were not lovers," he answered honestly, his words seeming loud in the empty vastness of the hall.

Her eyes narrowed. "You were never intimate?"

How easy it would be to lie! To deny everything. To be a duplicitous scoundrel, a man without honor and unworthy of respect or admiration. To tell her they were not intimate. Instead, he chose the more difficult way and gave her the truth. "We kissed."

Celeste sucked in her breath and the color left her cheeks. "How could you?" she demanded in a whisper, staring at him as if he were the devil incarnate.

She had started this and he would tell all, regardless of the cost. "We kissed after I had asked her to marry me and she had accepted."

Celeste staggered back a little, as if his words had been blows. "You asked and she accepted? You truly wanted to marry her? Or were you simply trying to seduce her?"

The old accusations, the same foul charge based on past behavior, but also lies and speculation.

Yet he would answer this honestly, too. "I never tried to seduce your sister. She offered to use her wealth to secure a title from the king and persuade him to give me Dunborough, and I was willing to marry her to make it so. It wouldn't have been a love match, but it would have been no worse a marriage than many another."

He might never even have realized what he lacked, because Celeste would not have come back into his life. Only now, because of her, did he know what love between a man and woman could be, when it was too late.

Celeste regarded him steadily, her expression unreadable. "She had no wealth to offer."

"What do you mean?" he asked, confused. "Of course she did. Your father was a rich man."

"*He* was, but she was deep in debt, as any of the merchants of the town could have told you."

His mind reeled. Celeste sounded so certain, yet how could that possibly be true? Audrey had lived as if she had vast riches at her disposal.

"How can that be?" he demanded. "You saw her clothes, the jewels, the furnishings in your father's house."

"Her jewels were paste, the furniture purchased by my parents. As for the gowns and everything else, she owes every merchant in Dunborough."

Celeste had to be mistaken. "Have you seen proof of these debts?"

"Yes. I found the bills and I've promised to pay them. Yet you knew nothing about this?"

Her skepticism was as painful as her anger.

"Why would I?" he replied. "Audrey never told me, never even hinted, that she lacked for money, and she always wore the finest clothes. I'm not her husband or her father or her brother, so no merchant would have said anything to me about her liabilities."

He saw doubt come into Celeste's eyes and pressed on. "I swear to you, I knew nothing of your sister's finances."

At last Celeste looked as if she believed him. Unfortunately, that was not the end of it.

"And if you had known," she charged, her voice still stern, "would you have married her regardless?"

"If I had discovered it after we were betrothed, yes, I would have married her regardless," he said with firm conviction, and even though he would have been caught in a trap of Audrey's making. "I had given my word. I'm not so lacking in honor as that."

He could only hope that Celeste would believe that honest answer, too.

And there was something else to consider, something she might not have thought of when it came to her sister's debts. "If another man had sought your sister's hand and then found out she wasn't as wealthy as she let on, he might have been angry enough to want her harmed, perhaps even killed. No man likes to be tricked. And if he wanted to justify his actions, thinking her a deceitful whore could do that. Men will often find ways to excuse their selfish decisions."

"As you did?"

The accusation hurt him. Nevertheless, he would answer this honestly, too. "Yes, as I made excuses for my excesses and poor judgment for years."

"Did Duncan know about your betrothal?" Celeste asked, her voice still hard, still merciless, still stubbornly determined.

"Just as I was ignorant of her debts, no one else was aware of the betrothal," he answered, fighting to keep his distress from his features. "That was only between Audrey and me."

"Or so you thought. If Duncan found out, that could have set him on his murderous path." Celeste blinked, and suddenly he saw the pain beneath her stoic mask, a misery as deep as his own. "Yet you never told me. When I talked of possible reasons someone might want to harm my sister, you left me in ignorance to try to find another cause."

If ever he had reason to loathe himself…

His heart breaking even more, he regarded her with remorse and regret. "Because I was ashamed. Aye, and greedy and ambitious, as your sister was. She wanted power and wealth and position, and so did I."

"That is no excuse for not being truthful about what happened between you," Celeste replied, her words more distressing than a slap. "Tell me, Gerrard, how far would you have gone in the wood if I hadn't stopped you? Would you have made love to me?"

"Since it's honesty you want, yes, I would have made

love to you. I wanted to make love to you as I've rarely wanted anything before."

"More than Dunborough?"

"Much more."

"And Audrey? Did you want to make love to her, too?"

His brows lowered as the interrogation continued, and his anguished frustration grew. "What do you really want to hear, Celeste? The truth? Then here it is—I would have made love to your sister if she'd let me. She never did. But I didn't set out to seduce Audrey or do anything that would get her killed. And if there was deception between us, she was just as guilty."

Celeste stepped back as if he'd struck her. "Nothing's ever your fault, is it, Gerrard? There is always someone else for you to blame."

"I'm *not* blaming Audrey," he cried with chagrin and despair. "I blame myself for letting my aspirations and envy and resentment cloud my better judgment."

"You should have told me of your betrothal. Instead, you kept it from me all this time. Worse, you made me believe you had changed until…until you tried to seduce me in the wood."

"*I* tried to seduce *you*?" he repeated incredulously. "Who grabbed *me* and kissed *me*? By God, Audrey may have been ambitious, but at least she was no hypocrite and didn't try to make a man feel ashamed of his desire."

Her cheeks aflame, Celeste regarded him with ire flashing in her eyes. "You think you knew her? She always said you'd never amount to much, and without your family's name and rank and power, you'd be worth even less." Celeste jabbed his chest, each poke sharp, as if her finger were a dagger. "You were nothing more than the poor third, the consolation prize, once Broderick and

Roland were out of her reach. And what was she to you except a bag of coins to get what you wanted? At least Duncan wanted *her*."

This was pointless. Because he had been less than forthright, she saw him as a villain and wanted to believe her sister was as innocent as an angel. Nothing he could say would ever change her mind.

He waved his hand dismissively. "Now that you've blackened my name even more, you can go."

"I will and gladly," she replied. "I hope I never see you, or Dunborough, ever again."

As she turned to leave, wincing a little, the doors to the hall opened and another woman swept into the chamber. She wore a black cloak lined with fox fur and a heavy black veil of fine wool over a wimple white as clean fleece. A golden crucifix that hung from her neck glinted in the firelight.

The mother superior of Saint Agatha's ran an imperious gaze over the two people facing her and, in tones as haughty as her posture, said, "So, Celeste, here you are. This deplorable disobedience is yet more evidence, if I required it, that you are not fit to be a bride of Christ."

All Celeste's righteous indignation drained away like water from a bucket with no bottom.

"What's that you said?" Gerrard asked as he came down from the dais. "Hasn't she taken her final vows?"

The mother superior ran a scornful gaze over him. "No, and clearly I was wise not to permit it. She is too wanton and disobedient *and* she's a thief besides. She stole that habit from Sister Sylvester."

"She *stole* it?" Gerrard repeated with an expression both incredulous and amazed.

Celeste blushed with shame, but only for taking Sister Sylvester's habit without permission. She did not regret disobeying the mother superior's command to stay in the convent. As for pretending to be a nun, she had done that for safety, even though it was a lie.

"I had a right to come home," she said, addressing the older woman and trying to ignore Gerrard. "You kept me in ignorance about my sister's death far too long as it was. And I thought traveling in a nun's habit would keep me safe."

"Your sister was a bold hussy and you are little better."

"While you are cruel and mean-spirited," Celeste retorted.

The mother superior's face twisted with rage. "You spawn of Satan, you devil's—"

Glaring, Gerrard stepped between them. "Watch your tongue, woman," he said to the mother superior, "or I might forget who and what you are and put you in the stocks."

Celeste flushed even more, her body hot as a summer's day. That he should come to her defense after what she had just said to him, the accusations she had made...

"I've heard about you, too, young man," the nun replied. "It is a miracle you haven't been excommunicated for your scandalous behavior."

"It's a miracle to me you are in charge of anything, yet so it is," Gerrard returned. "You can say what you have to say to Celeste with civility, or you are free to go."

The silence stretched out for what seemed an eternity before the mother superior waspishly replied, "As you wish."

"Good." He gestured toward his chair on the dais. "Won't you sit?"

Without a word in reply, the nun mounted the dais and sat. Gerrard set out another chair and then came to offer his arm to Celeste. She couldn't look at his face as she took it and let him lead her, grateful and limping slightly, to the seat. Then he got himself a chair and set it between them.

He regarded the mother superior steadily. "Now then," he began, "why have you come to Dunborough?"

"To bring Celeste back, of course," she replied as if he were an idiot.

"Why?"

Chapter Twenty

The single interrogative word hung in the air and Celeste scarcely dared to breathe.

"B-because she should come back," the mother superior spluttered at last.

"Again, I ask you, why?" Gerrard replied. "It appears to me that you don't want her there, nor care what happens to her, or you would have sought her long before now. And if she is not, in fact, a nun, you have no right to order her to do anything."

"I delayed chasing after her because I thought she would come to her senses and return," the mother superior replied.

She ran another critical gaze over Gerrard, then spoke to Celeste. "I gather I can add the sin of lust to your many faults."

"No one is without them," Celeste said in her own defense. "But I don't pretend otherwise, like others who mete out harsh and unjust punishments for the most minor of infractions while claiming it's for the good of people's souls."

"Your soul is obviously beyond redemption and you'll never be fit to wear a habit, stolen or otherwise."

"I will send it back," Celeste replied, "or pay for another for Sister Sylvester when I've gone to a different convent, one where no unjust mother superior will prevent me from taking my final vows."

The older nun's lips thinned. "I will see that you are never allowed that privilege. You are willful, stubborn and disobedient. I shall ensure that every nunnery, abbey and convent in England knows the sort of woman you are."

"Then I shall go abroad!"

"Stop!" Gerrard commanded, rising from his chair. "I have been party to enough arguments in my life." He addressed the mother superior. "Leave us. I wish to speak with Sister...with Celeste alone."

"I have no doubt you wish to be alone with her, although I doubt you'll do much talking!" the woman snapped as she got to her feet with outraged majesty. She said no more before she turned in a swirl of black fabric and jingling chain, then marched down the hall and out into air as cold and dry as she was.

Not sure what to do, Celeste twisted her fingers in her lap, waiting for Gerrard to speak. What could she say? She had lied to him and everyone in Dunborough about being a nun.

He should have told her about his betrothal to Audrey, but he hadn't denied it when she'd asked. He hadn't lied, as she had done for days.

For a long time he didn't speak. He stared at the floor, his expression hard and grim.

Did he hate her now? Celeste couldn't fault him if he did.

She never should have upbraided him for their intimate encounters, or accused him of seducing Audrey, or cast any blame on him for how her sister died. Celeste knew that now, when it was too late. "I'm sorry I deceived you, Gerrard, and I'm grateful for your defense. Forgive my accusations and please try to think well of me when I'm gone, even if I don't deserve it."

He raised his eyes to look at her. "I should have told you what had passed between Audrey and me. Finding out about our plans might have made MacHeath lose his temper and attack her, and I should have told you that, too. But I was too ashamed." He gave her a sorrowful smile, a ghost of his merry grin. "I wanted you to like me."

She reached out to take his hand, then drew back. "I do like you, Gerrard. I've always liked you."

And more, so much more. Especially now, when he was lost to her.

His grave eyes studied her features. "Do you really want to be a nun?"

What more could she hope for? "Yes, it's what I truly desire."

"Then I'll likely never see you again."

So this was how a broken heart felt. "No, I don't suppose you will. I wish you well, Gerrard."

"I hope you find peace, Celeste."

"And you, too," she softly replied, before she slowly left the hall of Dunborough and the man she loved.

It was all Gerrard could do not to run after Celeste and beg her to stay.

She had lied to him about being a nun. She had made him feel guilty and ashamed of his desire. She had tempted and tormented him and chastised him for not being completely honest, while she had been less than truthful herself.

And yet he loved her.

No other woman had come close to touching his heart, while she, with her kind compassion, her tender generosity, her bold defense of those weaker than herself, and yes, her stubbornness, as well as her strength and her passion, had taken possession of his heart long ago.

She *was* his heart. His conscience. His better self.

Yet for her sake, because of what she wanted, what would make her happy, he must let her go, even though he yearned to plead with her to let him try to show her he would do everything in his power to be a good and honest man if only she would stay.

She had been the first love of his boyish heart and she would be the last.

Once back at the house, Celeste sank onto a chair and covered her face with her hands. Never again would she consider a broken heart a minor complaint, an affliction of silly girls or foolish women. Losing Gerrard was a painful agony of a sort she'd never experienced before, not even when she'd been sent to the convent or been told of Audrey's death.

Gerrard had shown her the joys of passion, the thrill of being desired, the sort of happiness a woman beloved by a man could know. She would never again experience the delight she felt in his presence or the way he could lift her heart with a smile and a word.

She would have no one who shared their past, their mutual memories.

She would miss him, and everything about him, for the rest of her life.

"Sister Augustine?"

She looked up to find Lewis standing before her, regarding her with an eager, intense expression she found slightly disconcerting, and holding the ginger cat in his arms.

She'd forgotten she had left him there. By rights, he shouldn't call her that, but she was too tired and heartsick to tell him so, or why. "Yes?"

He put down Joseph quickly, almost tossing him away. The cat hissed, but he ignored it. "Are you still leaving Dunborough?"

"Yes, Lewis. As soon as I can."

"Not today, though. It's too late to travel today."

"Is it? Is it past the noon?"

"Almost."

Joseph came toward her and rubbed his face against a chair leg before she bent to pick him up. "Then perhaps not today," she said with a sigh.

"I'm going with you."

She stiffened, suddenly alert, and not only because of what he said. It was the fervent, determined way he said it.

"You have a place in the castle," she replied as she put the cat down.

Joseph sauntered to a corner, where he sat and watched them.

"I don't want to be a clerk. I *hate* it! And I hate it here. I'll hate it more when you're gone!"

The vehemence in his voice and the feverish look in his eyes made her wish she'd told him to leave before she went to the castle. She thought of Audrey and how she'd either missed or ignored any signs that MacHeath might be dangerous. Had she done the same with Lewis?

"Oh, Lewis, that's so kind and generous of you!" Celeste exclaimed. She would act the helpless maiden and lie if she must to get him to leave the house. "I'll feel so much safer with a protector! Do you have a horse? I have Audrey's mare and riding will make our journey so much easier and more comfortable, don't you think? She's at the castle, though." Or so Celeste assumed, for she had never asked. "I shall have to fetch her."

"We can take horses from my father's stable," he replied. "He owes me for all the years I slaved for him."

"No, no, let me take Daisy, and perhaps you can buy a horse. Otherwise your father might come after us."

"Matheus at the Cock's Crow has one he'll probably sell."

"Go and get Daisy from the castle and purchase a horse from Matheus. We'll begin our journey tomorrow," Celeste said, although she had no intention of being there.

When Ewald brought the money for the sale, she would ask him to settle Audrey's debts, send some to Saint Agatha's to pay for Sister Sylvester's habit and take what remained for her journey. She'd say she was heading south, then go north to Scotland.

Although gossip traveled among the clergy, too, there must be somewhere she could go and start afresh. It might have to be remote and without many comforts, but she would have peace, at least a little.

"Now that that's decided," she went on, "I should prepare some food to take on our journey, and you no doubt have things to prepare, as well."

She made her way to the door and opened it, signaling that it was time for him to leave.

With a look like an anxious puppy, he came to stand in front of her. "I don't want to go back to the castle."

"You can't stay here. It wouldn't be proper."

"I don't fear gossip."

"I do. Gossip has a way of following one, and if I'm to go to another convent—"

"You won't, will you?" he pleaded, reaching out to take her hands in a tight grasp, his gaze more intent. "You wouldn't do that, would you? You shouldn't. You're far too beautiful to shut yourself away."

She pulled her hands free. "It's what I want, Lewis."

"I don't want you to leave me. I love you!"

"I'm flattered, Lewis, truly," she began, backing slowly toward the stairs, "but—"

"You're the most beautiful, wonderful woman in the world and I love you with all my heart!" he declared, following her.

"I'm grateful that you care for me, Lewis, but I wish to be a nun with all *my* heart. You are young and—"

"I'm not a baby!" he cried, his expression hardening, his eyes glowing with a stronger emotion. "I'm a man!"

God help her, she *had* been as blind as Audrey! She should have noticed…seen…suspected. But she hadn't. Now, though, thanks to her sister's fate, she knew she must persuade Lewis to leave as quickly as possible, then get way from Dunborough before he realized she had gone. Later she would send word to Roland about the chandler's son and his worrisome behavior.

In the meantime, she must help herself.

She remembered that Sister Sylvester had quieted more than one novice who was overcome with emotions. She must remain calm. Serene. But also firm. "Yes, of course you are a man. And it's because you are that you cannot stay here tonight. If you were just a boy, it would be different."

At last Lewis went to the door of the chamber and put his hand on the latch.

Instead of leaving, he shot the bolt home.

"Lewis! What are you—"

"I *will* stay the night."

He didn't sound like a boy or a youth or a love-struck young man. He sounded hard. Ruthless. Determined.

And she was here alone, without a soldier or servant nearby.

Despite her fear and growing panic, she tried to keep her voice level. "I've told you why you cannot stay, Lewis. Please go."

Before she could move away, he crossed the room, grabbed her shoulders and pulled her close. "I love you and I want to be with you! We're going to be lovers, so why not begin now?"

"No, we are not!" she declared as she twisted free of his grasp and ran to the door despite the pain in her ankle. "I am going to be a nun and you are going to leave."

"No!" he shouted, getting to the door first. "You love me as I love you. You came to my aid and defended me from my father."

She backed against the table and reached for the candleholder. "I didn't want him to hurt you, and that's all."

Lewis smiled, a terrible smile that made her blood run cold. "You think I'm some love-struck boy, the way I thought you were virtuous. But I know what you're really like. I've seen the way you look at Gerrard, that disgusting, debauched reprobate. You're a whore, the same as your sister, no matter what clothes you wear or vows you've taken."

"No, I'm not," she retorted. "Now let me go or—"

"Or what? You think Gerrard will come to your aid? He's leaving."

"Lewis," she said, her desperation growing, "if you truly care for me—"

"I'll let you go?" he scornfully replied. "You'd rather

be with Gerrard, I suppose. You're just like every other woman anxious to spread her legs for him."

Celeste gripped the candleholder. "You're wrong."

"I thought you were different. Now I know otherwise, or you wouldn't have been so angry when you heard Gerrard was going to marry Audrey, as angry as Duncan was when your sister wouldn't have him. She saw Roland riding past, and Duncan tried to tell her to forget the lords of Dunborough. I saw the look on his face when she told him she was going to marry Gerrard."

Celeste gasped. "You were a witness to what happened?"

"I saw and heard *everything*," Lewis confirmed with smug satisfaction. "I watched through the window. I often watched her through the window, and you, too. Sometimes I came into the house. It's easy to open the latch on the kitchen shutters."

God help her, what kind of twisted…?

"You don't sleep much, though. And that Lizabet was always bustling about. Not like Martha. She preferred to sit in the kitchen by the fire. Or take her time outside. Nobody even realized I was here when Duncan raped and killed your sister. I saw him beat her, as she deserved," Lewis finished, his tone boastful and proud.

Celeste could hardly believe what she was hearing. "And you did nothing to help her?"

"Why should I? Your sister got what she deserved, and so did MacHeath. I followed him when he left here, too. I had to get my horse, so I didn't catch up to him until after he'd fought Roland. MacHeath was on the bank of the river. I was careful to tread where he had, and he didn't hear me. He was so weak, it was easy to push him in. He didn't have the strength to get out. I watched him drown. You would have liked that. It took a long time."

Celeste felt too sick to speak, to move, to do anything except stare at Lewis with horror. She was in the presence of a madman and she was all alone.

No, not all alone. "God, please help me!" she cried as she lunged for the door.

Chapter Twenty-One

When Lewis moved to stop her, Celeste raised the candleholder, intending to bring it down on his head.

She wasn't fast enough. He grabbed and held her arm tightly, squeezing until she was forced to drop the makeshift weapon.

"You stupid slut!" he snarled, his eyes full of rage as he picked up the candleholder and threw it against the wall, cracking a wooden panel. "You let Gerrard have you, so why not me?"

She slapped Lewis hard across the face with her free hand and tried to kick him, too. He struck her on the cheek, cutting her lip and knocking her down.

She tried to scramble away, the pain in her ankle excruciating. The ginger cat appeared out of nowhere and leaped at Lewis, scratching his arm in three long, bloody lines before landing on his feet and dashing from the room.

Celeste was nearly out the door when Lewis caught the back of her habit and dragged her into the room. Wrenching herself free, she knocked over a chair.

He tackled her and brought her down beneath him.

Breathless, she tried to buck him off, until he punched her by her ear, nearly knocking her senseless.

Only then did she lie still, panting, the taste of blood in her mouth.

"That's better," he muttered as he straddled her, kneeling on her upper arms to hold her in place, the resulting pain making tears start in her eyes.

Then she heard a sound that made her try to stand again. He was taking off his belt.

"Stop!" he ordered as he wrapped the belt around her right wrist and slid the leather strap through the buckle. After pulling it tight, he bound her other hand until both were tied behind her.

Her wrists and shoulders were in agony and she let out a low moan.

"It's your own fault," he snarled as he stood up. Grabbing the end of the belt, he hauled her to her feet. "I suppose I'll have to gag you, too."

Desperate that he shouldn't, she vigorously shook her head despite the pain it caused. "Please, Lewis, don't! I'll be quiet. I give you my word."

"You must be forgetting that I know what a deceitful whore you are."

He tore the veil from her head and then pulled out a dagger that had been hidden in the waist of his breeches.

"Are you going to kill me?" she barely managed to whisper, her throat dry and constricted with panic.

He appeared genuinely surprised. "Of course not. I've told you, I love you—in spite of your evil ways."

Her life might depend on appeasing him, so although her mind worked feverishly to come up with some way to escape, she didn't move while he cut a long strip of fabric from her veil and tossed the rest away.

Holding the knife and the length of cloth, he smiled

and ran a long, leering gaze over her, from the crown of her head to the hem of her tunic. "I wonder," he murmured, before he reached out and slipped the knife between the wimple and her cheek.

Trying not to move, she closed her eyes and held her breath as he sliced into the cloth, then pulled it away, along with her cap.

"No, no, no, this won't do," he muttered as he walked around her. "Your hair shouldn't be bound up like that."

She felt his terrible presence close behind her, yet did not move, not even when he began to undo her braid.

"They told me Gerrard cut your hair off once. He should have been drawn and quartered," Lewis said, pausing to take a handful of the loose curls and hold it to his face, breathing deeply. "Sandalwood, isn't it? How worldly!"

His attention was on her hair. This might be her best chance.

Turning swiftly, she shoved him with her shoulder, throwing him off balance, and ran.

"You bitch!" he cried, staggering.

Before she reached the door, he grabbed a fistful of her hair and yanked, sending her stumbling to the ground, crying out in agony.

He seized her arm and hauled her upright. Trying to keep her weight off her aching ankle, she could see the rage, the madness, as he forced the strip of fabric between her teeth.

"Don't try that again, or by God, you'll be sorry!" he snarled, pulling the gag ruthlessly tight.

Once it was tied, he put his arm under her shoulder and dragged her out of the room and toward the kitchen.

"You'll come to your senses soon enough," he muttered. "I'm doing this for you, after all. You want to leave Dunborough, and so we shall. We belong together. I thought it was Audrey I loved, but I know better now. You'll love me. I love you so much you'll have to love me."

She was not an easy burden for him, so they made slow progress through the kitchen while she desperately tried to come up with a plan of escape and silently prayed for aid.

She saw the basket of dried peas near the door and, like a sudden shaft of light in a dark tunnel, recalled a story from her childhood that Audrey used to tell her, about two children lost in the woods.

Celeste waited until they were nearly at the door, then let her knees give way, sinking down and nearly taking Lewis with her.

"Get up!" he ordered.

Using the basket to give her leverage, she lurched to her feet, her hands apparently balled into fists as he pulled her forward.

He didn't realize each hand was full of peas.

"Arnhelm!" Verdan called out when he saw his brother in the distance.

They were a few miles from Dunborough along the main road south to DeLac. Overhead, the sky was gray and dingy, with no sun to be seen. The dales here were barren, rocks protruding like sores, and a few birds wheeled high in the air.

Otherwise, the only living things to be seen were the two riders and their horses.

Arnhelm reined in and twisted to look behind him.

His eyes widened when he realized who was galloping toward him, his arm flapping like a scared chicken and no helmet on his head.

"What's wrong?" he demanded when his brother pulled his horse to a skittering halt, nearly coming down on its haunches on a patch of ice.

"You've got to come back! Now!" Verdan cried as he got his mount back under control. "Gerrard's leaving for DeLac and he wants you to go with him."

Arnhelm's horse began to prance nervously. "Gerrard's going to DeLac?"

"That what I said, isn't it? He's giving up Dunborough and going to tell Roland."

Arnhelm couldn't have looked more amazed if Verdan had announced he was really the king's illegitimate son. "Giving up Dunborough?"

"Aye, and goin' to DeLac to tell Roland. And he wants you to go with him."

Arnhelm frowned. "But I have to tell Sir Roland—"

"Doesn't matter now, does it?"

Arnhelm was thinking hard. "It might, depending on what happened with Sister Augustine."

"Well, you can tell Sir Roland when you get there with Gerrard. In private like. In the meantime, you ought to get back and go with him, or he might be thinking you're up to no good. I wouldn't want Gerrard cross with me, not for anything."

Arnhelm let out his breath slowly. "I suppose you're right. Best go back and see if I can find out more when I ride with him. Could be there'll be nothing to tell Sir Roland, but if there is, I'll have a better idea what."

"Aye," Verdan vigorously agreed.

The brothers wheeled their horses and galloped toward Dunborough, leaving the dales to the clouds and the birds.

It didn't take the two men long to get back.

"You don't suppose he's left already?" Verdan asked anxiously as they waited for Hedley to open the gate to the courtyard.

"Hope not."

At last it swung wide enough for them to enter and they urged their horses through. The brothers exchanged relieved glances at the sight of Snow with a large leather pouch tied to the saddle.

"Where were you?" Hedley demanded of Arnhelm.

"Never mind that now," he replied as he slid from his horse. "If Gerrard comes askin', tell him I'm in the stable. That'll be true enough," he added as he started to jog toward it with Oaken in tow.

His brows contracted, a puzzled Hedley regarded Verdan. "What's going on?"

"Nothin'," he said, before he, too, dismounted and led his horse toward the stable.

They had barely gotten their horses into the stalls and unsaddled when Gerrard strode inside, his mail jingling, his long cloak swirling about his legs.

"Ah, Arnhelm, here you are," he said. "Hedley told me I'd find you here."

The brothers came out of the stalls so fast they nearly knocked each other over.

Gerrard frowned. "What are you doing here, Verdan? Why didn't you tell your brother I was looking for him?"

"I did," he replied. "Seems his horse is still lame," he added, his face aflame as he lied.

Fortunately, it was dim in the stable, and Gerrard turned away to address Arnhelm before he got a good look at Verdan's flushed cheeks. "Take another," he said, "and be quick about it."

Gerrard had left the stable and was waiting for Arnhelm when Norbert burst through the wicket gate like someone being chased by a pack of ravenous wolves.

"Where is my scoundrel of a son?" he demanded as he trotted toward him.

"I have no idea," Gerrard calmly replied.

He hadn't seen Lewis since he'd made his announcement in the hall. Not that it mattered. The lad's whereabouts were no concern of Norbert's now. "He's safe from you, though."

"And learning sin from you, no doubt," the chandler retorted with astonishing disrespect as he came to a halt. "He's taken my two best horses and I want them back!"

"So why have you come here?"

"Where else would he have taken them?" the angry man demanded.

"There are no horses in the stable except those that belong to Dunborough."

"I'll look for myself!"

His ire rising, Gerrard moved to intercept Norbert. "No, you won't. Your horses aren't there. Maybe Lewis took them, or maybe a thief stole them, but *they are not here.*"

"Might have walked off on their own," Verdan said under his breath. "I would, if I was his."

Although he shared the sentiment, Gerrard ignored the soldier's comment. "If your son has taken your horses without your permission, that is theft and punishable by hanging. Is that what you want, to see your son hanged?"

"Hanged?" Norbert repeated, his voice nearly a squeak. He shook his head. "No! No, no, no!"

"Then perhaps you should refrain from making hasty accusations."

"Gerrard!" Ewald's deep voice rang across the yard.

They turned to see him struggling through the wicket gate, out of breath and nearly falling. "Gerrard!" he called out again. "Something's happened! Sister Augustine— she's gone!"

A shaft of fear and dismay, worse than any blow from a spear, pierced Gerrard's heart. Ewald staggered to a halt and bent over, breathing hard, his hands on his knees.

"The house—chairs overturned, panel broken. Like Audrey," Ewald panted.

Not Celeste, too! Dear God, not Celeste!

Gerrard swung himself onto Snow. "Open the gate!" he shouted as he kicked his heels against the stallion's sides.

Hedley barely got the gate open before Gerrard charged through. He didn't wait to see if anyone followed, didn't care if they did. He had to get to the D'Orleau house.

As he galloped through the outer gate and down the main road of the village, men and women shouted warnings and got out of the way, then stood staring after him before they began to talk, gesture, exclaim and wonder.

Gerrard didn't dismount at the gate to the D'Orleau yard. Instead, he urged Snow over the fence, then reined in. After dismounting, he ran through the gaping door and into the main chamber, where he saw what Ewald had—the overturned chairs, the disarray and the fallen candleholder that had hit the panel, cracking it.

Calling out Celeste's name, Gerrard took the stairs two at a time and charged into her bedchamber.

It was empty save for the furnishings and a few

undergarments and a small cloth bag lying on the unused bed. Mercifully, there was no sign of a struggle here, or in the other bedchamber.

He ran back down to the main room.

It was then he saw the blood. God help him, there was fresh blood on the floor.

He took a step closer and saw more drops leading to the kitchen. He rushed there to find that the trail of blood ended at the threshold of the door into the garden. There was no sign of a struggle in this chamber, either, except for a handful of peas scattered on the floor next to the half-open door.

The biggest orange cat Gerrard had ever seen suddenly dashed into view, apparently chasing a pea. The animal careered into the door, which opened wider. The cat crouched on the threshold, looking at Gerrard, before batting the pea with his paw and sending it outside.

Ignoring the beast, Gerrard went out in turn, searching for more signs of blood or a struggle.

He saw neither, but he did see more peas. And not scattered about as they'd been in the kitchen. These looked to be in a line leading to the stable.

With a gasp, he ran toward the outbuilding.

Empty, save for that cat. And a few more peas.

There was one by the door that opened to the north. He went outside and spotted another closer to the road.

Dear God, could this be a sign?

A trail for him to follow?

"Gerrard!" Arnhelm called out. "Is she there?"

He quickly returned to the house, to find Arnhelm and Verdan, Hedley and several of the other soldiers crowding into the main room, every one of them staring at the blood.

"She's not in the house or stable," he informed them.

"Lewis ain't in the solar or his chamber in the castle, neither," Arnhelm said. "And he ain't in the kitchen or anywhere else."

"Maybe she fell, an accident like," Verdan said hopefully. "And maybe Lewis is somewhere in the village."

His brother darted him a sour look. "And maybe not. Remember what happened to Audrey?"

Gerrard didn't need that reminder. The vivid images were all too clear in his mind. But Celeste was not Audrey, and it seemed that even in her distress, she'd thought of a way to help them find her. "I think she's been taken, but has left us a trail to follow."

He led them to the kitchen and pointed at the peas. "They're in too straight a line to be random. I think she was trying to show us the direction they were going."

"S'truth!" Verdan murmured.

"Aye, she's a marvel," Gerrard said. "And she better be alive, by God, and unharmed when we find her, or whoever took her will be sorry he was ever born."

And if it was Lewis who had taken her, he would pay even more dearly for that crime, made worse because Celeste had tried to help him.

"Verdan, go to Ralph and have him get ten men mounted as quick as he can, to follow me along the north road. You and Arnhelm and Hedley should be in the party, too. And Ralph should organize more search parties for the other roads from Dunborough. Tell Peg to have the servants search the castle again, and Lewis's chamber especially. I want to know if there are any signs he's left the castle for good, and if so, any clue as to where he might be going."

After issuing his orders, Gerrard went back to the yard, threw himself on Snow and set off along the northern road.

Chapter Twenty-Two

In a clearing off the road some miles from Dunborough, Lewis threw his horse's reins over a low tree limb, then dragged Celeste, bound and gagged, from the other horse he'd stolen from his father. Blood had dried on her lip and chin. Her body, especially her ankle, ached from hours in the saddle. The cold made her shiver, for she had no cloak. Her wrists were bruised from the tight belt around them and she could hardly breathe because of the gag in her mouth.

Yet her physical discomfort was nothing compared to her dread of what might happen as Lewis took her farther and farther from Dunborough. It could be hours before someone realized they were gone, and she hoped the disarray in the house would tell Gerrard, or anyone, that she'd been taken by force.

Worst of all, she had dropped the last of peas some time ago. Hopefully, she'd left enough of a trail that they would realize what she'd done, and figure out which direction they'd gone.

Lewis pushed her down onto the ground near a tree. "We'll rest a bit. Are you thirsty?"

She nodded.

To her relief, he crouched down and began to remove her gag. "No one will hear you if you cry out here," he said, his breath hot on her ear.

And then he licked her.

Sickened, she turned away. He grabbed her chin and forced her to look at him. "You're going to love me," he said.

Although he spoke with the whining voice of a child, he glared at her with the hard, angry eyes of a man before, then let go abruptly and went to the horses. As he'd led her farther from Dunborough, he'd bragged about stealing them. Surely by now his father would have realized his animals were gone and started looking for them, and perhaps his errant son, as well.

Lewis untied a wineskin that had been affixed to his saddle and brought it to her. After pulling out the stopper, he held it to her lips. "Drink!"

She did, but he poured too fast and she began to choke, wine spilling over her clothes and making her shiver more. Ignoring her discomfort, Lewis took a drink. Maybe he would keep drinking until he fell asleep.

As he wiped his mouth with the back of his hand, his lustful gaze roved over her, making her tremble with fear as well as cold. She never should have accused Gerrard of looking at her that way. She knew now there had always been respect and admiration in his eyes as well as desire.

"I'm hungry, too," she said, hoping to turn her abductor's attention to different needs.

Putting the stopper back in the spout of the wineskin, Lewis frowned, then mercifully got to his feet and went back to the horses. While he rummaged in the pack tied to one saddle, she looked around, seeking anything she could use as a weapon. There was a stick nearby, too thin to be effective. Still, it would be better than nothing and she could jab it at his throat or eye.

Lewis pulled out something wrapped in a length of linen. It proved to be a small loaf of brown bread. He broke off a piece and put it into her mouth, forcing her to eat without using her hands.

"It would be easier if I were untied," she said as she chewed.

"I can't trust you," he replied with a weary, petulant sigh, as if she were the one at fault.

"I give you my word that I won't try to leave." She wouldn't use the word *escape*, or any other that might upset him. Nor would she consider herself bound by any promise she made to him. "I can hardly walk for my sore ankle."

He studied her a moment, then smiled. "All right. Even if you could run, you wouldn't get far."

No, she wouldn't, unless she could get on a horse.

She didn't answer as she leaned forward to let him reach the belt binding her hands, and uttered a silent prayer of thanks when he knelt behind her and began to loosen it. She'd planned to be patient and wait for her chance, yet once the belt was undone, his hand snaked around to cup her breast. Shocked and frightened, she instinctively pushed back with her elbow, hitting him hard in the neck.

He fell back, gasping.

This might be her only chance!

She clambered to her feet, nearly tripping on her habit. Lewis was between her and the horses. He could stop her if she went that way.

Gathering her skirt up in her arms, she ran in the other direction, ignoring the pain in her ankle and going as fast as she could. She paid no heed to the bare branches of trees and underbrush scratching her face, or the mud splattering her clothes and soaking her shoes.

Her breathing harsh and ragged, she saw a tangle of holly bushes ahead. A horse wouldn't be willing to follow her in there.

Falling to her knees, she threw the skirt of her habit over her head to protect it from the sharp points of the holly and pushed her way inside, shoving dead leaves behind her to hide any signs of her passing.

There was a bare spot in the middle of the bushes and she lay curled up on her side, clutching her swollen, aching ankle, trying to calm her breathing, listening for any sound of pursuit, while praying fervently to God to help her.

With growing desperation, Gerrard surveyed the brush and trees and ground around him. The trail of peas had stopped several yards before, and he and his men had fanned out in the wood, seeking any sign of Celeste and Lewis or their horses.

He'd followed some promising hoofprints this far. Now they were petering out.

"Anything?" he shouted to the others.

"Not yet, sir!" Hedley answered, followed by a chorus of "Nothing!" and "No, sir!"

"Keep looking!" Celeste couldn't have disappeared into thin air, and if they were looking for a body, there would be some sign of that, too.

Oh, God, not that! he prayed. She didn't deserve a terrible death any more than her sister had. If someone deserved to die, it was him. He'd made his useless, worthless life a disaster.

He scanned the undergrowth again and saw a broken branch. And then another. It could be from a deer. Nevertheless, he went that way.

"Where are you, Celeste?" Lewis called out in a singsong voice, as if they were playing some sort of game. "You might as well show yourself. I'm going to find you, and the longer I have to search, the more you're going to regret running away from me."

Her muscles sore, her face and hands scratched and bleeding, she could hear the anger and agitation in his voice, and that he was getting closer. Yet hard as it was to stay still, she didn't doubt that if she tried to flee again, he'd catch her. Her only hope was to hide and stay quiet, like when she'd been little and her father was on a rampage.

She'd had Audrey to cling to then. Audrey, who always seemed so brave and determined, who was so keen to make a better life for herself. Was it any wonder Gerrard had admired her? He and Audrey were alike in many ways. The truly great surprise should be that Audrey had apparently finally seen his merit, a worthiness Celeste had always known was there.

If only she had told Gerrard that she loved him, she thought, as the cold grew more and more unbearable. She had loved him before she left Dunborough. She loved him now. She would always love him.

Here, in her most desperate hour, she realized what she truly wanted, and it wasn't being shut out from the world in a convent, no matter how peaceful and secure such a life would be. She wanted to be Gerrard's wife, to live with him and bear his children and, yes, even quarrel with him. To share his bed and his concerns, to help and comfort him as she was sure he would help and comfort her. And he would make her smile, no matter what troubles they faced.

"Where are you?" Lewis called again, and from close by.

Stay still, she silently ordered herself. *Keep quiet. Don't even breathe.*

"There you are! Thought you were clever, did you?"

Gerrard's heart leaped to his throat at the sight of the horses through the bare trees.

Drawing his sword, he started to run. He was going to call out to his men until he realized that might alert Lewis. Better to keep quiet. He was stronger and better trained than the chandler's son. He could best him easily in a fight and he didn't want to take the risk that the desperate lout would harm Celeste.

Difficult though it was, Gerrard slowed to a walk when he drew closer to the horses, which were now shifting nervously.

"Shhh," he whispered, looking for any sign of their riders.

There! Footprints in a patch of mud where the leaves had been blown clear. Two sets, one large, one smaller.

Gripping his sword, he moved away from the horses and began to circle the area, looking for more footprints or any other sign of the people he sought. He spotted a long, narrow piece of damp black fabric at the base of a tree and bent to pick it up.

He felt the stickiness of blood on it.

His resolve hardened. Whatever had happened here, he would find Celeste and soon.

He *must* find her.

* * *

As Lewis started slashing at the holly, Celeste rose to her hands and knees and, grimacing, began to crawl away, until her hair got caught on some of the leaves. She desperately tried to pull it free, tearing at the holly with her bare hands, paying no heed to the painful nicks and cuts that gave her, until Lewis clutched her swollen ankle.

"Now I've got you!" he cried as she yelped in pain. He started to drag her out of the bushes.

Despite her agony, she did all she could to stop him—kicking, twisting, grabbing at sharp leaves and branches, digging into the ground with her fingers.

But he was too strong and she was too tired to prevent the slow, inexorable progress. Yet she wasn't going to give up. Once free of the holly, she flipped onto her back and kicked at him with her other foot. When he moved out of range, she struggled to her feet. He got hold of her shoulder and threw her to the ground. Then he stood over her, one foot on either side of her torso, his knife in his hands and ire in his eyes.

"Don't try that again or I'll gut you like a pig!" he warned as she lay panting beneath him.

She said nothing. All her effort was concentrated on trying to breathe and gather her strength. Tired and hurt though she was, she wasn't going to surrender. Not yet. Audrey had fought for her life and so would she.

Lewis took hold of the front of her scapula and pulled her up. He was no trained mercenary, not like Duncan, and she could see that he was tired, too.

"Is this any way to thank me?" he demanded, pushing her back against a tree. "Is this any way to repay my devotion? And saving you from a miserable life in a convent?"

She didn't answer as she gripped the trunk, grateful

for its support. Her mind still sought a way to defeat her enemy, to hurt or incapacitate him if she couldn't outrun him. Sister Sylvester had said something once about men's weaknesses. No matter how big and strong and apparently invincible they were, there were places where a well-aimed blow could hurt them.

What were they? Where?

The ears. And that spot at the bottom of his neck above the collarbone, where there would never be muscle.

Like a snake striking, Celeste suddenly and swiftly raised her arms and smacked Lewis's ears with her palms.

He shrieked and fell back, unsteady, giving her enough time to shove her way past him.

"Bitch!" he snarled, again grabbing hold of her scapula.

She was ready for that this time and with the last of her strength managed to duck out of the garment. Her fear and desperation gave her the energy she needed to limp swiftly toward the trees.

Not fast enough. Lewis threw himself at her and sent her sprawling. She clawed at the dirt, trying to stand, until he struck her shoulder hard with his fist. The blow sent her facedown into the mud and leaves. He put his foot on her back and held her there as she gasped for breath.

"You stupid woman!" he snarled. "I would have made you happy."

Never. The only man in the world who could make her truly happy was back in Dunborough.

"Leave her alone, you dog!"

Gerrard! Oh, thank God, thank God!

She managed to raise her head to look over her shoulder. His sword drawn, Gerrard was racing toward them as fleet as a stag fleeing the hunter's hounds.

"By God, I'll kill you!" he shouted as Lewis took off through the trees.

She tried to get up. Before she could stand she felt a pair of strong arms raising her and heard Gerrard whisper her name.

Then pain overwhelmed her and darkness closed in.

Carrying Celeste in his arms, Gerrard jogged toward the small clearing where he'd found the horses. His breathing was hoarse and rasping, his arms and calves were burning, yet his discomfort meant nothing. He had to get Celeste back to Dunborough, although that meant letting Lewis escape.

For now.

There! There were the horses, placidly munching a few bits of grass.

One of them suddenly raised its head and looked not toward Gerrard, but something else.

Verdan.

Gerrard tried to call out to him, but the only sound that escaped his throat was a hoarse croak. Nevertheless his progress was far from quiet and Verdan heard him. In the next moment, the soldier was lumbering toward him.

"S'truth, is she...?" he gasped, sliding on some damp leaves as he stopped.

"She lives," Gerrard managed to say. "Get me a horse."

Verdan did so at once. Meanwhile, Gerrard looked down at Celeste's pale face. Her lip was cut and bleeding, her cheeks scratched and bruised.

But she was breathing.

For the first time, he noticed her hair, long and curling just as he remembered. *She* was just as he remembered and more. She was his past, his present, his future, his redemption and his life.

He hugged her close and blinked back tears. "Live, Celeste, live!" he whispered. "Live for me, I beg you!"

She stirred and her eyes opened and she gave him a weak smile. "Gerrard...my hero...you saved me," she whispered, before her eyes closed again.

"No, Celeste, it's you who saved me," he murmured.

"Here, sir, let me take her while you get on the mare," Verdan said with quiet reverence, as if she were dead.

She couldn't die. She must not, or his heart would die, too.

When he had Celeste cradled in his arms again, he lifted the reins. He was about to turn his mount toward the road when he paused and grimly said, "Fifty marks to the man who catches Lewis, and my eternal gratitude."

Lizabet and the rest of the household were waiting anxiously in the courtyard when Gerrard rode through the gate with Celeste in his arms. He quickly told the maidservant to prepare her bed and warm the chamber.

He half expected Celeste to rally enough to tell him she wouldn't sleep in the castle as long as he was there.

She didn't. She didn't wake at all, not even when Gerrard handed her down to Ralph and one of the other men. Nor did she wake when he took her in his arms again and carried her inside.

That frightened him most of all.

After he'd laid her on the bed, and Lizabet and Peg had come to tend to her, he went back to the hall and found Ralph waiting. Gerrard sent him to fetch the apothecary with all haste, then threw himself into a chair and leaned forward, his hands on his knees.

And began to pray.

Chapter Twenty-Three

"There he is! There on the bridge!" Hedley called out.

The other soldiers within range of his voice joined him as he ran to the mossy stone bridge over the rushing waters of the river that fed into the Ure.

"Stay back! Keep away!" Lewis shouted in warning. His hair was wild and full of bits of leaves, his cloak torn and muddy. His hands gripped the stone railing as he leaned over it, anxiously scanning the trees along the bank, where the soldiers had congregated.

Verdan started forward, until Arnhelm held him back. "Best not."

"But the reward—"

"Is already Hedley's," Arnhelm replied, addressing his brother, as well as the other men who'd joined them. "I don't like the looks of that lad, and the river's deep. Let me try to talk him into coming quiet."

"The river or the noose, what's it matter?" Ralph asked. "He's dead either way."

"It's not our place to pass judgment on him," Arnhelm reminded the sergeant at arms. "That's for the lord of Dunborough."

"Go on, then," Ralph replied. "See if you can get him off the bridge. The rest of you, stay here unless he runs."

Most of the men were willing to obey, and those who weren't would have had to get past Ralph, so they grudgingly stayed where they were.

"Lewis!" Arnhelm called, stepping out of the grove of trees. He threw his sword onto the bank and held up his empty hands. "It's over, lad. Best come back with us and seek mercy."

Lewis laughed, a high-pitched, sickening sound. "Mercy?" he scoffed. "From a son of Sir Blane?"

"Better one of them than their father," Arnhelm noted, walking slowly toward the bridge. "You ain't done murder, after all. Sister Augustine's all right."

"So instead of being executed, I might merely be imprisoned for the rest of my life and left to rot or starve to death."

Arnhelm was at the foot of the bridge by then. "You don't know that."

"Don't I?" He raised his voice. "Don't the rest of you? Any son of Sir Blane won't be merciful. They don't know how.

"Keep back!" he ordered Arnhelm. "If you come any closer, I'll jump!"

The soldier dutifully retreated a few steps. "You don't want to do that."

"How do you know what I want? I wanted Esmerelda, yet the slut would rather risk her life meeting with Gerrard. I wanted Audrey until she proved to be a worthless whore who deserved to die. I thought Celeste was different. Better. Purer. What a fool! All women are sluts and whores."

"Could be you're right. Come back and you can tell everybody in Dunborough that."

Lewis regarded the soldier with outright disgust. "I may be a fool when it comes to women, but I'm not stupid. I'm not going to let you take me so Gerrard can have the satisfaction of torturing and killing me."

He began to climb onto the wide stone railing.

"Lewis!" Arnhelm cried, starting toward him.

"I told you to stay back!" the young man exclaimed as he stood on the ledge, the cold north wind blowing his cloak around him like a fluttering flag.

He looked over at Arnhelm, who dared to take a few steps closer.

Tears slid down Lewis's cheeks. They might have been from the wind, though, for his voice was proud and defiant. "Tell my father that I'll see him next in hell!"

Arnhelm rushed forward to try to grab the youth before he fell into the swirling water below.

He was too late.

The flames in the central hearth of the great hall flickered in the darkness. Shadows shrouded the corners of the vast chamber and stretched out behind the pillars. Dusk had turned into night, and the few men and servants lingering there talked quietly among themselves. They cast occasional glances at Gerrard on the dais, a cup of untouched wine at his elbow.

Norbert, pale and shaking, crept into the hall. His cloak was soaking from the rain that had started to fall and his boots were thick with mud. He came forward slowly, keeping to the shadows, but Gerrard saw him nonetheless. "What do you want, Norbert? Your horses? One is in the stable, the other with my men."

"S-sir, I'm so… I beg your pardon, s-sir," Norbert stammered, his eyes wide with dismay. "Sister Augustine, how is she?"

"Alive. The apothecary is with her." And had been for what seemed an endless age.

"I'm glad she's… I'm glad," Norbert replied.

"And now you can go. I never want to see you again."

The chandler didn't move.

Trying to keep a rein on his temper, Gerrard got to his feet. "Did you hear me, man?" He pointed at the door. "Go!"

Norbert winced, yet made no effort to leave. Instead, he fell to his knees and held up his hands in supplication. "Have mercy, Gerrard!" he cried. "He's my only son, my only child!"

Gerrard regarded the man steadily. He would never, as long as he lived, forget the sight of Celeste on the ground, her clothes torn and muddy, dried blood on her lip, her hands cut and bleeding and her long hair tangled with leaves. "Your son has sealed his fate. He will be caught, imprisoned, tried and, I have no doubt, executed for what he did."

Norbert covered his thin face with his hands and wailed as if he were the one doomed to die.

Gerrard had heard cries of anguish before, when his father had passed judgment. Lewis did deserve to die for what he'd done, but Gerrard was not Sir Blane and his heart wasn't made of stone.

He came down from the dais and raised the grief-stricken man to his unsteady feet. "Your son has committed a serious crime, Norbert, and he must be punished. That cannot be denied. Perhaps God will forgive Lewis if he repents before—"

"Sir!"

Their expressions grave, their cloaks and helmets dripping, Arnhelm and Verdan marched up the center of the hall.

"We've got Lewis, sir," Arnhelm said grimly. "We saw him on the stone bridge where the road forks, and he saw us. I tried to talk him into coming back but, well, he jumped. He's dead."

Norbert shrieked as if he'd been impaled, then fell to the floor. "Oh, no! Forgive me, my son, forgive me!"

As the chandler's wails became choked sobs, Gerrard took the soldiers aside. "Where is Lewis now?" he asked quietly.

"Took us a while to find his body," Arnhelm answered. "We did at last. It... He's in the stable, sir."

"Take Norbert to his son."

After Arnhelm and Verdan helped Norbert from the hall, Gerrard started to go back to his chair on the dais, then changed his mind and headed to the stairs leading to the bedchambers.

What was happening in Roland's chamber? Was Celeste seriously injured? The apothecary had been with her for so long...

Gerrard went up the steps and peered down the corridor. All was quiet, with none of the bustle usually found when there was a seriously injured person being tended. Was that good, or...not?

He ventured along the hall, pausing outside the door of his father's bedchamber, a room that had been forbidden to him and his brothers all their lives.

A room he had never wanted to enter, even after his father had died.

He opened the door and stepped across the threshold. A broken shutter allowed moonlight to shine across the floor and fall onto the bed. It was still covered with dusty linen and surrounded by equally dusty bed curtains. A heavy brazier, ashes in its bowl, stood nearby.

His father's chest of clothing had likewise been left untouched and was covered with a thick layer of dust.

So much for the man who had terrorized him and his brothers. Who had meted out harsh punishments and cruel judgments. Who had used women as toys for his amusement.

Given the way he'd thought to use Audrey, was he really any better?

Tomorrow, after selecting an escort to take Celeste to the convent or wherever else she wished to go, he would leave Dunborough and ride to DeLac, as he'd planned. He would refuse Roland's offer and seek his fortune elsewhere.

With a heavy sigh, but his decision made, he left the chamber.

And came face-to-face with Celeste.

He gasped and took a step back. It was like encountering an angel. Not only was her presence unexpected, but she wore a plain white shift and her hair fell long and loose about her, just as it had when she was young and innocent. When they both were.

But she was no young and innocent child. She was a woman who had been abducted, injured and upset, and she should be in bed. "What are you doing here? What about your ankle? Where's the apothecary?"

"He's gone. He went down the servants' stairs with Lizabet and Peg." Celeste raised the hem of her shift and held out her bandaged foot. "He put something on it and wrapped it well. It's much better, and so am I. All I need is rest, he says, and I was resting, until I heard the door to that chamber open and thought it must be you." She clasped her hands together, her eyes as pleading as a penitent's. "I want to thank you, Gerrard, for saving me."

"You've done so already. Now you should go back to bed."

"Will you still be here in the morning?"

"Until the dawn at least."

"Then you will go."

"Yes."

She raised her cut and bruised right hand and placed it lightly on his chest. "Don't."

He swallowed hard, for her touch set his blood running hot and full of need, a need that she would never fulfill. "It is for the best."

And then, because he couldn't keep the words from being spoken, he said, "Besides, you will soon be gone."

Her eyes glistened in the light from the torch in the sconce nearby. "Only if you tell me to go."

His brows lowered, for he scarcely dared to hope that he had heard aright. He could more easily believe her words were the product of his own fervent longing.

Celeste drew in a long, quivering breath as she looked into his confused, dark eyes. She was taking a great risk, yet in her heart, she knew not speaking would be worse, no matter what the result. She had discovered what she truly desired, what would make her happy and content, secure and peaceful, and it was not life in a convent. She wanted to spend the rest of her life with Gerrard, to love and cherish him, come what may, and, God willing, bear his children.

"I mean," she said, stepping closer, "that I will stay here if you ask me to. Or I will go with you if you ask me to. I want to be with you, wherever you go and whatever you do. I love you, Gerrard. I've always loved you, even when you cut off my hair."

His eyes widened. He couldn't have looked more astonished if the gates of heaven had opened before him.

That expression lasted only a moment before doubt darkened his handsome visage. "Do you truly mean that, Celeste? I want to believe it, but perhaps what you feel is merely gratitude." He lowered his head. "After all, I'm not a good man. I have lied and cheated and sinned. I am not nearly good enough for you."

She reached out and took his hands firmly in hers, now more certain of her feelings for him than she had ever been about anything.

"You *are* a good man, Gerrard," she assured him. "Perhaps you wandered from the path before, but you've changed. You're the man I always hoped and dreamed you would be, in spite of your upbringing. You're a man I can admire and respect, as well as love." She smiled then, and let him see the fullness of her heart.

Then she raised herself on her toes and kissed him.

Instead of responding, he stood stiff and still, and she feared she'd made a terrible mistake, until with a sudden sigh of exultation, he gathered her into his arms and clasped her tightly. "I will never let you go again! I love you, Celeste. I've loved you from boyhood, and long before I truly knew what love could be."

He kissed her passionately, his embrace telling her better than his words how much he loved her, and that she hadn't been wrong to hope that he cared for her.

He broke the kiss and, still holding her close, whispered in her ear, "I loved you even when you broke my collarbone. I'll always love you. If you would be my wife…"

"Yes!" she cried, happy beyond measure, until a harsh reality intruded into her joy. "Are you sure, Gerrard? You'll be marrying the daughter of a merchant, and one who'll have a very small dowry, or perhaps nothing at all once Audrey's debts are paid."

He grinned. "As if I cared about that! Good God, I should have gone to that convent and proposed to you years ago."

"We would surely have encountered opposition from your family then."

"There's no one to oppose us now," he noted, pulling her back into his arms and pressing featherlight kisses on her cheeks.

"What about Roland?" she asked breathlessly, not quite distracted by his kisses, or the ache beginning in her ankle. "You might not care about my rank or lack of riches, but your brother may."

Gerrard laughed then, a rich, lovely sound that lessened her worries at once, although not as much as what he said next. "He can't protest my marriage over a lack of dowry. His own wife lost most of hers in a fire and came here with just the clothes on her back and a bag of coins. And I'm no lord or even a knight."

Gerrard's words lifted Celeste's spirits and she held him close, her face against his chest. "If only my father really *had* left a treasure in the house, as he always said he had. Then I would have more to give you."

Gerrard pulled back, a confused frown wrinkling his brow. "*Your father* said there was a treasure?"

"Every time he shouted at my mother. He would claim there were gold and jewels hidden in the house, but she would never have any of it. I thought Audrey had found it, until I learned she was in debt. I've been searching for it ever since I came here, to no avail."

"Is that why I saw a light in your house for so long last night?"

Now *she* was confused. "How could you—"

"That tree near your south fence is not a comfortable perch for a watchman."

"You were *there*?"

"All night," he admitted.

"Oh, Gerrard, my love!"

"I couldn't have slept anyway, thinking you were alone and unprotected."

"And yet there are those who say you care nothing for anyone save yourself."

"Not anymore," he murmured, leaning down to kiss her again.

He drew back before he did so, concern on his features once more. "What have *I* to offer *you*? I don't have anything but a horse and a few coins to my name, unless I accept Roland's offer and take Dunborough." He smiled, but it didn't reach his eyes. "Yes, of course, that's what I'll do."

She wasn't fooled by that smile. There was dismay in those dark eyes of his.

"Accept only if you *truly* wish to," she said firmly. "I understand that you don't want to be beholden to your brother for the rest of your life. If you'd rather not accept his gift, I'll go with you wherever you wish. All that matters to me is that I'll be your wife."

His gaze softened and he stroked her cheek. "My pride has been my downfall too often. It's time I thought of someone other than myself and what suits me." His mischievous grin returned. "After all, I would be lying if I said I didn't want to be the master of Dunborough. I do, and I think I can rule it well with such a wife to help me. Therefore, my beloved, I'll tell Roland I will take what he offers and be grateful, and do my best.

"And as for my poor, untitled bride, her love makes

me rich beyond compare," he said softly before he captured her mouth with his.

She returned his kiss with fervent longing, her whole body heating as it had that day beneath the tree.

She wanted to feel more of what she had then, although this time, he must feel the same. Moving back, she took his hand and started toward the open door of the bedchamber, limping just a little.

In the next moment, Gerrard swept her up into his arms. "Your ankle *is* bothering you."

"A little," she said. However, the state of her ankle was not uppermost in her mind as she looked into his handsome, concerned face. "You may take me to my bed and stay with me."

He started toward the chamber. "I'll sit by your side all night if you like."

The time had come to be bold, and in truth, her ankle wasn't so very sore. "That isn't what I meant."

He halted, still as a statue, and regarded her warily.

She ran her finger down his cheek, then his neck and finally his collarbone. "I want you to be with me, Gerrard, tonight and every night."

"We aren't yet wed."

She flushed, for he was right. It would be a sin in the eyes of God and the law. And if she needed any other sign that he wasn't the rogue and wastrel people claimed, here it was.

Then his eyes lit up and he grinned that delightful, merry, mischievous Gerrard grin. He carried her swiftly into the chamber and set her on the bed.

"Wait here!" he ordered, and then hurried from the room.

Chapter Twenty-Four

Celeste felt as if she'd suddenly been stranded on a deserted island. She gingerly got under the covers and waited, although for what, she wasn't sure, until she heard a commotion in the corridor and Gerrard rushed back into the room, practically dragging Arnhelm. The soldier looked as puzzled as it was possible for a man to be. Behind him came an equally baffled Verdan holding Lizabet's hand. Peg, frowning, brought up the rear.

Celeste pulled the coverlet up to her neck. What in the name of the saints…?

"Here are our witnesses!" Gerrard exclaimed with proud satisfaction.

"Witnesses to what?" she asked cautiously.

"Aye, to what?" Arnhelm echoed.

"Our marriage!"

"S'truth!" Verdan muttered, clearly as taken aback as the others, including the bride-to-be.

"As much as I want to marry you, Gerrard," she began, "there's no priest to bless—"

Gerrard's earthy curse showed that he was not yet completely virtuous. "I'll go fetch Father Denzail."

"But it's night!"

Grinning again, Gerrard shook his head, and he was again that bold, brave rascal of a boy she'd adored all these years. "Day or night, I've waited too long as it is and will not wait any longer." His grin began to fade. "Unless you wish to?"

There was only one thing that she wished for now, and his urgency matched her own. "Go and fetch the priest, my love. We shall be ready when you return."

He started to go, then turned back and smiled at the soldiers and their sweethearts. "What say we make it three weddings, eh?"

Arnhelm and Verdan looked at the blushing maid-servants, then each other.

"Ma might never change her mind," Verdan said to his older brother.

"You're right," Arnhelm agreed. "Well, Peg?"

"You'd best make an honest woman out of me," she replied, her cheeks pink and her eyes sparkling.

"What do you think, Lizabet?" Verdan asked, his boyish bashfulness at distinct odds with his size.

She threw herself into his arms. "O'course I will!"

"Father Denzail! Wake up!" a voice shouted, followed by the sound of pounding on the rectory door. "Father Denzail!"

Tempted though the priest was to curse, for as the son of a seaman he knew some very colorful expressions, the middle-aged man crossed himself instead and muttered a prayer for forbearance. It must be Bardolf, come because his father was dying at last, although this wouldn't be the first time old Talby fooled them all and rallied.

Nevertheless, it was his duty to tend to the sick and

dying, so Father Denzail pulled on his robe and went to answer the door.

Before he got there, his unwelcome guest stuck her head out of the room next to his and glared at him.

"No need to trouble yourself," he said, waving his hand at the nun. "One of my parish is near death. I'm sure—"

"Father Denzail!" the man called again.

"Unless I'm very much mistaken, that's the young man from the castle," the mother superior said sharply and with an accusing expression, as if this nighttime visit meant Father Denzail was somehow in league with him.

The priest did not like Gerrard. However, he liked her less. She had treated him like a lackey, and a dim-witted one at that, since she had arrived.

Father Denzail drew himself up to his full height of five foot two and spoke with priestly authority. "If it *is* Gerrard, there must be some trouble at the castle and it's my duty to answer his call."

"I'm sure there's trouble there, all right," the woman retorted. "I'm sure they're all going to the devil."

"Be that as it may, this is my parish, so you may go back to bed."

"I think not," the mother superior declared, and much to Father Denzail's chagrin, she followed him down the stairs.

Between her, his interrupted sleep and the continual pounding and shouting, he was already getting a head-ache.

He hurried to open the outer door, ignoring the woman on his heels, except to note that her thick velvet bed robe was very fine for someone who had supposedly taken a vow of poverty.

"Now then, what's amiss?" he began, opening the door and shivering in the sudden blast of cold air.

He was not happy to find Gerrard on the doorstep, any more than he was to have that censorious nun behind him.

"I have a request, Father Denzail, that only you can fulfill," Gerrard said with a broad smile.

It might have been a fine midsummer morning for all the young man seemed to care about the darkness, the wind tugging at his cloak or the rain soaking his head.

Or perhaps there was another reason he seemed impervious to the late hour and the elements. "Are you drunk?"

"Not at all!" Gerrard replied. "Well, drunk with happiness, perhaps. I want to get married and I need you to say the blessing."

"Are you mad?" the mother superior demanded. "It's the middle of the night!"

Father Denzail said another prayer for patience as he tried to decide if Gerrard was being sincere or if this was some kind of jest.

"I want to get married," Gerrard repeated in such a way that, astonished though he was, Father Denzail believed him. "Celeste wants a priest to bless us."

"Celeste?" The mother superior shoved her way past the priest, nearly knocking him over. "You can't mean that!"

"I assure you, I do," Gerrard replied. "Since her fate is no longer in your hands, you can go back to bed. Or to hell, for all I care."

Father Denzail nearly laughed aloud at the startled look on the woman's face. It had likely been years since anybody had spoken to her in such a way, if ever, and for once, he sympathized with Gerrard. Nevertheless, she was a member of the clergy, so he cleared his throat and said with some severity, "That is no way to speak to the mother superior."

The young man who had led so sinful a life immediately grew remorseful, and spoke with such apparent sincerity, Father Denzail was amazed. "Forgive me, Father. And you, too, Reverend Mother, if you please. I can only say that my delight in having Celeste for a bride has made me thoughtless." He looked at the priest beseechingly. "I hope you won't hold that, or anything I've done in the past, against me, Father. With Celeste by my side, and with your help, too, I'm going to try to be a better man."

The fellow sounded as sincere as he appeared, and Father Denzail couldn't ignore the appeal. Nor could he help thinking it would do Gerrard good to have a wife who'd almost been a nun. "I shall be delighted to say a wedding blessing."

He turned to the red-faced, irate nun. "And like Gerrard says, you should go to bed."

Shifting his weight anxiously from foot to foot, Gerrard stood on the dais waiting for his bride. Soldiers and servants of the household had gathered in the hall, muttering with astonishment, confusion and suppressed excitement. Father Denzail, standing beside him, tried to stifle a yawn.

What was taking the women so long? They'd had plenty of time to get ready while he'd fetched Father Denzail.

Tapping his foot with impatience, Gerrard glanced at the little priest. He did have some backbone, after all, the way he'd stood up to the mother superior. Father Denzail was more familiar with the villagers and their needs, too, so he should treat the man with more respect, and ask him for his help if he was to govern the townsfolk and tenants wisely and well. Perhaps he should start going to mass. It would please Celeste and he had to admit that, resistant as he'd been, he'd experienced a certain comfort being part of the congregation.

More important than being a good overlord or his own comfort, though, was making Celeste happy. He would try his best, he silently vowed. Surely the dread of losing her respect and love would help him stay on the righteous path he'd begun to walk before she'd returned.

Nevertheless, doubts began to assail him. He was, after all, Gerrard of Dunborough, son of the loathed Sir Blane. He was no virtuous knight, but a man more familiar with vice and sin and the weaknesses of the flesh.

The laughter of women interrupted his worrisome thoughts, and he turned to see his bride approaching, with Lizabet and Peg beside her. One holding each forearm, the women offered their support as Celeste limped closer, wearing that magnificent gown of embroidered silk.

Then he noticed Bartholemew and Marmaduke behind her, beaming as if they were giving away the bride.

Yet it wasn't the gown, or her company, that garnered Gerrard's attention after the first thrilling moment. It was the smile on her face and the love shining in her eyes.

Somehow—and he could only think it must be through the grace of a merciful God—he had found this incredible woman who loved and trusted him. He would, please God, be worthy of that love and faith all the days of his life.

His bride reached the dais. With the priest between them, he took her hand and made his vow. "I, Gerrard of Dunborough, take you for my wife. I will respect you and honor you, provide for you and keep you safe for the rest of my life. I will be faithful to you always, and I will love you forever."

She solemnly took both his hands in hers. "I, Celeste D'Orleau, take you for my husband. I will respect and honor you, and provide a loving home for you. I will be faithful to you always, as I will love you until the day I die, and in the life to come."

Arnhelm and Peg, Verdan and Lizabet likewise made their vows of love and fidelity, and when they were done, Father Denzail said a blessing over all of them. His final words, however, were drowned out by the rousing cheers and clapping of the soldiers and servants of Dunborough, as well as Bartholemew and Marmaduke, who seemed nearly faint with joy.

Gerrard turned to his bride and spoke in her ear so that only she could hear him above the cacophony. "I believe you were ordered to rest. I don't want you to fall ill."

"I *am* feeling rather weary," she replied, although that was far from true. Rarely in her life had she felt more vital and alive. Nevertheless, she should rest, or at least go to bed. "I should retire. With you, if you wish it."

His expression was all the answer she required.

He took hold of her hand and announced, "Thank you, one and all, for your good wishes. Since it's too late for a wedding feast today—" he glanced at Florian, the cook, who couldn't have looked more relieved if he'd been spared the rack "—and my brother and his wife should be here to help us celebrate, as well as Arnhelm and Verdan's mother, too, if she'll come, we shall postpone that happy event for the time being.

"Now I believe we should all retire," he finished, before he swept his bride into his arms and carried her up the stairs.

Chapter Twenty-Five

Celeste thought it was like a dream come true as Gerrard carried her over the threshold and into his bedchamber, except for one thing: her sore and bandaged ankle.

As he slowly set her down, that minor problem was quickly forgotten, overwhelmed by happiness and excitement and the sight of the bed made up with fresh linens. Lizabet and Peg, in spite of their own giddy delight, had seen to that. They'd also sent the spit boy rushing to the village to fetch Bartholemew and Marmaduke, and the red silk dress she'd hoped they hadn't sold.

Still in Gerrard's strong arms, Celeste raised her face to kiss him. Yet when she saw the desire burning in his dark eyes, she suddenly felt shy. To be sure, they had shared some intimate embraces, but she had never been alone in a man's bedchamber before. "What will you say to Roland about our marriage?" she asked instead.

Gerrard smiled before he lightly kissed her cheek. Even that sent her blood racing. "That his reprobate brother achieved a miracle and wed an angel."

"That is casting me in rather a grand and blasphemous light."

"He likes you. You never called him names and, I seem to recall, always took his side when there was a difference of opinion."

"He was always right."

"Mostly," Gerrard allowed. "He could be very stubborn, too, like someone else I love."

He kissed her then and would have done more, except that she turned her face away. "If Roland will accept our marriage despite my lack of wealth, then all I have to regret is that I'm not rich enough to persuade the bishop to move the mother superior."

Gerrard frowned. "Must we talk about her?"

"I'm sorry." Celeste leaned her head against his shoulder. "It's just that I'm so happy, and yet when I think of the other novices still at Saint Agatha's under her thumb…"

"Perhaps a few words from the master of Dunborough and the lord of DeLac to the bishop will prove persuasive."

"You'll do that? You'll intercede? And Roland, too?"

"I think my brother will be willing once he hears why. Even on short acquaintance, I'm sure that woman should not be in charge of anything." Gerrard tilted his head to one side and raised his brows. "Now, wife of mine, is there anything else you care to discuss?"

"Not at present," she replied, feeling more at ease. She gave him a mischievous grin of her own. "Right now I find I have other things on my mind."

"Really?" he replied, running his hands up her arms and sending shivers of delight across her flesh. "Such as?"

"This," she answered, rising to kiss him lightly on the lips.

"And this," she added as she splayed her hands on his chest.

"Then this," she murmured, sliding her arms around him.

His lips captured hers in a passionate kiss, but she was not quite ready for more. Not yet.

She pulled away and, her gaze holding his, reached back to untie the laces of her gown. It wasn't easy with his hot, yearning eyes watching her, so she turned her back to him.

His fingers took over the task. Once the knot was undone, he kissed the nape of her neck and slid his hands inside her dress, his palms grazing her shift as he reached around to knead her breasts.

She had envisioned being in his arms many times, yet never like this. All she could do was close her eyes, sigh and relax against him at first, until the urge to feel his lips on hers proved overwhelming. She turned and took his mouth with hers. Then, still kissing him, she helped him push her gown lower, until she could step free. She took another moment to lift off his tunic and the shirt beneath, so that his chest was bare.

She gasped when she saw the several scars. Although none were very large, there were many.

"My father and Broderick," he replied in answer to her unspoken question. "And some my own foolishness." He pointed to a mark on his collarbone. "This one is from you."

"I'm so sorry, Gerrard!"

He grinned. "I'm not. It was a reminder of you when you were gone, and one I'm glad I had."

"Otherwise you would have forgotten me."

"Otherwise I would have forgotten what I'd done to get it. I never again falsely accused Roland, or any man, of cheating. You see, even when you weren't here, you were guiding me."

He frowned as he pointed at the scar on her own shoulder. "And that?" he asked. "Is that from that terrible woman at the convent? If so, I'll—"

She took hold of his hand and lowered it. "That was from my father before I was sent away, and one reason I was so glad to go, at least at first."

"I promise you, Celeste, that I will never lay a hand on you or our children."

"And I promise you, Gerrard, that I will give you the love you deserve, the love you have always deserved."

His breath caught and his eyes glistened with sudden moisture. He tried to laugh as he swiped at them. "Say no more or you'll have me weeping like a child, and a man on his wedding night should be very manly indeed."

She touched his cheek lightly with her lips. "I know what you've endured, Gerrard, and it would be no weakness to me if you did weep."

"Let's try to put those times behind us, and forget."

"I doubt we can, but we can begin a new life today, one with more joyful memories."

"I love you, Celeste D'Orleau," he whispered as he gently pulled her into his arms and kissed her with all the passionate longing of a loving heart that had been lonely for so long.

"As I love you," she replied.

No more needed to be said as they kissed and caressed, letting the past retreat, overcome by the needs of the present and the yearning that both had tried to ignore and deny for so long. When their clothes became a nuisance, Celeste lifted her shift over her head and stood naked before him, one arm over her breasts, her other hand between her thighs. She was too modest to do more, until she saw the hunger in his eyes, the rapid rise and fall of his chest.

"You're so beautiful," he murmured. "To think you are my wife!"

Yes, she was his wife, and his words emboldened her. She lowered her arms.

His gaze upon her, he pulled off his boots and stockings and kicked them aside. He untied the drawstring of his breeches and tugged them off, so that he was standing naked before her, too. Magnificently, marvelously naked, from the top of his head with its shoulder-length hair, to his broad shoulders, flat stomach, narrow hips and long, lean legs.

"You're like a statue of a god," she murmured. An aroused god.

"I'm a man of flesh and blood," he said, moving closer. "A man eager to love his wife," he added before he took her in his arms and carried her to the bed.

She pulled him down atop her, welcoming the weight of him. Her hands slid over his naked skin, feeling its warmth, letting her own excitement guide her as they kissed deeply.

Instinctively she parted her legs and gasped when he put his hand between them, stroking her. She gripped his shoulders as sensations she had felt once before began to overtake her.

His finger slipped inside her and she raised her hips, wanting more. Needing more.

When he withdrew his finger, she whimpered with disappointment, until he entered her. As her mind reeled and her body welcomed, he began to thrust, slowly at first, then with increasing speed. She broke the kiss to speak, although no words came, only panting breaths and gasps and little moans, while the tension built and excitement grew and she arched upward until…until… Release! Glorious, throbbing, rocking release, so powerful she didn't hear Gerrard groan deeply before he laid his head upon her sweat-slicked breasts.

"To think I didn't know what I was going to give up if I left you," she murmured, stroking his head as the pulsing ebbed.

"To think I was going to let you go," he said in return before he looked at her. "I've been a fool plenty of times in my life, but never more than when I thought I could live without you."

"Now you won't have to," she said, smiling, "and I won't have to try to live without you…or *this*."

He raised a brow. *"This?"* He frowned. "Perhaps that's why you married me, for *this*."

"If you think that, you're very much mistaken. How could I miss something I'd never experienced before?" She grew serious. "There's never been any other man I wanted to kiss, let alone do *that* with."

"If you think that was exciting, let me assure you, it's just the beginning," he said, sounding like temptation in the flesh.

Then he frowned again. "What about your ankle?"

"It's only a little sore."

"The apothecary said you ought to rest."

"I'm in bed, aren't I?"

The early-morning light crept into the bridal chamber like an unwanted guest at a feast. Celeste woke first and lay still, listening to the calm, easy breathing of the man beside her. Her husband. Her beloved husband sleeping as peacefully as a babe, with a loose lock of hair on his brow. He looked so much like the boy she'd known, she could almost forget he was the man who'd made love to her with such passion.

Almost, she thought with a smile, brushing the lock off his forehead.

She nestled closer, wincing a little from the slight pain in her ankle. She wished they could stay this way all day, or even a few more hours. Unfortunately, the sounds of the castle stirring told her that was probably impossible.

"Hmm?" Gerrard murmured, opening his eyes and smiling sleepily. He rolled onto his side and put his arm around her. "Is it morning already? I feel like I hardly slept a wink, while you look fresh as the morning dew."

"It *is* morning, and neither of us slept very much. We were, you may recall, otherwise occupied."

"Indeed, I do recall," he said. "I recall a lot of things we did last night," he added with a grin that made her laugh and blush and cover her face with her hands.

He reached up and pulled one hand away, his expression unexpectedly serious. "You're not ashamed of what we did, are you?"

"Oh, no!" she hurried to assure him. "I just… I mean, I never knew that it…what we did…that it could be so wonderful!"

He fell flat on his back and laughed. "Thank God! I feared you were going to tell me you didn't like it and never wanted me to touch you again."

"I do want you to touch me," she said, her voice low and sultry. She slid her hand below his waist, determined to do more than tell him how much she enjoyed making love with him. "I want to touch you, too."

"What about your ankle?"

"It's all right," she assured him, inching closer. She leaned down to lave his pebbled nipple with her tongue while her hand stroked and aroused. When he tried to caress her, she gently pushed his arm away and told him to lie still.

His eyes flew open and he couldn't have looked more taken aback if she'd announced she was Venus come to call.

"I want to pleasure you, Gerrard," she whispered. "Let me pleasure you."

"As long as I get to return the favor," he huskily replied.

She smiled then, and nodded, and drew back the covers to expose his naked body. With tender, loving passion, she used her lips and hands until he was twisting and moaning and practically begging her to let him make love to her.

Only then did she shift to straddle him, taking care that her ankle was not too painfully positioned before guiding him into her. With her hands on his shoulders, she leaned down and kissed him deeply as she began to move, rocking back and forth, letting his response tell her whether to go faster or more slowly.

He began to knead her breasts and her own need overtook her. Faster she went, and faster, her breathing erratic, the tension building. He groaned, a sound more like a growl from deep within his chest, and he bucked like a wild horse new to the saddle. At nearly the same time, her whole body seemed to clench. She held on tightly to his shoulders in her ecstasy, until he gasped and said, between his panting breaths and laughter, "Have mercy, wife! I fear you're going to break my collarbone again."

Flushed and sweat-slicked, she gingerly moved off him and lay back down at his side. "I didn't know what I was doing."

"If that is what you do in ignorance, I can hardly wait to see what you do when we've been married for a few years," he said, smiling before he kissed her.

"I wanted to show you that I enjoy being intimate with you."

"In that, beloved, you've succeeded admirably." He toyed with a lock of her hair. "I was hoping your hair was long again beneath that veil and cap and wimple. I was afraid they'd made you cut it off."

"The mother superior did try more than once, especially the time I had a fever. That was an excuse, though, and we both knew it. Fortunately, Sister Sylvester forbade it, saying it might upset me too much and make the illness worse. I don't think she really thought so, though. I think she was as aware as I that the mother superior sought to punish me that way. I'd spilled her wine when I was serving the evening meal the day before."

"She wanted to cut your hair off because of an accident? God's wounds, she's worse than I thought!"

Celeste colored and snuggled against him, and in a small voice said, "It might not have been an accident."

"You spilled her wine *deliberately*?"

Celeste raised her head to look up at him. "She'd been very cruel to one of the new girls that day."

He laughed again, louder this time. "I have indeed married a marvel of a woman. And now I know what it means should you spill *my* wine."

"I won't have to do that if I think you've done wrong. I'll tell you."

With love shining in his eyes, he smiled. "Good. As I'll tell you if I think you've done something…not quite right. Now, since we are both so determined to be good, I reluctantly suggest we climb out of bed, dress and get to the hall before somebody comes up here to see if we're still alive."

"And I'm starving," Celeste said, rising from the bed. "No doubt you are, too, after all your exertions."

He didn't answer as she limped to the washstand.

Instead, he hurried to her and said, "I was right! We did too much and now your ankle's worse."

"Not worse," she said. "It's well bandaged and the liniment worked wonders. Still, I think I should rest for a few more days. In bed." She sighed with false dismay. "I hope I won't be too bored."

He laughed, just as she'd intended. "I'll also require some assistance getting dressed," she noted.

"It will be my pleasure," he replied with equally bogus gravity.

It took them some time to dress, and not because of her ankle. However, she was eventually garbed in another gown Bartholemew and Marmaduke had thoughtfully provided. It, too, had been Audrey's and was one of the few simple ones she'd possessed, of light green wool. Gerrard donned his usual shirt, tunic, breeches and boots.

When they were ready to join the household in the hall, he swept her into his arms again. He raised his brows as if expecting her to protest, but instead she wrapped her arms around his neck. "This once," she said, kissing him lightly, "because of my ankle. In future, I don't expect to be carried everywhere."

"Not even if I enjoy it?"

"It's not exactly dignified, and the wife of the lord of Dunborough should be dignified, don't you think?"

"Only in public," he said with a seductive look that made her blush before he carried her down the steps and into the hall.

Where Sir Roland of Dunborough and DeLac sat waiting on the dais, looking as grim as a judge about to pass sentence for a heinous crime.

Chapter Twenty-Six

Celeste felt a lurch of dread when she saw Gerrard's stern twin, and she gripped her husband tighter. Roland was dressed all in black, without a hint of color at collar, cuff or hem of his long tunic. Even his sword belt was black, and his expression was as stoic as it had ever been, without a hint that he even knew how to smile. How any woman could have fallen in love with him remained a mystery, no matter what people said.

"Greetings, Roland," Gerrard said as calmly as if he always arrived in the hall with a woman in his arms. "Remember Celeste? *My wife*, Celeste."

She expected Roland to scowl or frown. Instead, to her amazement, he smiled. It made all the difference in the world, and for the first time, he resembled Gerrard more than she would have thought possible. "So I've been informed," Roland said, walking toward them, limping slightly.

"Put me down," she whispered to Gerrard, who did as she asked. He might appear composed, but she saw the dread lurking in his eyes and remembered the quarrels and harsh words that had passed between them.

More no doubt had been said and done since she'd been gone, so it was no wonder Gerrard looked worried.

But Roland was still smiling as he took her hands in his and kissed her on both cheeks. "Greetings, sister-in-law." He reached for his brother's hand and engulfed it with his. "Of all the things you could have done to show me that you've changed, Gerrard," he said with true good humor, "marrying is the best, and especially such a worthy bride."

"Thank you," Gerrard said. "What brings you here?"

Before Roland could answer, Arnhelm and Peg appeared at the kitchen entrance, a petite, gray-haired woman between them. Behind them came Verdan and Lizabet. The brides appeared pleased. The grooms looked thrilled and more than a little relieved.

"As you can see, sir," Verdan called out, "Ma's come to Yorkshire at last. She's goin' to stay, too."

"Excellent," Gerrard replied.

By now, several servants and soldiers had come into the hall. Some hurried to offer their greetings and good wishes to Verdan and Arnhelm, others were watching the people on the dais.

Roland turned to his brother. "Although this is a joyful day, we have important matters to discuss and I would rather do so in private."

"Aye," Gerrard replied. "Let's go to the solar."

"May I join you?" Celeste asked, although in truth, she had no intention of being left behind.

Roland's lips turned up in a little smile. "I would expect nothing less. You were always wanting to see."

Gerrard looked less convinced and she feared he was going to refuse. Then he said, "Can you manage the stairs with your ankle?"

If that was his only concern... "I think so."

He nodded and she was glad he wasn't going to refuse.

Looking pleased and proud, he held out his arm to escort her. "Then let us go."

When they reached the solar, Roland entered first and moved a chair closer to the table for Celeste. Gerrard was fetching one for himself, leaving the largest one for his twin, when Roland spotted a familiar letter and another barely started in his brother's nearly illegible scrawl.

He pointed at it and, with his usual grave expression, said, "Now you know why I decided to come. I've been waiting weeks for an answer."

"You know I'm not good at letter writing," Gerrard replied with a shrug of his right shoulder, "and I hadn't yet made up my mind about your generous offer."

"You could have sent word you were getting married," Roland said, his dark brows drawing together in a frown. "As your older brother—"

"By less than an hour, and you never sent word to me that you were getting married, either," Gerrard retorted, half rising from his chair.

Celeste began to fear that another quarrel was in the offing, until Roland suddenly smiled. "No, and now I think you can understand why I didn't want to wait."

Gerrard lowered himself back into the seat and laughed, a merry, rollicking sound that cleared the air of any tension. "I should say I do!"

More relaxed as well, Roland addressed a relieved Celeste. "I suppose this means you've forgiven him for cutting off your hair."

"We, too, have made peace," she solemnly agreed, although a smile played about her lips.

"And then some," Gerrard added with a grin. "I'm glad your leg is mended enough to ride, brother."

"Aye, it's well enough," Roland agreed, sitting behind the table. "I'll stay a few days before I return, though, if you'll permit it."

"If *I'll* permit it? You're still the overlord here."

Considering his next words, Roland's pleasant mood and manner were even more surprising. "That is no longer true. It seems the king has decided two estates such as DeLac and Dunborough are too much for one man. He has decided to take Dunborough away from me and give it to you. Apparently he believes we're sworn enemies and thinks that's better for him. I fear the poor man is going to be disillusioned. In the meantime, Dunborough is yours by the king's command, as well as with my blessing."

Gerrard stared at him incredulously. "*John* has given me Dunborough?"

"Yes, and he's also decided to confer a knighthood upon you. I suspect he thinks that will increase our enmity and deepen the division between us."

"Who's been telling the king that you and Gerrard are enemies?" Celeste asked warily.

"I have no idea who's been spreading such rumors," Roland replied, his expression fraudulently innocent, "unless it's Sir Melvin. Have you ever met him, Gerrard? His estate is some miles from here."

Sir Melvin?

"No, I don't believe I have," Gerrard replied.

"I have!" Celeste exclaimed. "He and his wife gave me a meal and shelter on my journey here. He's a generous, kindhearted man but, alas, has no good opinion of you, Gerrard." She blushed as she recalled their hospitality and the way she had deceived them. "They may not have a good one of me, either, when they find out I'm not a nun."

"It seems none of us made a very good impression the first time we met Sir Melvin and his wife, except for Mavis," Roland ruefully replied. "They are good people for all that and hopefully will be willing to admit they may have been mistaken about our animosity, should we decide we want the king to think all is well between us."

Gerrard regarded his brother with wry respect. "I am to believe, then, that I must accept Dunborough with no thanks to you?"

"You *should* believe it, or else you'll give me more credit than I deserve. I have no head for machinations and strategy, as you should know."

That was indeed true, Celeste realized. Roland had never come up with plans when they were children. He merely criticized or condemned and stayed strictly within the rules.

"Or perhaps it was your wife who influenced the king," Gerrard proposed.

Again that look of bogus innocence came to Roland's features. "Mavis? She's a woman."

"A very clever woman," Gerrard declared. "God save me, two clever women in the family! We had best take care, Roland, or they'll be running DeLac and Dunborough instead of us."

"I welcome Mavis's help and guidance," Roland sincerely replied. "Nay, I need it. She knows more about running an estate than I do."

"I know nothing of running a noble household," Celeste admitted.

"You can drive a hard bargain, or so I hear, and that's a talent I sorely lack," Gerrard said.

"Have you given any thought to a wedding feast?" Roland asked. "Mavis will want to come."

"Will she be well enough to travel, in her condition?" Gerrard asked.

"If I know my wife, and as long as it's soon," Roland said with a grin that was the mirror of Gerrard's, "nothing I say will stop her."

A few days later, when Celeste's ankle was better, and a fortnight before their wedding feast, Celeste and her husband strolled hand in hand through the village. The people called out greetings and congratulations and waved as they passed.

"It seems our marriage has pleased the villagers and tenants," she remarked.

"Not as much as it pleases me," he said, patting her hand on his forearm and smiling warmly.

"Or me," she replied, leaning her head against his broad shoulder. "I wish everyone could be as happy as I am today. Love is an amazing thing, isn't it, Gerrard? It can make grim, stern men like Roland pleasant and easygoing. I must confess, I never thought he could be lighthearted."

"I agree that the change that's come over him is amazing, and so is his wife," Gerrard replied, lifting her hand for a kiss. "You'll like Mavis, I'm sure. She's a fine woman."

"She must be, if she can soften Roland's heart."

They reached the chandler's shop and paused. The shutters were still over the windows and there was no sign of life.

"He's gone," Bartholemew said from behind them.

They turned to see the cloth merchants standing side

by side, sad expressions on their faces. "He left the day after his son died, at dawn," Marmaduke added.

"He loaded up a cart and drove off without a word to anyone," said Bartholemew. "He didn't even wait for his son to be buried."

"No doubt he couldn't bear to stay after…" Marmaduke began, before his voice faded to sorrowful silence.

Celeste let go of her husband's arm. "Do you know where Ewald is?"

The two men exchanged uneasy glances. "I think," Bartholemew said, "that he's waiting for you at the house."

He didn't have to say which house, or why. The sale had been concluded, and once the deed was exchanged, it would be his, with all its memories, good and bad. "Thank you."

Gerrard stepped forward and his smile put them all at ease again before he said, "Perhaps later you can come to the hall. I believe my bride is going to need some new clothes."

The two men eagerly bobbed their heads. "We'll be delighted!" Marmaduke cried.

"It will be an honor!" Bartholemew seconded.

Although she did need clothes and the prospect of pretty new gowns was pleasing, Celeste couldn't help feeling the money could be better spent elsewhere.

"I won't need much," she said, after they had bade farewell to the two men and continued on their way.

Gerrard came to an abrupt halt and regarded her with outraged majesty. "My dear, you are the wife of the lord of Dunborough. You must be appropriately attired!"

She regarded him with a straight face and steady gaze. "As long as you allow me to decide what is 'appropriate.'"

His frown was as bogus as his outrage as he started

walking again. "I won't have you wearing sackcloth and ashes, or nothing but black."

She smiled then. "Somehow, I don't think Bartholemew and Marmaduke would allow that, either."

"Make way there! Make way!" a man cried out behind them. He was driving a heavy covered carriage, one Celeste recognized.

"It's the mother superior," she said to Gerrard.

He grinned with devilish merriment and, before she could stop him, darted forward and leaped onto the side of the wagon, one foot on the step and his hands grasping the grilled window. "Leaving without a farewell, Reverend Mother?"

Celeste could have sworn the woman cursed, and Gerrard's next words confirmed it. "Such language from a holy woman! Tsk, tsk, what will the bishop say? Well, he'll likely add it to the list of sins that will ensure you leave the convent of Saint Agatha's for somewhere more…penitential."

If the mother superior replied, her words were drowned out by the creaking wagon wheels as the carriage rolled past Celeste. She could hear Gerrard's response, though, for it was loud and clear. "You may think you have the man wrapped around your aristocratic finger. I suspect he'll find his backbone if he's given enough incentive. Monetary incentive."

She could hear the mother superior's answer to that and gasped at the rough, uncouth language. Meanwhile, Gerrard merely laughed and jumped lightly to the ground.

"Dear me," he said with bogus dismay as he joined Celeste once again, "I've never heard such language from a woman! Wherever did she learn it? Not at her mother's knee, I trust."

"She'll go to the bishop right away, you realize," Celeste warned him. "She'll think that will give her the advantage."

"She can think what she likes," Gerrard said, not a whit concerned. "Between Roland, his wife, her cousin and her husband, and yours truly, we wield enough power and influence to outweigh whatever complaints she makes. I gave her a little parting gift, too."

"A gift? You gave that woman a gift?"

"Indeed," he said virtuously. "I went after a certain old servant and brought her back to serve the mother superior. Father Denzail has assured the mother superior that while not young, the serving woman is competent and well trained. Unfortunately, she'd fallen on hard times and grown weak, but she'll soon be back to her old self. Alas, I fear that nun is not quite prepared for a servant who possesses such a sharp tongue."

Celeste's eyes widened as she realized what he meant. "You gave her *Eua*?"

"Father Denzail and I agreed that it would be a fine idea to pay Eua to serve the mother superior. Eua will surely make life less than delightful for that woman."

"And you claim you have no gift for governance!"

He tried to look modest and didn't succeed. "It was one of my better ideas," he agreed. "The other was asking you to be my wife."

"I love you, Gerrard," she said, taking hold of his arm and leaning against him. "I only wish I could have seen the mother superior's face when you jumped onto her carriage like a monkey."

He widened his eyes and made his mouth a round O, making Celeste giggle with delight.

"Now, there's a sound I hope to hear more of," he noted as they reached the gate to the yard of her family's house.

"Eua looked as if she'd never seen me before in her life," he added somewhat wistfully.

"She had to or the mother superior might have been suspicious and not taken her to the convent," Celeste said comfortingly, and with renewed determination to make her husband feel loved and cherished for the rest of his days.

In the next moment, though, her thoughts were on what they had to do now. It was strange to think that her family's house was going to belong to Ewald.

"Take heart, my love," Gerrard said softly, rightly understanding how she was feeling. "After today, you'll be with someone who loves you with all his heart."

She gave him a smile and continued to the door, where she reached into her cuff and produced the key.

Even with Gerrard beside her, she couldn't help trembling a little as she recalled the last time she'd been there. Lewis's attack, the struggle…

"It's just as well this will be someone else's house," she said as they entered the main room.

The furniture was as it had been, and to her surprise, the ginger cat was sitting in front of the panel that had been broken in the struggle. Joseph looked as if he'd been waiting for her.

"Will you come back to the castle with us, Joseph, or would you rather stay here?" she murmured, crouching down to stroke the cat's broad back.

"That is a rather miraculous creature," Gerrard noted. "He showed me the peas that led me to you."

"Truly?"

"Truly."

"Then we should take him with us, to bring us good— Gerrard!" She slid forward, staring with awe at the space behind the broken panel. "Gerrard, look!"

She pulled out a leather bag covered in dust. It was large enough to hold a loaf of bread and clinked suggestively. "Oh, Gerrard, I think… It must be…"

She undid the leather drawstring and poured the contents into her lap—gold and silver coins, a necklace of gold links, an emerald ring and a ruby necklace.

Her father's hidden hoard.

"So it was here, after all," Gerrard said quietly.

"And Audrey never found it."

"She never spoke of it, so perhaps she doubted its existence, as I did."

"Yet it could have meant freedom for her, or at least a chance to choose a husband she could love," Celeste replied as she began to gather up the treasure and put it back into the pouch.

"What will you do with it now?"

She raised her eyes to look at him and got to her feet. "Since you're my husband, by law it all belongs to you."

Gerrard shook his head. "No, not mine. Yours, to do with as you will."

"Then I should like to make sure Audrey's debts are all paid, and since it's doubtful the mother superior will be at Saint Agatha's much longer, I'd like to give some to Sister Sylvester for the medicines she needs, and more food and wine for the nuns and novices. The rest should be for the people of Dunborough. Your father spent all his money and tithes building the castle. I would have this spent on the village and maybe a new church, if you are willing."

"Indeed I am. The people of Dunborough are owed for all they gave my father and a new church is a fine idea. Perhaps it could have a bell and a stained glass window, too, something Father Denzail would like."

Clutching the pouch, Celeste felt her eyes fill with

tears and she held him close. She had always known he was a brave and bold fellow. Lately she had learned he was honorable and worthy of admiration. Now she knew that he was truly kind and generous, and willing to change his ways if he was shown better ones. "Thank you, Gerrard."

As they embraced, she dropped the pouch, and some of the jewels and coins spilled onto the floor. One of the baubles caught Joseph's attention and he began to pat it with his paw.

"Dear God in heaven and all the saints, too!"

Startled, they jumped apart. Ewald stood in the doorway staring with stunned surprise not at them, but at the treasure on the floor. "Is that… Are they…*real*?"

As Celeste put the money and jewelry back into the pouch, Gerrard picked up a gold coin and dramatically bit it, then held it out to Ewald, the dent clearly visible. "It seems the rumors were true and there was a treasure hidden here."

"S'blood!" the merchant murmured, for once unable to say more.

"I'll fetch the deed, Ewald," Celeste said.

That woke him up from his stupor. He reached into his belt and drew out a purse considerably smaller than Celeste's pouch. "I've brought the money." His eyes locked onto the pouch in her hand as if by an invisible force. "Do you suppose there's any more hidden somewhere else?"

"I don't think so," she answered honestly. "But since this house is yours, you can search all you like."

"Does your husband agree?" Ewald asked.

"The sale was Celeste's to make, so I have no objection," Gerrard replied.

"Excellent!" the merchant exclaimed, regarding the

room with renewed interest and a gleam of avarice in his eyes that made her think the walls would soon be torn asunder.

She had a moment's regret about selling the house, until she thought of her new home and life with Gerrard.

She retrieved the deed and returned to find Gerrard holding Joseph. The cat jumped out of his arms and, tail swishing, sat beside him.

When she handed Ewald the deed in exchange for the coins, he gave a perfunctory nod of acknowledgment, then immediately went to a panel and began to pull it from the wall.

With tears in her eyes, Celeste hurried from the house, followed by the cat and her husband, who drew her into his arms.

She wept a little, then sniffled and looked up into Gerrard's sympathetic eyes. "I shouldn't be so sad. I'm sure Audrey would be happy for me. And her spirit isn't in that house." Celeste touched her chest. "It's here, with me, always."

He nodded and kissed her gently, holding her close.

The November air was cold, and soon it would be dark and colder still. But here, as they started their lives together, it was spring.

And it always would be.

* * * * *

COMING NEXT MONTH FROM

⊕ HARLEQUIN®

ℋISTORICAL

Available January 19, 2016

WANT AD WIFE (Western)
Wild West Weddings
by Katy Madison
Abandoned as a child, John Bench has always craved a family of his own.
Even if that means advertising for a mail-order bride from back East...

MARRIAGE MADE IN REBELLION (Regency)
The Penniless Lords
by Sophia James
Severely wounded, Captain Lucien Howard, Earl of Ross, holds the
beautiful Alejandra in his arms. Could there be a way to make their time
together last forever?

A TOO CONVENIENT MARRIAGE (Regency)
by Georgie Lee
As wedding bells begin to chime, Susanna Lambert discovers she's
carrying a huge secret...one that could put at risk her future happiness
as Justin Connor's wife!

SAVING MARINA (Americana)
by Lauri Robinson
Sea captain Richard Tarr arrives in Salem to claim his child. So he's shocked
to discover his daughter in the care of Marina Lindqvist—a rumored witch!

Available via Reader Service and online:

REDEMPTION OF THE RAKE (Regency)
A Year of Scandal
by Elizabeth Beacon
When James Winterley's dangerous past catches up to him, he must protect
widowed Rowena Westhope. Will he renounce his rakish ways and marry her?

THE NOTORIOUS COUNTESS (Regency)
by Liz Tyner
When notorious Lady Riverton is caught in a *most* compromising position
with Andrew Robson, for the first time, the truth is even more scandalous
than the rumors!

REQUEST YOUR FREE BOOKS!

HARLEQUIN®

HISTORICAL

Where love is timeless

2 FREE NOVELS PLUS 2 FREE GIFTS!

YES! Please send me 2 FREE Harlequin® Historical novels and my 2 FREE gifts (gifts are worth about $10). After receiving them, if I don't wish to receive any more books, I can return the shipping statement marked "cancel." If I don't cancel, I will receive 6 brand-new novels every month and be billed just $5.69 per book in the U.S. or $5.99 per book in Canada. That's a savings of at least 12% off the cover price! It's quite a bargain! Shipping and handling is just 50¢ per book in the U.S. and 75¢ per book in Canada.* I understand that accepting the 2 free books and gifts places me under no obligation to buy anything. I can always return a shipment and cancel at any time. Even if I never buy another book, the two free books and gifts are mine to keep forever.

246/349 HDN GH2Z

Name _____ (PLEASE PRINT)

Address _____ Apt. #

City _____ State/Prov. _____ Zip/Postal Code

Signature (if under 18, a parent or guardian must sign)

Mail to the **Reader Service:**
IN U.S.A.: P.O. Box 1867, Buffalo, NY 14240-1867
IN CANADA: P.O. Box 609, Fort Erie, Ontario L2A 5X3

Want to try two free books from another line?
Call 1-800-873-8635 or visit www.ReaderService.com.

* Terms and prices subject to change without notice. Prices do not include applicable taxes. Sales tax applicable in N.Y. Canadian residents will be charged applicable taxes. Offer not valid in Quebec. This offer is limited to one order per household. Not valid for current subscribers to Harlequin Historical books. All orders subject to credit approval. Credit or debit balances in a customer's account(s) may be offset by any other outstanding balance owed by or to the customer. Please allow 4 to 6 weeks for delivery. Offer available while quantities last.

Your Privacy—The Reader Service is committed to protecting your privacy. Our Privacy Policy is available online at www.ReaderService.com or upon request from the Reader Service.

We make a portion of our mailing list available to reputable third parties that offer products we believe may interest you. If you prefer that we not exchange your name with third parties, or if you wish to clarify or modify your communication preferences, please visit us at www.ReaderService.com/consumerchoice or write to us at Reader Service Preference Service, P.O. Box 9062, Buffalo, NY 14240-9062. Include your complete name and address.

She laughed and he thought he should like to hear her do it more, her throaty humour catching. Tomorrow he would be gone, away from Spain, away from these nights of talk and quiet closeness.

"Being happy suits you, Alejandra Fernandez y Santo Domingo." Lucien would have liked to add that her name suited her, too, with its soft syllables and music. Her left wrist with the sleeve of the jacket pulled back was dainty, a silver band he had not noticed before encircling the thinness.

"There has been little cause for joy here, Capitán. You said you survived as a soldier by living in the moment and not thinking about tomorrow or yesterday?" She waited as he nodded, the question hanging there.

"There is a certain lure to that. For a woman, you understand."

"Lure?" Were the connotations of the word in Spanish different from what they were in English?

"Addiction. Compulsion even. The art of throwing caution to the wind and taking what you desire because the consequences are distant."

Her dark eyes held his without any sense of embarrassment; a woman who was well aware of her worth and her attraction to the opposite sex.

Lucien felt the stirring in his groin, rushing past the sickness and the lethargy into a fully formed hard ache of want.

Was she saying what he thought she was, here on their last night together? Was she asking him to bed her?

"I will be gone in the morning." He tried for logic.

"Which is a great part of your attraction. I am practical, Capitán, and a realist. We only know each other in small ways, but…it would be enough for me. It isn't commitment I am after and I certainly do not expect promises."

"What is it you do want, then?"

She breathed out and her eyes in the moonlight were sultry.

"I want to survive, Capitán. You said you did this best by not thinking about the past or the future. I want the same. Just this moment. Only now."

Don't miss
MARRIAGE MADE IN REBELLION
by Sophia James, available February 2016 wherever
Harlequin® Historical books and ebooks are sold.

www.Harlequin.com